THE MAFIA AND HIS ANGEL

PART 2

Tainted Hearts Series

By Lylah James

THE MAFIA AND HIS ANGEL PART 2

Copyright © 2017 by Lylah James.
All rights reserved.
First Print Edition: October 2017

Limitless Publishing, LLC
Kailua, HI 96734
www.limitlesspublishing.com

Formatting: Limitless Publishing

ISBN-13: 978-1-64034-241-5
ISBN-10: 1-64034-241-9

No part of this book may be reproduced, scanned, or distributed in any printed or electronic form without permission. Please do not participate in or encourage piracy of copyrighted materials in violation of the author's rights. Thank you for respecting the hard work of this author.

This is a work of fiction. Names, characters, places, and incidents either are the product of the author's imagination or are used fictitiously, and any resemblance to locales, events, business establishments, or actual persons—living or dead—is entirely coincidental.

Dedication

For my Lovelies.
You never stopped begging for the next chapter.
And as always, your wish is my command.
I am raising a flute of champagne—To you. To us.

CONTENT WARNING

Not intended for readers younger than 18.

This book contains dark—and sometimes violent—depictions of the world of organized crime, sexual assault, and suicide, and some events might be triggers for some readers. *This is book 2 of 3. The Mafia and His Angel. Part 1 should be read before, to fully understand the story.*

Prologue

Ayla

There usually comes a time when the darkness becomes too much and you succumb to it. You drown in it, suffocate until you are breathless.

The darkness never truly leaves you. It's always there, waiting for the right moment to strike.

And just like that, the darkness never truly left me. It had been months since I ran away from the nightmare that was slowly killing me. I ran for my life. I ran for my freedom.

Until I had stumbled upon a man I thought would be worse than my nightmare.

Oh, little did I know…

He became my savior, and I was still basking in our blissful times.

Chapter 1

Maddie and I were walking back to my room after dinner when she suddenly stopped on the top stair. Stopping in my tracks, I looked at her sideways. "What's wrong?"

Instead of answering, she called out, "Alessio."

My head snapped in the opposite direction, and I saw Alessio's back to us. He was walking toward his office. At the sound of Maddie's voice, he turned around, his eyebrows furrowed in question.

"What is it?" he mumbled, approaching us.

Maddie dragged me up the last step and stopped in front of Alessio. "I was thinking of taking Ayla out shopping tomorrow. She's been living with us for some time now and doesn't have any clothes except for her maid dresses and the one outfit Mum got her on the first day."

Shopping? Shocked, I stared at Maddie. She didn't tell me anything about this.

From the corner of my eyes, I saw Alessio looking at me. I glanced up, and our eyes met.

Licking my lips nervously, I played with the hem of my dress as his penetrating gaze sent a shiver down my body.

"Of course. You can take her," Alessio said, keeping his blue eyes on me. "But why are you asking me?" he questioned, now looking at Maddie suspiciously.

Maddie rolled her eyes. Letting out a huff of annoyance, she crossed her arms over her chest. "I'm not asking you, I'm telling you. There's a difference. I'm just letting you know so you don't go batshit crazy and start panicking when you don't see Ayla."

I didn't pay attention to Maddie's words because my mind was still trying to register what Alessio said.

I was allowed to go out. Alessio was letting me go out. I stared at Alessio, speechless, my body trembling slightly.

I was never allowed to leave my father's estate, not even a step outside of the gates. The furthest I had ever gone was to our back garden. I wasn't allowed to roam free. Ever. All my days and nights were spent locked in my room or the piano room. I didn't know much about the outside world.

But now, I could go see the world.

I could go shopping...something I never had a chance to do. Alberto was the one who chose all my clothing. I just had to wear what he gave me, a doll he liked to dress and own.

Alessio and Maddie were talking, but their voices sounded like they were coming from under water. I could only focus on Alessio's face. He was slowly giving me things I had lost. Alessio was giving me back my life.

Freedom. I was finally truly free.

The one thing I had always wanted, hoped, and prayed for every night as I cried myself to sleep, my soul breaking. After every torturous night, that was what I dreamed of.

Alessio eyes were on me again. I saw his forehead crease in worry. "Ayla?"

I snapped out of my daze and then nodded my head. "Yeah?"

"Are you okay with going shopping tomorrow?" he asked softly.

I nodded again, but this time my lips stretched in a smile. "Yup."

"Good." He gave me a small smile, then turned around and walked away. Swiveling around, I grabbed Maddie's hands, excitement coursing through my body until I vibrated with it.

"I can go shopping?" I asked, staring into her eyes, my heart feeling hopeful.

"Of course, babe. Why not? You desperately need clothes." She laughed.

We resumed our walk to my bedroom. I was giddy, like a child getting a new toy for the first time. "When are we going?"

"Maybe after lunch? Tomorrow?" she suggested.

"That sounds good. I can't wait," I muttered, closing the door behind us.

Maddie jumped on the bed and took the remote in her hand. "So? What movie?"

I shrugged and joined her on the bed. Propping myself on the pillow, I looked at the TV as she searched for some movies. "I don't know. Maybe something funny." I paused and then looked at Maddie from the corner on my eyes. "And romantic?" I finished.

She laughed. "Gotcha, babe. *The Notebook* it is."

"*The Notebook*?" I questioned as she started the movie.

"Get your tissues ready, Ayla. You're going to love this."

***

I woke up from a kiss behind my ear. The ticklish feeling brought me back from my deep slumber, and I let out a yawn. I moaned, stretching out as the sunlight shone brightly behind my closed eyes. I could feel its warmth bathing my face, and I smiled.

My eyes opened, only to see Alessio sitting next to me. He was already dressed in his suit, his hair a little wet with a few strands sticking to his forehead.

"Good morning," he murmured, gently moving my hair from my face.

"Good morning," I whispered back sleepily.

"I'll see you at breakfast," Alessio said as he got up. Nodding, I watched him smile before he left the room. When the door closed behind him, I turned around and burrowed further into my pillow.

Today was the day. I was going shopping.

Letting out a small, excited laugh, I got up and went to the bathroom. After freshening up, I changed into my black maid dress. Instead of braiding my hair like I usually did, I left it down. It fell in small waves behind my back, just the way Alessio loved it.

My smile dropped when I caught sight of my scars in the mirror. Swallowing hard, I looked down at my arms and traced the pink lines with my fingers. I thought of Alberto.

Slowly, I lost the little hope that was blooming in my chest. My heart clenched.

I couldn't go shopping.

That wasn't possible. Not when Alberto was still looking for me. If I went out, his men would find me and I would be taken back to the hell I had been in. I would have to live my nightmare again.

I didn't think I was strong enough to go through it again. After finding such happiness, if I had to go back, this time…I wouldn't make it out alive.

I had just found my heart; I wasn't ready to lose it.

Taking several deep breaths, I tried to calm the panic rising inside of me. I placed a hand over my chest and controlled my breathing like Sam taught me.

The world eventually stopped twirling, and my vision wasn't blurry anymore. With a shake of my head, I walked out of the bathroom and Alessio's room, closing the door behind me.

How was I going to explain this to Maddie? She was really excited to go shopping with me.

She had everything planned: the shopping and even going as far as making plans to watch a movie afterward and then having dinner before returning home.

I felt guilty, knowing I had to ruin her little

THE MAFIA AND HIS ANGEL PART 2

happy moment.

After serving lunch, I quickly made an excuse about not feeling okay, hoping it would come across as natural.

"I think I'm going to lay down. I don't feel so good," I said quietly beside Maddie.

She glanced at me, and her lips twisted sadly. "Okay. Go take a break," she replied before turning back to the table.

I felt Alessio's eyes on my back as I headed upstairs, but I didn't look back. In my room, I fell on my bed with my face buried in my pillow, feeling completely emotionally and physically drained.

Both of my lives kept intersecting. My past and my present. There was no leaving the past behind.

When I heard Maddie's voice, I quickly sat up. "Ayla, it's me. Can I come in?"

Pressing a trembling hand over my forehead, I shook with tension. I swallowed hard against the ball of nervousness and stood up, taking careful steps toward the door.

Think. Think, Ayla. Think of something.

"I'm coming," I called out in a trembling voice.

I rested a hand on the doorknob and held my stomach with the other, biting on my lips as my shoulders strained with the tension. Opening the door, I gave Maddie a forced smile.

"Hey, are you okay?" she asked worriedly, pushing the door wider to step inside.

"No. I don't feel so good. I have a headache, and my stomach hurts a little," I mumbled, holding my stomach as I leaned against the wall.

Maddie gave me a pitied look before nodding sadly. "It's that time of the month, isn't it? I know it's a pain in the ass. Or vagina, I should say."

I nodded back. At least that was true, so it worked with my fabricated lie.

"We can go shopping another time. No worries. We can shop online today, if you want," she suggested.

"Okay," I replied with a smile. That sounded better, even though I didn't know we could shop online. How much did I actually miss while living with my father and Alberto?

"I'll be right back. Let me get my laptop." Maddie left the room quickly.

I walked back to my bed and sat down. Rubbing my hands over the satin comforter, I found the softness calming. Closing my eyes, I tried to get rid of the negative, painful thoughts. I needed to stop thinking about the past.

"I'm back!" Maddie announced as she came back into the room. "Okay. Let's shop!" She placed the laptop between us.

I couldn't help but laugh at her enthusiasm. She knew how to make a situation lighter. Most importantly, she knew how to make *me* laugh, and that was exactly what I needed.

We shopped for a while. Okay, it was definitely hours. Maddie was a beast at shopping. She was definitely possessed. "Shop till you drop," she muttered, finally shutting her laptop.

"How much was that? You paid for me," I asked quickly. Maddie shrugged and turned on her side to look at me.

"It's okay. You can use your salary the next time we go shopping."

"But how much was that? We bought a lot, Maddie. And that blue dress was expensive," I argued.

"I don't know. It was two thousand something," she mumbled under her breath. "And before you start, I have the money. I might be a *maid*," she stressed the word maid while rolling her eyes, "but Alessio pays me a lot. Allowance and all."

"Sister benefits?"

She nodded with a laugh. "Damn, that makes me sound like a horrible person."

"No. He loves you like a sister and Lena like a mother. It's very obvious. I'm sure the other men feel the same way," I said, lying down on my back beside Maddie. They all respected Maddie and Lena.

The bonding of this family always left me speechless. They were the true definition of *family*. Not by blood, but by choice. Something I never had with my own blood, but with the Ivanshovs, I found a family.

Maddie and I were both silent for some time, both staring at the ceiling, lost in our thoughts. When she finally broke the silence, it wasn't something I ever expected her to say.

"Ayla?"

"Hmm…yeah?"

"I'm weird, aren't I?"

At the question, I grew confused. Turning on my side, I pushed myself on my elbows, facing her as she continued to stare at the ceiling.

"No. Not at all. Why are you asking this?" I questioned.

"They always say that I'm weird. I should be more mature and blah blah blah."

"Who says that? That's horrible." I was outraged at the thought. She was the sweetest person I knew.

"My *friends*," she quoted again, still staring at the ceilings. "I don't have a lot of friends. I lost a lot of them over the years."

"What do you mean?" I asked, my heart growing tighter at the forlorn, distant expression on her face. She was silent for a few minutes, the tension around us growing thicker, as if a dark cloud had settled over us.

"I was sick," she admitted finally. It was a quiet admission, and I stared at her, confused.

"Sick? As in badly sick?" I questioned, moving closer to her.

Maddie nodded. "I had *Hepatitis C* when I was nineteen. After I was cured, I got Leukemia a year after. It's now two years since I have been cancer free."

Her admission left me shell shocked. I didn't know what to say. Not once would I have guessed that she had been deathly sick.

"You know sometimes when you come close to death, you realize what you're missing and what you have been taking for granted. And I was taking my life for granted. After I was cured, I decided that I was going to live my life as if it was my last day. I was going to be happy so that I didn't have any regrets later on."

She paused, a tear slipping down from the corner

of her eyes. Bringing my hand up, I swiped it away. Before I could pull away, she grabbed my hand. "But when I got out of the hospital, after years of fighting to stay alive, I found that I had lost my friends. They'd moved on. I tried to get back into my life, trying to fit in again, but you just *know* when someone doesn't want you anymore. That's how I felt. Unwanted. I was unhappy."

My fingers tightened around hers, giving her strength to continue. Her words brought tears to my eyes. I knew what it was like to feel unwanted. To feel unhappy. So I lent her a tiny bit of strength from me.

"So I left school. I always wanted a degree. Wanted to be a lawyer. That was always my plan, but I couldn't do it anymore. I was already twenty-five, lost with no goal for my life. It felt suffocating. I felt weak and not needed. So I came back to live here with Mum and the others."

Maddie let out a small laugh before turning on her side to face me. "I didn't know I would find happiness here, but I did." She shrugged before continuing. "This is my life now, but I don't want to live it maturely. I want to live it freely."

"I'm glad you were able to move on," I whispered, swiping away the tears on her face. "I don't think you're weird. I think you're the best."

"Truthfully, you are my first friend in so long. That sounds pretty pathetic, doesn't it?"

Letting out a laugh, I shook my head. "No. Because you're my first friend, too."

"Wow," she whispered.

"Yeah."

"Your turn now," Maddie said, pointing at my chest.

"Huh?" I asked confused.

"I shared something. It's your turn."

I let go of her hand and laid down on my back again. Share something? What did I have to share? My truth…they were all messed up. And I couldn't even tell her the whole truth.

But maybe some of it…

"I'm engaged," I whispered to the ceiling.

Maddie was silent beside me. Then she sat up quickly. "Wha-what?" she sputtered.

The words tumbled out of my mouth before I could stop them. I was in a daze, my mind lost as I went back into my past. Images after images, memories after memories flashed in front of my eyes.

"He wasn't a good man. He beat me up. I was raped—lots of times. I don't know anything about others because he never let me go outside. He was really controlling. When I couldn't take it anymore, I ran away, and that was how I found Alessio. I hid in his car to escape *him*."

"Ayla," Maddie gasped, her hands folding over mine.

"He said he loved me. He loved me too much. His love became his obsession."

"That wasn't love, Ayla," Maddie said, her hands squeezing mine in comfort.

"I know," I whispered. Now that I thought of it, I knew Maddie was right. Alberto never loved me. To him, I was just an item to be possessed. Not a human…not someone he *loved*. Alberto played a big part in my undoing. I was his obsession, and he was my downfall. My nightmare.

Now, I knew what love really meant.

Love meant soft kisses, gentle caresses, sweet words, and loving eyes.

And Alberto was none of that…

But I found it here.

"Who is he? Alessio is going to kill that little shit of a human being. God, I don't even know what to call him. I can't wait for Alessio to get his hands on him. He will wish he never laid eyes on you," Maddie growled angrily, her hands tightening around mine.

When I was silent, Maddie came closer, placing a hand over my shoulder. "Ayla, does Alessio know? Did you tell him?"

I shook my head mutely, my throat closing up against my words.

"You have to tell him. He needs to know."

"He knows that I have been raped, but I'm not ready to tell him the other things. I will, but not now. I don't think I'll ever be ready, but I know I have to tell him one day."

"Ayla—"

"And you can't tell him either. Please, Maddie," I begged, quickly sitting up and grasping her hands in mine.

"That's not my story to tell. You have to tell him yourself. But you can't keep this from him for too long. In the end, you'll only hurt him and you. Alessio needs to know."

"I will…I will tell him. But not now." I was delaying the truth, hoping it would buy me time. I

was just trying to find the courage.
 I didn't want to lose what I had just found.
 Not yet.

Chapter 2

"Ayla, be careful. You're going to fall on those rocks," Alessio called out from behind me.

I laughed freely, jumping from one rock to the other before landing in the cold stream. The cold water rushed across my bare feet and came up a little bit above my ankle. "So cold," I called out.

"Yet you still insist on getting your feet wet," he mumbled, coming closer.

"It feels good. You should try it too," I suggested, turning toward him with a smile.

"No, I'm good," Alessio said, stopping at the stream's edge, his hands buried in the pockets of his black slacks.

It had been a week since my conversation with Maddie. Every day, I was tempted to tell Alessio the truth, but my fear for his reaction stopped me every single time. I didn't want to see the hate or disgust in his eyes.

I wanted him to keep looking at me with the same loving, gentle, soft eyes. I wanted his smiles. His soft words and gentle caresses. I wanted them *forever*.

Every day with Alessio felt like heaven. It was a breath of fresh air. A glow of happiness. *He* was my happiness. And I had come to the point where I craved his attention.

He was like a drug, my addiction.

"You don't want to get into the water?" I asked with a pout. Alessio shook his head mutely. The little grey speckles in his blue eyes were twinkling brightly in the sunlight.

Sending him a smile, I bent down and scooped some water in my palms. My steps were slow as I walked toward him, shoving my hands into this face. "Here." I giggled.

Before he could do anything, I threw the cold water in his face. Alessio flinched and reared back in surprise. "What the—" Alessio growled, swiping his hands over his wet face.

Hiding a laugh behind my hands, I took a few cautious steps back. "Oops." I stuck my tongue out at him.

Alessio raised a questioning eyebrow, a smirk on his face. His eyes twinkled mischievously as he cocked his head to the side. Without saying anything, he removed his suit jacket and threw it on the grass. As he rolled the sleeves of his white shirt up, he shook his head.

"I'm giving you a head start, kitten," he said, his voice deep and playful.

My eyes widened, and I let out a small laugh. "You won't be able to catch me," I teased before jumping out of the water and running past him.

"Let's see about that," he yelled. Looking behind

THE MAFIA AND HIS ANGEL PART 2

my back, I saw him coming at me in full force.

Letting out a yelp, I ran faster, turning in circles and running toward the stream again. I felt him coming closer, and as soon as I was on the edge of creek, his arm lashed out and wrapped tightly around my waist, pulling me back.

Alessio picked me up and spun me around in circles, my laughter echoing around the creek.

"Got you," Alessio whispered in my ears. He placed a kiss on the back of my neck. "I'll always catch you, kitten." I melted in his arms, pressing my back against his front. "You've been very bad. Such a little minx."

"Alessio," I breathed as he placed a kiss behind my ear.

I was about to turn around in his embrace, but my feet slipped on the wet grass. My eyes went wide as I let out a yelp, my hands going to Alessio's collar to hold on.

"Fuck," he swore.

Everything happened so fast. First, I was falling, and then I wasn't. But as soon as I had straightened myself, I heard a splash of water and a spring of curses coming from Alessio. Quickly swiveling around, I faced the stream, only to let out a booming laugh when I saw him.

He was sprawled in the water, completely wet, his face a mask of astonishment.

I quickly lost my smile when I saw his face turn expressionless. Standing frozen in my spot, I bit on my lips nervously, scared that he was going to be angry. There was only silence for a few moments.

But then a sudden laugh startled me, and I

jumped slightly.

I stared at Alessio, shocked. He was laughing. Alessio Ivanshov was laughing.

I had never seen or heard him laugh before. He was always a brooding man, his face impassive and hard. Occasionally, he would have a full smile on his face but never a laugh. It was as if it was forbidden in some way.

Such a joyous sound coming from Alessio sounded so foreign. His laugh was deep and rich. His whole face was lit up with it. As his whole body shook, all I could do was stare at him in amazement.

Such a beautiful sound coming from a broken man. When was the last time he laughed so freely?

This…whatever I was feeling in my heart as my chest grew fuller with unnamed emotions…*this* was heaven. *This* was true happiness.

A smile spread across my lips until my cheeks hurt from it. "I've never heard you laugh before," I whispered, kneeling down on the edge.

Alessio quickly lost his laughter, and he looked confused for a second, like he couldn't believe he was actually laughing. He cocked his head to the side, looking at me with a strange expression on his face.

And then he smiled. "I don't think I ever had a reason to laugh before," he whispered back.

We were lost in each other's eyes. Blue to green. Not once did we look away, both of us refusing to break this connection.

When I finally blinked away, I looked down at the rushing water. "You said you didn't want to get into the water, right?" I teased.

Alessio let out a small chuckle. "How the fuck did I fall and you didn't?" he muttered under his breath.

I shrugged at his question. "Give me a hand," he said, holding out his hand. Instead, I rolled my eyes and shook my head.

"I know what you are doing, Alessio. I'm not going to fall for that."

He dramatically placed a hand over his heart. "You wound me, kitten."

Shaking my head at his teasing expression, I stood up. "You should get out of the water or you'll get sick. It's too cold."

"I really need a hand, Ayla. I think I hurt my back."

At his words, I let out a gasp. "What?"

With my heart filled with panic, I ran into the stream and bent down, giving him a hand. "Oh my God. I'm so sorry. Where?"

When I realized my mistake, it was too late. His hurt expression turned into a smirk. Alessio grabbed my hand and pulled. The next thing I knew, I was half sprawled over his chest.

"Oops," he mimicked my words from before.

Slapping him gently on the arm, I looked down at him. "Alessio," I scolded.

"What?" He feigned innocence.

"You're so bad," I murmured, shaking my head.

I felt his hand on the back of my head, his fingers tangling in the dark strands. He pulled my head down until our lips were mere inches apart.

"I never said I was good," he replied, his voice dropping to a huskier tone. And then he claimed my lips in a hard, bruising kiss.

This kiss wasn't gentle or sweet. It was possessive. His tongue licked at my lips, coaxing me to open to his demanding advances. I readily complied, parting my lips to allow him entry. His other hand framed my face to pull me harder into him.

There was so much feeling behind this kiss that I wanted it to last forever.

Starved for air, I broke away long enough to gulp in a breath before Alessio took my lips again. His tongue danced with mine, touching, licking, claiming me.

His lips moved to the corner of my mouth, and he placed a kiss there before dragging his lips down my jaw and the side of my neck. Throwing my head back, I gave him better access, completely lost in him, his kisses and touch driving me insane.

Alessio sat up and shifted me around until my legs were wrapped around his waist. He stood up, his lips never once leaving my skin as he walked out of the water.

Then I was slammed against a tree. His fingers dug into my hips as he brought his lips to mine again. My hair was wrapped tightly into his fist, pulling my head back. I felt his hard length resting between my legs, and my fingers tightened around his shoulders.

Alessio suddenly pulled away harshly. My eyes snapped open in surprise. Both of us were gasping for breath when he laid his forehead against mine. "We need to stop here," he said gruffly, his eyes still closed.

Thank you.

My hands moved from his shoulders to his neck, and I held on, as if he was my saving grace. "Okay," I whispered back.

He took a deep breath and opened his eyes. *Lust*. That was what I saw. His *need* for me. His blue eyes glinted with it.

"Alessio."

He shook his head. "I just need a minute," he said before closing his eyes again, his breathing harsh.

Alessio always stopped himself. For me. He put *his* need aside, giving me what *I* needed. Always thinking of me first. After my breakdown, he never pushed for more. This was the first time he lost control like that, yet he didn't let it go too far.

Palming his face, I gently rubbed my fingers over his cheeks. I placed a kiss on the tip of his nose and then gave him a quick peck on the lips. "Thank you," I whispered against his lips.

Chapter 3

I was lying back against the tub, my eyes closed, my hands running over the warm water. It was late at night, and after playing the piano for Alessio, I couldn't sleep.

All I could think about was the moment at the creek that morning. Every time, the same images flashed behind my eyes. Alessio kissing me. Our *need* for each other.

And then I would remember how it was when he had made love to my body.

My body warmed up under the thoughts of his lips and hands on me again. Letting out a tired sigh, I opened my eyes and stepped out of the water, drying myself with the big white towel. But instead of putting on my nightdress, I wrapped the towel over my shoulder, staring at myself in the mirror.

"What am I doing?" I whispered to my reflection. "Can I do this?"

Alessio wanted me…and I wanted him too.

I craved his touch.

Placing a hand over my chest, I felt my pounding

heart. "I don't want to be scared anymore."

I wanted to be free. I wanted to live. I wanted to feel…everything.

I wanted Alessio.

I opened my eyes, making direct contact with my own green eyes in the reflection.

Holding the towel tighter around me, I glanced at the mirror one final time before turning around. My hand rested on the knob for several minutes, pulling at the strength and courage inside of me to open the door and go to Alessio.

I was at a constant battle in my mind. Fear on one side, while the other demanded freedom and happiness.

With my final decision made, I took a deep breath and opened the door. Alessio was sitting on the bed, leaning against the headboard with only his black sweatpants on. He was looking down at his phone but quickly looked up when I walked into the room.

"Ayla?" he questioned, his eyebrows furrowed at the sight of me. "Why are you only in your towel?"

Sitting forward in bed, he placed the phone on the nightstand. "Are you okay?" he asked worriedly, tension cording the muscles of his shoulders.

My eyes met his, and I held on. He gave me strength. "I don't want to be scared anymore," I told him.

"Ayla," he started, confusion clear in his voice and expression.

Quickly dropping the towel to reveal my bare body, I took a nervous step forward. My hands fisted to my side as I walked toward the bed, stopping beside Alessio.

He must have understood what I meant, because his eyes softened. "Ayla," he sighed. Pushing his arm toward me with his palm up, he gave me his hand. "Come here."

Swallowing hard, I put my hand in his and he grasped mine tightly. My hand trembled, but Alessio gave me a gentle squeeze before pulling me forward. I climbed onto the bed, and he shifted me around, pulling me onto his lap so that I straddled him, my knees on either side of his hips.

Bringing his other hand up, he softly rubbed his thumb over my lips. "Are you sure?"

I nodded mutely, finding it hard to voice out anything. "Ayla, I need the words. I need to know you are one hundred percent sure about this."

"I'm sure," I replied, my voice barely audible. Placing his forehead against mine, he let out another sigh.

"Okay. We'll do it like this. With you on top," he said.

Me? On top?

Panic filled me, and my hand tightened around his. "I…"

But he quickly shushed me. "I know. It's okay."

I didn't know how to do anything. I had never done this.

"Here." He lifted me from his lap and placed me on the bed beside him. Alessio quickly removed his sweatpants and boxers, throwing them on the floor so that he was naked too. He pulled me on his lap again, in the same position as before.

THE MAFIA AND HIS ANGEL PART 2

"Alessio, I don't know…" I murmured.

He smiled and shook his head. "You do. Let your mind and body go. Your body knows what to do. You are in charge, Ayla. Do whatever you want."

I was in control. For the first time.

Sending him a shaky smile, I placed my hands over his chest and pushed until he was reclined on the bed. I wasn't sure what to do afterward, but when I felt his length twitch between my legs, I trembled and shifted slightly, causing his tip to rub against my sensitive core.

He touched me last time, but I never had a chance to explore him. My hands moved over his chest and his stomach, feeling his muscles ripple under my wandering touch.

When my hands reached his pelvis, just above his hardened length, I stopped. My head snapped up toward Alessio, looking for help, not knowing what to do.

His hand grasped mine, and he placed it over the rigid head, wrapping my fingers around the length. Our eyes stayed connected as he moved my hands up and down. And then he let go.

Looking down, I rubbed my thumb over the tip and gave him a small squeeze. "Fuck," Alessio swore. Believing that I did something wrong, I quickly looked up, only to find his eyes hooded with lust.

Feeling confident in my actions, I moved my hands again, squeezing the length at the same time. Alessio's finger dug into my hips, and he let out a growl.

"Like this," he muttered, curling his hand over mine again, tightening my grasp. He worked from top to bottom, tightening and loosening our grip until moisture formed at the tiny slit. Rubbing my thumb over it, I coated the tip fully.

"Ayla, if you keep doing this, I'm going to come."

"Isn't that a good thing?" I asked.

"Little minx," he replied, his voice slightly hoarse.

With my hand still wrapped around him, I leaned forward, tilting my hips up slightly, my breasts bobbing forward toward Alessio. I wasn't sure what to do, feeling lost.

I was about to lower myself, but Alessio's hands were like a band of steel around my hips, stopping my movement. "You are not ready for this yet."

"Huh?" I asked, confused. Smiling, he pulled me from his hardness and moved me over his chest.

"Alessio, what are you doing?" I asked, pressing my hands to his chest as I stared down at him with wide eyes.

"I'm getting you ready, kitten. Move up. Straddle my face," he ordered.

Straddle his face? His hands came down to my thighs, holding me still. Nervous, I slowly moved into the position he told me. With my knees on either side of his face, I held onto the headboard.

His breath feathered over my clenching core. My head fell back at the strange sensation. When I felt his tongue at my entrance, I let out a moan.

As my body responded with a rush of wetness, Alessio's fingers tightened on my thighs. He ran his tongue over my wet lips, lapping at the wetness there. He licked, teased, sucked, and drove me insane with his tongue until I was shaking uncontrollably. My body clenched, desperate for my release.

"Alessio," I moaned, my knuckles going almost white at how hard I was holding the headboard. My hips rocked against his mouth, grinding into his face. I sighed and whimpered against his torturous ministration.

I was so close, dangling over the edge yet not falling over.

He pushed his tongue inside me and groaned, and my eyes closing at the sensation building in my lower region. He was relentless, pushing me over the edge so many times but refusing to let me fall. I let go a sharp cry when he brought a hand up and pressed a finger against my tiny nub.

"Alessio!" As my orgasm rushed through me, my thighs tightened around his head.

I was still lost in the intense ecstasy surrounding my mind and body when Alessio lifted me from his face and pushed me over his cock again.

"Wait," he muttered, leaning over to the side to open the drawer and removing a box. I stared at him as he took the condom out and rolled it over himself.

He smirked. "Now you are ready. Take me, Ayla." His words were deep and filled with need.

My entrance was right over his tip, and I swallowed nervously, my thighs still shaking from my orgasm. Alessio's eyes glinted, and he grasped my hips again, lifting me up slightly. His rigid length strained upward as he fitted me over his cock and began to pull me down. "Like this."

We both gasped when he sank slowly into me, my eyes almost closing at the wondrous feeling. I paused as he reached my depth, my body spasming around him.

But when the sudden dark memories started to surround me, I went still. Alessio's hands tightened around me. "Ayla, open your eyes," he demanded quickly.

My eyes snapped open at his command, and I looked at him for help, scared that I would fall back into the darkness.

"Keep your eyes on me, Ayla. Just me. Look at me. Only me. It's only *me*, Ayla," he whispered gently, his thumb gently caressing my sides.

Only him. It was only Alessio. Just him.

"There you are. Keep looking at me. Don't take your eyes off me," he continued in the same deep voice.

Alessio raised a hand and removed my hair from my bun, letting it fall over my back and shoulders. He stroked my hair gently, soothing me with a soft smile. "Easy and slow. We're taking it slow."

Letting my hair go, he grasped my hips again and helped me with the movement. Slowly lifting me up, I began a slow descent again, my whole body trembling with the sensation.

Only *Alessio*. He surrounded me. He overwhelmed my senses until he was the only one I could sense, see, feel, or hear. He was everything.

As I sheathed his cock inside me, going as deep as I could, I continued to stare down at him. His breathing was ragged, almost painful. Sweat formed over his forehead, same as me.

"Alessio," I breathed. His fingers dug in my skin, giving me confidence to continue moving again. I gave a tentative twist, and he groaned, his hips arching off the bed.

"Ayla."

I couldn't help but smile. He liked it. Growing coy under his gaze, I placed my hands over his chest, levering myself up, his hardness gliding inside my wet heat. Slowly moving up and down, I watched his every reaction. When I twisted my hips over him, his hips rose to meet mine, the action pushing him further inside me.

I moaned louder, and he swore. "Fuck."

Alessio slowly took control, thrusting his hips upward, slow and deep each time. "Ayla, I'm going to switch us around," he said, his voice hoarse.

When I nodded, he quickly rolled us over until I was on my back and he was positioned between my legs over me.

When I let go a gasp, he placed a kiss on my lips. "Keep your eyes on me. It's only me. No one else but me."

I nodded, keeping our eyes connected as he thrust inside of me again. His groan vibrated from his chest, and I soaked it all up.

My hands frantically flew to his shoulders, holding on as my body trembled with the ferocity of the sensation coursing through my body.

Alessio paused, our gazes held. "Okay?"

"Okay."

"Hold on to me, Ayla. Don't let me go."

Nodding again, I twined my hands behind his head. As he withdrew, my fingers curled around his neck. "Oh…Alessio."

And then he pushed again, stretching me with his fullness. I felt my pussy stretch to accommodate him, the pressure inside of me building faster than before.

He pulled back slightly and pushed back in. Instinctively, I tilted my hips up, and he thrust hard inside. I let out a gasp, followed by an unashamed loud moan, and my nails bit into his back.

Alessio started to move, finding a rhythm as our eyes stayed glued on each other. In and out. Slowly at first and then a little faster. Harder. Deeper. My body swelled and quivered. There was no space between us. Our bodies moved fluidly as if they knew each other for years.

No words were spoken. Only our bodies spoke, moving with each other's in ease. Our harsh breathing filled the room, and our eyes stayed on each other through it all.

Leaning his forehead on mine, he grasped my thighs and pushed them upward until I was opened to him.

"I got you," he muttered.

I was balancing over the edge, ready to fall, and I begged Alessio silently. My body was strung tight, my muscles corded together. I needed relief. I needed *him*.

I knew he was close when his thrust became faster. Alessio reached underneath me and cupped my back, tilting me upward as he plunged forward again.

As soon as he rested deep inside me, my orgasm exploded with such ferocity. My vision blurred as my body went limp under Alessio. My body wasn't my own anymore. It was broken into tiny pieces. I was floating, a limp mess.

He thrust into me one final time. Deeper and harder. And I heard him groan loud and deep, his face twisted almost painfully as he twitched above me with his orgasm. His hips jerked against mine. He quivered with his release as we came together.

In that moment, I was his. Only his.

Our eyes were connected, but our souls came together too, bonding, holding tight, refusing to ever let go.

Alessio let go and laid on top of my shaking body, heaving desperately for breath as I did the same. I couldn't process what just happened. My mind was fuzzy, my heart full as I wrapped my arms around Alessio's shoulders.

Was this how it felt? To be with someone…like this?

Tears blinded my vision as I quickly blinked them away. Alessio buried his face in my neck, and he placed a kiss there.

Finally lifting his head, he looked at me with soft blue eyes. "Are you okay?"

"Mhm…"

"Sure?"

"Mhm."

He let out a small laugh. "Is that all you can say?"

"Mhm."

I really couldn't say anything else. My body was

sore and languid. I could barely keep my eyes open.

"Have I worn you out, kitten?" he whispered before taking my lips in a sweet kiss.

"Mhm."

Pulling back, he chuckled at my lack of words. He gave me a quick peck on the nose before rolling off me.

I closed my eyes, my body still spread over the bed, too tired to move. I heard the water run in the washroom, and then a few minutes later, I felt something warm between my legs.

My eyes opened to see Alessio cleaning me with a warm towel. "I got you," he whispered the same words again.

He went back to the bathroom to dispose of the towel before walking out in all his nakedness again. Alessio joined me on the bed and pulled the cover over us. Lying on his back, he pulled me into him until I was half on top of him. My head rested on his chest, my arms thrown over his waist, and my legs tangled with his.

I sighed and snuggled tighter into his warm and safe embrace.

Alessio placed a kiss on my forehead, his arms tightening around my back in a protective manner. "Sleep, Ayla."

With the sound of his beating heart to my ear, I let sleep take over, letting my mind and body go.

But before I fell asleep, a thought registered into my mind. I smiled sleepily, my heart dancing with happiness.

Alessio didn't fuck me.

He made love to me.

Chapter 4

Alessio

Ayla made a slow descent over my cock, and as soon I rested deep inside her, I saw panic flash in her eyes, her body freezing for a second. My fingers instinctively tightened on her hips.

I could sense her spiraling down toward the darkness, but I wasn't going to let her lose herself again.

"Ayla, open your eyes," I demanded quickly. Her eyes snapped open instantly, fear glistening in her pleading green eyes. She wanted this, as much as me, yet she was scared of falling back into the darkness.

I tried to soothe her, and slowly, the fear started to disappear from her eyes.

"Easy and slow. We're taking it slow," I soothed with my words.

Slow. A strange word to describe sex. I've never done *slow* before. It used to be just raw fucking. But with Ayla, it was different.

Ayla seemed to accept my words, and her body relaxed.

There was only me and her.

Not my past or hers. It was just *us*. Alessio and Ayla. Both of us lost in each other's eyes. Both of us lost in each other.

I never thought it was possible to feel that way. To feel so deeply connected to one person, but with Ayla, I felt it. Her fear, her pain…it was my own. In this moment, I felt everything.

A moan escaped past her lips, and that was enough to snap the little shred of control I had. "Ayla, I'm going to switch us around." I groaned as her pussy clenched around my cock.

When she nodded, I quickly rolled us around and positioned myself between her spread thighs before thrusting deep inside of her. A gasp whispered across her parted lips, and I placed a kiss there. "Keep your eyes on me. It's only me. Just me. No one else but me."

I gave a tentative push, and she moaned, her back arching up. "Don't let go of me," I whispered. Ayla nodded, and her hands frantically moved to my shoulders as I thrust inside of her again. Resting deep inside her tight pussy, my muscles tightened with the need to come.

I pulled back slightly before pushing back in. Taking her legs, I pushed them upward until the soles of her feet rested on the bed and she was wide open to me. I picked up the pace, my movement urgent as we both raced toward our release. Faster and deeper, we found a rhythm, our bodies moving together.

I wanted this to last longer, but I knew she was close. I was too, my cock swelling inside her, stretching her tight walls.

She moaned, her nails biting into my back. Her body was strung tight, her muscles corded together with tension and intense pleasure. Her eyes begged me for release, and I gladly gave it to her.

Grasping her ass, I tilted her hips upward, slamming inside of her, my pelvis pressing against her clit. She gasped, and then I felt her clench tightly around me as she came. Her body quivered with her release, and her face softened, her eyes turning glassy.

Her tight pussy sucked me deeper into her, driving me insane. Thrusting into her one last time, I found my release too. I jerked inside her, my fingers tightening on her thighs in a bruising grip. Our eyes stayed connected as we came, and that was the most intimate moment in my life.

This was more than just fucking. It was more. It meant more. I didn't fuck her. I made love to her, something I've never done before.

But Ayla was everything.

She was an Angel. She deserved more than just a simple fuck. She deserved sweet loving.

I didn't think I could feel this way, but with Ayla, I had no control of my feelings. She overwhelmed my senses, surrounding me with her sweet, gentle soul. She made me *feel*.

Collapsing on top of her soft body, I buried my face in her neck as we both rode our orgasms, both of us lost in this raw bliss. No words were spoken. They weren't needed.

My breathing was harsh to my own ears as my heart pounded rapidly and loudly against my ribcage, matching Ayla's. Placing a kiss over her bare shoulder, I lifted my head and stared down into her hazy green eyes. "Are you okay?"

She hummed. I had worn her out.

Letting out a chuckle at her lack of words, I eased out of her, and her eyes closed with a sigh, her body going limp. Smiling, I gave her a quick peck on the nose and rolled off the bed.

I made my way to the washroom and rolled the condom off me, dropping it into the bin beside the counter. I soaked a towel and cleaned myself before returning to the room with another warm towel.

Ayla was still in the same position I left her, and I couldn't help but smile. I could go all night, but she wasn't ready for that yet.

Kneeling on the bed beside her, I cleaned the mess we made between her thighs. She smiled groggily at me before closing them again. Shaking my head with a low chuckle, I went to the bathroom and threw the towel into the basket.

I joined her in bed again and wrapped my arms around Ayla, pulling her into my body. Her body cocooned into mine, and my heart thumped to a strange beat. "Sleep, Ayla," I told her softly.

I watched Ayla's eyes flutter closed, and almost immediately she was asleep, her breathing soft and even. My arm tightened around her waist, and she snuggled tighter into me, a sigh of contentment escaping past her lips.

I stroked a hand through her hair, my fingers softly gliding behind her back. After everything she had been through, she trusted me. But there was a fear instilled inside of me. I had no control over what I felt for Ayla.

The thought of having any type of feelings for any woman almost paralyzed me. I couldn't allow it. It couldn't happen. History couldn't repeat itself.

But it was too late.

Ayla had become my weakness. My *only* weakness. A weakness I couldn't have.

Even though this fear was constant in my mind, it was a fight I couldn't win. I had tried to steel myself, building a wall between Ayla and myself. But she had broken those walls.

Without even doing much, she had made her way into my heart. Ayla had won. No matter how hard I tried to hold back, I was lost in her. Completely and deeply lost in her.

Chapter 5

I walked into the kitchen the next morning to find Maddie and Lena finishing up with breakfast. As soon as Maddie saw me, she waved. "Good morning. Where's Ayla?"

"She's still sleeping. I'm going to take our breakfast upstairs," I said, nodding toward the tray.

"Oh." Maddie raised an eyebrow at me, her eyes glistening mischievously, but I just glared. She shrugged. "I'll set a tray for you," she mumbled, tilting her face down as she hid her smile. Leaning against the wall, I waited for her. "There you go," she said, giving me the tray.

Taking it from her hand, I turned around to leave. "Thank you," I said before leaving the kitchen and making my way upstairs.

Closing the door behind me, I walked further into the room to find the bed empty. I frowned and placed the tray on the coffee table, looking around the room for Ayla.

"Ayla?" I called out.

When I heard the bathroom door open, I quickly

swiveled around and saw Ayla coming out with a towel in her hand. She was dressed in her maid outfit.

"Alessio," she breathed at the sight of me. "I thought you left."

"I went to get us breakfast," I muttered, walking toward her.

"Oh," she whispered, looking down almost shyly. I found it endearing that she was feeling shy even after last night.

Placing a finger under her chin, I tilted her head up. "Why do you always look away from me?"

She bit down on her lips nervously, and I wrapped my arms around her, pulling her closer. With her soft body plastered against mine, I felt myself harden as I remembered the night before.

Ayla shrugged at my question and placed her hands over my chest. She licked her plump lips, and before I could stop myself, my lips were on hers.

Her lips were soft like velvet, and I licked the seams, demanding entrance. She gave in to my demands, and our tongues moved together in a fiery dance. She met my kiss with the same intensity, pushing her body closer to mine.

Ayla consumed me. Mind, body, and soul. She was right; she was fire, and I was going to burn. We were both going to burn.

Gasping for breath, we broke the kiss. Her fingers tightened around my suit jacket, and she sighed.

"Are you hungry?" I asked, pulling away.

She nodded with a smile and placed a hand over her stomach. "Famished."

Taking her hand in mine, I walked us toward the sofa. I sat down and grasped her hips, pulling her to my lap. Ayla laughed and snuggled into my embrace.

"Are you going to feed me?" she teased, raising an eyebrow at me.

"Do you want me to feed you?"

"No." She laughed.

I had to smile. The free and happy expression on her face was something I wanted to savor and never forget. Her laughter did something to my heart.

Her happiness made me happy. She calmed me. In the same way that I brought her peace, she brought me peace too. I haven't felt peace since my mother's death. It was now a foreign emotion. But with Ayla, I could forget all the darkness inside of me.

Placing a kiss on her forehead, I leaned forward and picked up a piece of biscuit and held it to her lips.

Ayla looked at me strangely and hesitated for a second before taking a bite. I alternated between feeding her bites of eggs, toast, and some fruit. "Do you want juice?" I asked, brushing away the crumbs that rested on the corner of her lips.

"Hmm…"

I was about to grab the glass when Ayla stopped me with a hand on my arm. "You haven't eaten anything yet," she murmured.

I chuckled low under my breath. I didn't even realize that. Ayla smiled and then leaned forward, taking a piece of toast in her hand and slowly pressing it to my lips.

Surprise filled me, and I opened my mouth, letting her feed me the piece. Encouraged by my response, this time she took her turn to feed me. It was something unusual, but it felt intimate. This moment shared between us was something special.

As she brought the glass of juice to my lips, I stopped her. "What are you doing, Ayla?"

"I'm feeding you," she replied, cocking her head to the side.

"Why?"

"Because I want to." Ayla brought her other hand up and placed it over my cheek, rubbing her thumb back and forth. "I don't know how to repay you for this, Alessio. For everything you've done for me. I guess I just want to do the little things I can, to let you know how I feel."

She lightly caressed over my jawline and then pressed her fingers to my lips. "Sometimes words aren't enough," she whispered.

Her words did crazy things to my heart.

Ayla moved the glass closer, and I parted my lips for her. Our gaze never left each other as I drank from the glass. When I was done, she took a sip and then placed the glass on the tray.

She never ceased to amaze me.

Ayla stared at me for a few seconds, her expression changing from happy to uncertain. I saw her swallow hard, and then she leaned forward, quickly placing a kiss on my lips before moving back.

I felt an eyebrow arch in question, and she ducked her head timidly. I lifted her chin up and dipped my head, moving down until our lips were mere inches apart. Ayla's eyes flared in surprise, and she leaned forward again until our lips were joined together.

The first touch of our lips felt electrifying, almost like the first time I kissed her. Every time I kissed her was like the first. Our kiss was light and exquisitely gentle. She sighed almost dreamily into my lips as we broke off the kiss.

Ayla made a little contented sound and snuggled deeper into my chest. She placed a kiss on my shoulder and rested her head there.

A sense of comfort filled my heart as I wrapped my arms around her. I never thought I would need this. Holding someone, just being like this. Silent but still connected. This wasn't what I was looking for, but Ayla came crashing into my life and gave me something I didn't even know I needed.

My father was right.

An angel is someone who is sweet, kind, caring, calm, and mellow. The most beautiful woman on the planet. Someone who is amazing in every way. She is the girl who makes your heart beat faster when she walks into the room. The girl you will need wherever you go. The girl who makes you want to be better. Angel is someone who is your rock.

I gave up hope of finding my Angel a long time ago. After I lost my mother, the only person who was my everything, I believed that Angels didn't exist. I thought it was all a lie.

But Ayla…she truly was an Angel.

***

Walking into my office, I saw my men already waiting for me. Seeing them reminded me of who I actually was. For the past few days, I had been so lost in Ayla, only focusing on her. But now it was time to be *Alessio Ivanshov*. It wasn't easy, leading almost a double life…an experienced and well-known businessman by day and a crime lord by night. But this was second nature for me. I was bred to do so since my first breath.

"Give me a brief summary of everything," I demanded as I took a seat behind my table.

Nikolay leaned away from the wall and started. "I've done rounds through the clubs. Fifteen in all. Alberto has been quiet around them, and there has not been much activity from his men. The women are safe. As safe as they can be in a place like that."

I nodded and looked at Artur. "What happened to the other women?"

He shook his head, dejection clear on his face. "We didn't get there in time. There were kids with them too."

Pounding a fist on the table, I stood up as fierce anger assaulted me. "How the fuck didn't you get there in time? You knew about this for a week."

"Boss, he knew we were spying. His men took a different route to deliver the women and the kids to the buyer."

"Fuck!" I swore, raking my fingers through my hair in frustration. "How many?"

"About twenty women," he said, looking down in defeat.

Alberto was part of a human trafficking ring. Because of his alliance with the Mexican cartel, it was too strong to stop.

I had just failed twenty women. Twenty women and kids I could have saved.

"You're no longer in control of this job," I growled at Artur. His head snapped up, and he stared at me in shock.

"Nikolay is taking over," I said through gritted teeth. "Next time, I don't want a fucking mistake on this."

"Boss," Nikolay nodded, his face filled with conviction.

"Viktor," I snapped toward him.

"I've been keeping tabs on Alberto, and Mark called back with details," he started calmly and then paused.

"Alberto is weak on his own, but if he had the other's alliance, then he is much stronger. He's in deep with the Mexican cartel. He wants to expand his empire. He knows the only way to weaken you is by getting the others on his side, business-wise."

Sitting down, I rubbed a hand over my face, my body vibrating with rage and a thirst for my enemies' blood. Squeezing my hands in first, I closed my eyes. I thought about asking for support from the other Families.

Even though I was the *Pakhan*, the Boss—the Russian Mafia consisted of four families in all. They would come to my help if asked…but I had to deal with this shit on my own. For now.

When I heard the door, my eyes snapped open to see Phoenix coming in. "Boss," he greeted with a nod.

"What the fuck happened to you?" Viktor asked,

looking at Phoenix in astonishment. I was wondering the same thing.

The right side of Phoenix's face was red, quickly turning purple and forming a bruise, and his nose was bleeding a little.

"Maddie punched me," he stated calmly, his face expressionless.

Artur's face turned stoic at the mention of Maddie's name, and he turned to Phoenix, moving into his face. "What did you do to her?"

Phoenix stood up straighter, his shoulders bunching tensely. His eyes turned a shade darker as he replied, acting almost nonchalant. "Why don't you ask her?"

Artur's expression was almost murderous, but Nikolay quickly stepped in. "Phoenix, what is the meaning of this?"

Instead of answering, he turned to me and reported back. "There was a fight at one the clubs. Two were badly injured. The mess was cleaned up before the police came. Everything is clear."

I nodded. "What about the underground rings?"

"The underground rings are running perfectly. We got two more fighters. They're really good. The best, I would say," Phoenix replied. "They fight for blood." And that was exactly what the underground rings were about. Blood. Either death or win. We could make millions in one night. Easy fucking money.

Nodding, I closed my eyes and leaned back against my chair. I didn't have to say anything else. They knew the meeting was finished. I heard my men shuffling around and the door opening.

"Viktor," I called out without opening my eyes.

"Yeah?"

"Call Lyov and Isaak."

Maybe I needed their help.

Viktor swore under his breath but didn't say anything else. The door closed and then silence.

The silence was almost suffocating, and my skin prickled with tension. I clenched my hands in fists and then unclenched them again. Doing that for some time, I tried to control the monster inside of me.

Ayla's face suddenly flashed behind my closed eyes. Just the thought of her calmed me, and I felt the rage slowly diminish.

Angel.

Chapter 6

Maddie

My muscles ached as I quickly undressed. I needed sleep. Like now. But I knew Artur was supposed to visit me, so I waited.

I was combing my hair when I saw the door open in the mirror's reflection. He closed the door behind him and walked toward me. "Hmm…that's what I like to see," he murmured, his lustful eyes raking over my naked body. Artur stood behind me and wrapped an arm around my waist, pulling me to him. "Do you know how beautiful you are?" he asked, placing a kiss on my shoulder.

"You tell me every day, but I'm not complaining. I wouldn't mind if you say it one more time," I replied, placing my hand over his arm.

"You are so beautiful that you take my breath away. The sexiest woman I've ever seen," he muttered, his arms tightening around my waist in an almost bruising grip. "And all mine," he growled possessively.

"Yours," I moaned.

His hand wandered toward my already weeping pussy, and I felt myself clench in anticipation. But then he stopped. I moaned in protest, my head falling back against his shoulder. "Damn it. Artur, stop teasing me."

My eyes opened, and I stared at our reflection in the mirror. I saw him frowning, his eyebrows pulled together thoughtfully.

"I was wondering. Why did you punch Phoenix?"

My eyes widened at his question, and I froze. How did he know that?

"Wha-What?" I sputtered.

"Phoenix's face was a mess this morning. And he said you punched him. What did he do? Is he being a problem?" he asked, placing his chin on my shoulder as he looked into my eyes through the reflection.

My throat went dry at the question, my hands clenched in fist, my nails digging into my skin.

My legs were wrapped around Artur's hips as he pressed me against the wall. His lips claimed mine in a bruising kiss. "Good morning," he muttered.

"I like how you say good morning," I laughed against his lips. His fingers tightened on my hips, and I kissed him again.

When I pulled back, I caught a glimpse of Phoenix standing behind Artur, his expression almost painful and murderous.

"Artur, Boss is looking for you," he snapped.

Artur pulled away from me and glanced behind

his back at Phoenix. "Okay." Putting me down, he gave me a quick peck on the lips. "I'll see you tonight."

"Okay," I replied, smiling up at me. He turned around and gave Phoenix a nod before going upstairs.

Phoenix didn't move. He kept his eyes locked on mine. I saw his hands fisted at his sides.

"What the hell is your problem?" I asked almost angrily. "Every time you see me with Artur, you act like some type of caveman. This has gone on for too long now."

He silently took a step forward, and I paused in my furious rant. Phoenix stalked toward me and stopped when our bodies were just inches apart and I was forced against the wall.

Swallowing nervously at his close proximity, I took a deep breath and then glared up at him. "Move away, asshole. Ever heard of personal space?"

When he didn't, I placed my hands over his chest to push him away. "What the fuck is your problem?" I hissed, but he didn't move.

Instead, he grabbed my hands and held them to his chest. Before I could blink or think, his other arm quickly snaked around my waist. He pulled me into his body, his hold unyielding.

"What th—" I started to say, but he cut me off.

"Shut up."

And then he slammed his lips on mine. I gasped in shock, and he took the opportunity to slide his tongue in my mouth. I didn't move at first, but instinctively, I surrendered to his kiss. My lips moved over his, tentatively at first. He growled low in his chest and deepened the kiss.

He pulled back and glared down at me. "This. This is my fucking problem," he said, brushing his thumb over my sensitive lips.

Gasping, I pushed him away and stumbled back into the wall. "You bastard," I whispered, wiping my lips with the back of my hand. "How dare you?"

"You kissed me back. You want this."

"I'm with Artur," I murmured in shock.

"He doesn't matter," he replied, his face expressionless.

"Fuck you!" I said through gritted teeth, my breathing harsh to my own ears.

"That's what I'm saying."

Moving forward in a flash, I reared back and punched him in the face. He swore loudly and held his nose.

"Keep your hands off me. I swear to God, you come near me again, I will hurt you."

I walked away, leaving him behind. But as I went, my eyes prickled with hot tears. Blinking them away, I refused to let them fall.

How dare he?

After everything…after so long…why now?

The sound of my name brought me back to the present. I blinked in shock and stared at Artur through the mirror. He gave me a confused look and turned me around in his arms. "Are you okay?"

"Yeah. I'm fine. Phoenix was just teasing me and being annoying. I got mad and kinda punched him in the face. You know how I am."

"He isn't going to be a problem? I can talk to him if you want," Artur suggested, giving me a quick peck on the lips.

"No, it's okay. I have everything under control," I replied with a shake of my head. Artur still gave me a suspicious look. I sweetly smiled up at him, trying to distract him.

I didn't want him to think about Phoenix.

And *I* didn't want to think about Phoenix. He wasn't important. *Not anymore.* It was just me and Artur. And I wanted to get lost in the man who was standing in front of me, looking down at me as if I was his everything.

Running my hands over his chest and hard stomach, I made my way down until I palmed his cock through his black pants. I gave him a squeeze, and he hissed, instantly hardening under my teasing touch.

"So where were we? I believe you owe me an orgasm, Mister. Or maybe several," I teased.

"Fuck," he muttered. Grabbing me around the waist, he threw me on the bed before falling on top of me. Spreading my thighs, he settled between them.

"This is going to be a long night, baby."

"Oh, I was hoping it would be," I replied coyly, moving my hands to his shoulders.

Chapter 7

Ayla

1 week later

I was quickly getting dressed when I saw Alessio coming out of the bathroom with only a towel wrapped around this waist. My eyes followed his movement across the room, and I saw him smirk when he caught my eyes on him.

Stopping in front of me, he arched an eyebrow at me mischievously. "Like what you see?"

Letting out a sigh, I shook my head in exasperation. Alessio could be infuriating sometimes. He was calm and outright arrogant. Not to forget confident in everything. But those were the few things I liked about him. He wasn't borderline or rude.

Alessio knew he was hot and used it to his advantage every time.

"You know I do," I mumbled under my breath with a roll of my eyes.

"Louder. I didn't hear that," he said, moving closer to me.

Shaking my head, I laughed. "Nope. I'm not saying it louder. You clearly heard it."

"Kitten," Alessio warned.

I shivered at his nickname for me. I wasn't in denial anymore. I loved it when he called me that. There was something so primitive, intense, and enticing about the way he said it.

"Alessio, I'm going to be late. I need to help Maddie and Lena with breakfast," I admonished, taking a step away from him.

He crossed his arms, staring at me expectantly. Shaking my head, I smiled. He was so hard to resist. "No."

Giving him another look, I turned around and went to the bathroom to fix my hair. I was pulling my hair up in a ponytail when I saw Alessio walking in, already dressed in his black suit.

He walked toward me and wrapped his arm around my waist, pulling me into his body until my back was to his front. "You didn't kiss me *good morning*," he muttered, staring at me through the mirror.

Oh, I forgot. He was also very demanding.

Pushing my hair to the side, Alessio placed wet kisses along the length of my neck. He bit, sucked, and licked until I was putty in his arms.

I melted into his embrace, pushing my body into his. He found my sweet spot behind my ear and teased me with his tongue. Grazing the sensitive skin with his teeth, he chuckled when I trembled against his teasing touch.

My head fell back against his chest as he dragged his lips to the base of my neck and nipped at my shoulder before sucking on the tortured skin.

I let out a moan, pushing back into his hard body. "Alessio…"

He hummed against my skin, his arms tightening around me.

"We can't…I'm going to be…late…" I breathed as he continued to tease me with his torturous ministration. My body quivered when I felt his fingers at the end of my dress, slowly pushing upward, baring my thighs.

He was slowly seducing me, and I didn't have the strength to say *no*. His fingers moved to my panties, and he pressed against the fabric, right over my heated core. I whimpered as he teased me through my satin cloth. I squirmed in his embrace, feeling his length harden against my back.

"I can feel how wet you are, and I've barely touched you, kitten," he growled against my ear.

Placing a kiss there, he removed his hand from under my dress, leaving me feeling strangely empty. "You are going to be late, right?" he murmured. "We don't want Maddie angry."

I let out a sigh and turned around in his arms. After a week, I knew him well enough to know Alessio was teasing me. He loved leaving me over the edge, dangling, begging for release. Only then would he give me what I wanted.

"You are so bad for me," I muttered, resting my hands over his chest.

"I know," he replied. "You are bad for me too."

Giggling at his response, I placed a kiss over his

chest. Alessio grasped my hands and held them over his chest. Placing a finger under my chin, he lifted my head up and dipped his before claiming my lips. The kiss started slow and gentle at first, but then he kissed me like he was starving.

The kiss was brutal and possessive. He kissed me like I was his everything.

Alessio's hold was unyielding around my waist as he pulled me closer. He let go of my hands and wrapped his fingers around my hair, twisting my ponytail tightly into his fist, until his knuckles dug into my scalp. Tilting my head upward, he kissed me soundly. Instead of refusing him, I melted into his embrace, taking his kiss and demanding more in return.

"I don't think I'll ever get enough of you," he breathed out against my lips.

"Hmm…" I whispered in a complete daze.

His chest vibrated with a low chuckle, and he slowly let go of me. "I'll see you for breakfast." Giving me a quick peck on the nose, he smiled and then left.

Smiling at his retreating back, I leaned against the counter, feeling blissful. I turned toward the mirror and removed my hair tie to redo my ponytail again. But something else caught my eyes.

Letting out a gasp, I leaned forward, moving closer to the mirror and slightly turning my body to the side. There it was, on the base of my neck.

A red spot from where Alessio had bitten and sucked at the skin. He left a hickey.

Shaking my head at my reflection, I smiled. Infuriating man.

I placed the hair tie on the counter, deciding to leave my hair down. It was the only way to hide the mark Alessio left me.

At the thought, my smile widened. Alessio had laid his claim.

Giving myself a final look in the mirror, I walked out of the bathroom and Alessio's—*our* room. I mostly used Alessio's room. He said what was the point of going back and forth between rooms when I was already sleeping in his. In other words, he was claiming it was our room. He was the first one to call it that. *Our* room.

I skipped downstairs to see Maddie setting the table. "You are late, missy. Again," she grumbled at the sight of me.

I gave her a sheepish look. "Sorry." Maddie and I went back and forth from the kitchen and the dining room, placing the dishes on the table.

"Can you tell Milena and Sophia that it's their turn to serve today? They're in the garden," Maddie said as she placed the last plate.

I nodded in response, walking backward.

But I almost tripped over my feet when my back hit something. Or someone. My eyes widened in surprise, and I quickly swiveled around.

The first thing that came to my mind was that he was tall. The top of my head reached only to his chest. Glancing upward, I froze.

Grey eyes stared down at me. But in those grey eyes were small flecks of blue. Those eyes almost reminded me of Alessio's.

Taking a step back, I closed my eyes and quickly apologized. "I'm sorry. I didn't mean…I should have been looking…I'm sorry."

When I didn't hear an answer, I opened my eyes. I took a few steps away from him, finally seeing the man clearly for the first time. All I could do was stare at him in complete astonishment.

He looked like Alessio. Almost exactly like him. There were a few wrinkles in the corner of his eyes and lips, the only indication that he was older. Was he related to Alessio?

My eyes were still glued to him when I saw another man step forward until he was standing beside Alessio's lookalike.

With both men standing together, I trembled under their unflinching, tense gaze. I heard a loud gasp resonate from behind me, but I was too fixated on what I saw in front of me.

The other man's eyes shifted away from mine, and I saw him look behind my back. He nodded. "Lena."

"Isaak," I heard Lena say.

Alessio's lookalike gave me a final look before staring behind me too. "Lena," he greeted, his voice gruff and deep.

"Lyov," she breathed, shock evident in her voice.

Lyov. The name sounded so familiar.

When realization dawned, I took a step back, my hands shaking at my sides.

I now understood why he looked so much like Alessio.

Lyov was Alessio's father.

Chapter 8

As soon as I realized who was standing in front of me, I froze.

When I felt an arm wrap around my shoulders, I flinched in fright but quickly calmed down when I realized it was Alessio. He gave me a comforting squeeze.

Lyov's eyes moved to Alessio's arm around my shoulder, his stare burning holes into my skin. His gaze moved to mine, and I almost flinched at the glare he sent me. Moving further against Alessio's body, I sought comfort from his touch.

"Isaak." Alessio nodded toward the other man.

Turning to his father, he did the same thing. "Lyov." His voice was cold and void of emotion, a strange way to address his father.

"We'll have breakfast and then discuss the matter," Alessio continued.

Lyov walked around me without a second glance, while Isaak's eyes moved to mine again. He stared at me for a few chilling seconds, his gaze penetrating and almost frightening. There was a strange look on his face, but then he shook his head, as if he was clearing his mind. Without sparing us another glance, he followed Lyov.

As soon as they were out of sight, my shoulders sagged in relief, and I took a deep breath, trying to calm my wildly racing heart. Swallowing nervously, I peeked over my shoulder to see them walking upstairs.

"You don't have to worry about them. They won't hurt you," Alessio muttered in my ears.

"They look scary," I whispered back. His chest rippled with a low chuckle, his arms tightening around me in the process. He placed a kiss on my temple, and I turned around in his arms, facing him.

"Scarier than me?" he teased.

"No. You are worse," I admitted truthfully. All the men living in this house were dangerous and had a dark, tense vibe around them, but Alessio had the most chilling aura.

"And are you scared? Of me?" Alessio asked, pulling me closer.

Shaking my head, I placed a kiss in the middle of his chest. "No. I know you won't hurt me." Leaning on my tip-toes, I gave him a quick kiss and pulled away. "I'll see you later."

Alessio let me go with a nod. Sending him a smile, I walked away toward the back garden. The fresh morning air hit my face in a soothing manner, and I closed my eyes. How could I face Lyov without breaking down?

My father killed his wife. Mercilessly and cruelly.

Every single time it came back to this…I was an

Abandonato. The daughter of the man who destroyed a once-perfect family.

I wished there was a way to erase my past. Everything would have been easier if I wasn't an Abandonato. The guilt of lying to everyone was slowly eating me alive. My heart ached at my own betrayal.

How long can I keep this secret before everything crumbles under my feet?

***

I didn't see Alessio or the others for the rest of the day. I was tense, as if any moment now everything would end.

"Nikolay and Phoenix were living on the streets when Alessio found them." Maddie's voice snapped me out of my thoughts. Right. We were talking about Nikolay.

"I don't know much of their history, but Alessio does. All I know is that they are cousins and they had deadbeat parents," she explained.

"Was Nikolay always brooding like this?" I asked.

She nodded before taking a bite of her apple. "Oh yeah, definitely. He doesn't talk much."

Placing the last plate in the cabinet, I turned toward Maddie. "And Phoenix?"

Her expression changed the slightest bit, and she shrugged. "He's quiet but is much more easy-going than Nikolay. When he was a new recruit, he was with Viktor a lot. So you can say he is a second Viktor now."

THE MAFIA AND HIS ANGEL PART 2

Whenever the conversation would change to Phoenix, Maddie would shut down and change the topic. I was curious why, but she wouldn't say anything.

"They are all really close. Viktor, Artur, Phoenix, Nikolay, and Alessio. The loyalty they have toward Alessio is really endearing," I said, leaning against the counter.

"He trusts them a lot," Maddie agreed with a nod.

Getting up from the stool, Maddie walked away. "I'll go change, then we can watch something."

"Okay. I'll wait for you in my room." I nodded at her. I watched her leave the room.

Giving the cleaned kitchen a final glance, I walked out with a smile, but my steps faltered on the first step of the stairs when I saw Isaak coming down, his phone to his ear.

When he caught sight of me, he stopped mid-stride, his gaze roaming over my face. My throat was suddenly dry with nervousness, and I looked down quickly before continuing my way upstairs. As I got closer to where he was standing, my body went cold, the tiny hairs at the back of my neck standing in fear and panic.

I buried my trembling hands in the skirt of my dress as I passed by Isaak, my shoulders sagging in relief when I walked ahead of him.

But my relief was short-lived. His voice stopped me in my tracks, my body freezing at his words. "Have we met before?"

Closing my eyes tightly in horror, I swallowed several times. Did he figure out my truth?

I took a deep breath and made sure my face was a mask of indifference before turning around to face him.

Giving Isaak a blank look, I shook my head, trying to look convincing and not guilty. "No. That wouldn't be possible. I don't remember meeting you," I replied. At least that wasn't a lie. The truth was easier to speak.

Isaak cocked his head to the side and took a step up. His eyes skimmed over my face before nodding. "You remind me a lot of someone I knew," he elaborated.

His words were a surprise, and I stayed frozen as he stopped in front of me. Even though I was a stair above him, we were almost the same height.

Isaak brought a hand up to my face, his finger moving under my eyes, but he didn't touch me. As if he realized what he was doing, his arm fell down. His face presented a resigned and almost painful expression.

"You have my Leila's eyes," he murmured so low that I almost missed it.

I sucked in a harsh breath at the name. *Leila*. That was my mother's name. How was this possible? But then I realized he said *my* Leila. The person couldn't be my mother.

"She had a daughter name Ayla too," he continued in the same bleak tone.

A coincidence like this was impossible. My mother died when I was just a baby. Isaak was the enemy, so how would he know my mother? He called Leila *his*, claiming her as his woman.

"I'm sorry. My mother's name is not Leila." The

THE MAFIA AND HIS ANGEL PART 2

lie slipped past my lips effortlessly, but panic welled inside of me. Taking a deep breath, I continued. "She couldn't be me."

Isaak stared at me for another second before letting out a harsh and emotionless laugh. "Of course she isn't you," he agreed without a second thought, surprising me even further.

My fingers tightened around the fabric of my dress, and I sent him a shaky smile. He took a step down, putting his hands in the pocket of his black slacks.

But his next words were enough to send a chill down my spine. "The other Ayla is dead."

What? My mind screamed at this new revelation.

I stared at him in shock, but he didn't notice. Isaak was already turning around and walking down the stairs, but not before I caught a flash of pain in his expression. I stared at Isaak's retreating back, feeling completely horrified and appalled at his words.

His last words to me kept ringing in my ears as I walked into my room.

The other Ayla is dead.

I didn't know anything about my mother. No one ever talked about her. It was like she never even existed. But was it possible? Did Isaak know my mother?

"No, it couldn't be," I whispered. He said the other Ayla was dead. And I was alive. It was all a big misunderstanding. I tried to soothe myself with that thought.

I wished I knew more about my past. About my own family. But I knew nothing. I lived my life as a ghost, completely forgotten by my own father and everyone else. Only Alberto was a constant in my life.

But he did nothing except ruin me even more. Every day spent with him, I lost a piece of myself until I had nothing left.

Could Isaak be the key to my past? Was my mother *his* Leila?

I wanted to know, but I couldn't afford to reveal myself. My identity needed to stay hidden, and the only way to continue this façade was to be indifferent. I shouldn't care. For all I knew, it was just a big coincidence.

But Isaak's words were etched deep into my mind.

Everything was so uncertain.

Even my fate.

Chapter 9

Alessio

"Who is she?"

That was the first thing Lyov asked when he walked into my office. I knew who he was talking about, but I ignored his question. I was standing on the top of the stairs when Lyov and Isaak made their first appearance. I saw Ayla freeze from a distance. My first instinct was to go to her. And I did…without a second thought.

But I realized too late what I had done.

"Alessio, I asked you a question," Lyov growled.

"And I chose to ignore it. Now, can we discuss why you are here?"

My head snapped up when he slammed his fists on the desk. "Are you fucking stupid? After everything that happened, you let yourself get fucking weak over some girl?"

"That's none of your business," I hissed. Pushing my chair away, I stood up and glared at him. I saw

Isaak and Viktor standing at the door, both their arms crossed over their chests, an impassive expression on their faces. Like father, like son.

Walking around the desk, I pushed Lyov away. "Stay the fuck out of this. I'm serious about this, Lyov. Don't tell me what to do."

"I taught you better than this. I drilled it in your head before I left. No weakness. Make sure you don't have any weakness because that's the first thing your enemies will go after," he snapped, moving in my face.

Grabbing his collar in my fist, I pushed him way before yelling, "I know!"

Lyov laughed at my answer. "You know?" he mocked me, his laughter harsh around the walls of my office and to my ears. "Then explain that look in your eyes when you stared at her."

I paused at his question, feeling the anger coursing through my body. He was pushing me, forcing me to think about what I tried to bury deep inside of me.

"You know damn well what the outcome of this will be, but you still let yourself get weak," he continued in the same agitated tone, his face completely red with rage. My fists clenched at his words.

He was wrong. History wouldn't repeat itself. I wouldn't let it.

"I handed this empire, this *family* to you because I thought you wouldn't make the same mistake I did," Lyov said, his chest heaving with fury.

"I'm not you!" I roared, lurching toward him in anger. My fists made contact with his face in a loud crunch, and he fell backward against the coffee table.

From the corner of my eye, I saw Isaak moving toward us, but Lyov raised a hand to stop him. He got up and wiped his cracked, bleeding lips with his sleeves.

"That was *your* mistake. It was *your* fault. Not mine," I hissed. "You loved Mom. You brought her into this fucked-up world, and *you* got her killed."

His eyes went wild with rage, and he came toward me in full force. His fingers grabbed around my shirt and pushed me into the wall behind me. "You are right. It was my mistake, and you are making the same fucking mistake."

Letting me go, he took a step away. "After everything, I thought you would know better. You'll get her killed. Then you'll lose yourself. And in the end, you'll bring this whole family down with you."

That was what happened in the past. Lyov almost ruined this empire, and I was the one who saved it. But I wasn't going to make the same mistake as him.

"Stop comparing me with you!"

We both moved toward each other at the same time. I didn't have a chance to move away before he landed a punch in my stomach. I quickly retaliated, punching him in the shoulder.

I bore an anger that had no boundaries. Lyov had snapped the last thread of my control. We rolled on the ground, both of us lost in our years of held-in fury.

His fingers wrapped around my neck, squeezing.

His hold slipped when I punched him in the face. I felt someone pulling me back, but I struggled against their hold.

"Alessio, let go of him. Damn it, Alessio. Let go!" Viktor snapped, pulling me away.

Isaak helped Lyov to his feet and held him back when he tried to come at me again. Viktor was holding me back too. Our harsh breathing filled the room, the air around us chilling and tensed.

"You are right. You taught me better than this. I'm not going to make the same mistake," I snarled, glaring at Lyov.

"Did you hear that, Isaak? He isn't going to make the same damn mistake." Lyov laughed without looking away from me. "You are a fool and completely delusional. What you don't realize is that you already made the same mistake. She is already your weakness. Stop living in denial."

I could only glare at him. At my expression, he shrugged off Isaak and moved forward. "Come to your senses before it's too late. Get rid of her. Build that fucking wall around your heart again. Don't do the same thing I did."

With a dejected sigh, he shook his head. "I don't want you to go through the same thing, Alessio," he whispered. "I'm saving you from years of heartache."

He took a step away from me and turned around, walking away without a second glance. Isaak followed behind him without any words.

Opening the door, he stopped in the doorway. His next words were a blow to my chest. I closed my eyes and swiveled around, facing away from him.

"*Angels* don't belong in our world."

With that as his final words to me, I heard the door close, and then it was only silence. An unbearable and painful silence. I felt suddenly empty, my heart aching at the thought of Ayla.

"Alessio…" Viktor started, but I quickly cut him off.

"Leave. Just…leave."

He sighed but left without uttering anything else. I walked around the desk and fell on my chair, staring at the ceiling.

Lyov's words echoed in my ears. I wanted to say he was wrong, but he wasn't. I was living in denial. I didn't want to think of Ayla as my weakness, but she was.

The fear of losing her was instilled inside of me…but I was powerless. Instead of pushing her away, I was holding her closer every day.

Ayla consumed every fiber of my being. Ayla was everything I couldn't have but everything I needed.

She was my light. I'd let her into my heart where she had showered me with her sweet venom.

I was so lost in her, forgetting that I couldn't feel what I was feeling. It was all a temporary bliss and happiness, but now reality tasted sour.

Ayla was *my* Angel, but I couldn't have her.

***

I didn't know how long I stayed like this. Hours maybe, but I couldn't move. Eventually, a knock sounded on my door, and I opened my eyes. "Come in," I ordered. The door opened to reveal Sasha, one of the maids, holding a tray.

"Mr. Ivanshov, Viktor told me to bring your dinner to your office," she said.

Dinner? Looking at the clock on the wall, I saw that it was already past seven.

"Place it on the coffee table," I replied before closing my eyes again. I expected to hear the door close, but when none of that happened, my eyes snapped open.

Sasha was standing in front of my desk. Her eyes roamed over my chest, and she bit down on her lower lip. "Alessio," she started, her voice turning more sultry and softer. "You look really stressed out. Can I help in any way?"

With a sigh, I closed my eyes again. I used to fuck her. A pastime when I needed the distraction. But since Ayla came into my life, not once did I think of going back to Sasha. Ayla had my absolute attention.

I felt something on my crotch, and my hand quickly snaked around Sasha's wandering fingers, stopping her movement. "Get the fuck out of here," I snapped, pushing her hand away.

"I can make you feel good. Like always," she whispered in my ear.

"No. Leave."

I heard her frustrated sigh as she moved away. But Lyov's words echoed in my ears, and my fists clenched in anger as I fought for control.

Come to your senses before it's too late. Get rid of her. Build that fucking wall around your heart

again. Don't do the same thing I did.
Angels don't belong in our world.

My eyes snapped open, and I moved my chair back. Standing up, I quickly grabbed Sasha's hand, and I pulled her toward me.

I placed a hand on her back and pushed her front against the desk, bending her forward so her ass was pushed back. I heard her gasp of surprise, but then she moaned, moving her ass against my cock.

"Fuck me, Alessio."

I grabbed a handful of her hair and pulled her head back. "Don't tell me what to do," I hissed in her ear.

"Hmm, okay. Do whatever you want," she murmured huskily. Releasing her hair, I moved her dress upward until her red lace thong was visible.

Angels don't belong in our world.

I squeezed my eyes shut against the words, my fingers digging into Sasha's hips. Blindly moving my hand to her thong, I ripped it away and dropped it on the floor. I let go of her to unbutton my slacks and pulled my cock out.

Angels don't belong in our world.

I kicked her legs open, my body pressed against hers. Without touching her, I already knew she was wet and ready for me. The tip of the soft cock brushed against her inner thigh. Sasha let out a moan and wiggled closer to me.

At the sound of her moan, my eyes snapped open. Fuck. No.

What the fuck am I doing?

Pushing away from her body, I stumbled back, completely horrified at what I was about to do. I couldn't this. Not to *my* Ayla. She trusted me. She gave me herself. I couldn't betray her like this.

Shame filled my body, and I sucked in a painful breath. "Get out. Get the fuck out now," I growled, zipping my pants again.

"But…" She glanced over her shoulders, her face a mask of confusion. Just then, the door crashed open, and I saw Viktor coming in. He took his gun out and pointed it at Sasha.

"Get out before I blow your fucking brains out," he snapped. Sasha gasped in shock and fear before quickly bending down and grabbing her ripped panties. She ran out of the room, closing the door behind her with a bang.

"Are you serious?" Viktor roared at me, his eyes glistening with anger and disgust.

"Don't." I raised a hand, but he talked over me.

"Were you going to fuck her?"

"No!" I quickly answered. "I stopped."

Shaking his head, he walked toward me. "Are you really going to let your father's words take over your head? Are you going to let him control your life?"

"No," I growled.

Viktor shook his head. "What's Ayla to you?"

"It wasn't supposed to be like this, Viktor. None of this was supposed to happen. My plan was to get close to Ayla to make her reveal her truth. We had to know if she was a traitor. That was the fucking plan," I snapped, running my fingers to my hair in frustration.

That was the plan from the beginning. Get close to Ayla, gain her trust, and make her reveal her truth. But it didn't end that way.

"I wasn't meant to feel anything," I ended brokenly.

"I know," he agreed softly. "But that's not the plan anymore. That plan ended the same day it was made. It ended the moment you gave her your jacket and you felt her tears as if they were your own."

"He's right. Ayla will be my downfall," I whispered, turning around to face the window.

It was pitch black outside, so similar to the darkness inside of me. I closed my eyes and leaned my forehead against the glass. "I can't lose her, Viktor. She is everything."

"If something happens to her because of me…" I started but didn't finish the sentence. I couldn't bring myself to say the words. I couldn't imagine myself without Ayla. She was a part of me.

"I agree. Lyov was right. She is your weakness," Viktor replied coldly. I sucked in a harsh breath, my chest squeezing tightly in pain.

"But she is also your strength," he finished. My heart raced at his words, and I opened my eyes, swiveling around to face him.

He nodded with a sigh, his eyes turning slightly softer. "You've changed a lot since she came into our lives. Ayla is your strength. She is the one who's going to stop you from stumbling in the darkness every time. It's for you to choose if you'll let her be your weakness or your strength."

Sinking down on my chair, I placed my head in my hands. How was I going to protect Ayla?

"Don't hurt her, Alessio. After all she's been

through, she doesn't deserve to be hurt by you."

"I don't want to, Viktor. For the first time in my life, I don't know what to do." I spoke my harrowing thoughts, the words tasting bitter against my lips.

"Only you can answer that. Just remember one thing, though." Viktor paused, and I looked up, waiting for him continue. "She is your Angel."

With that, he gave me a nod and walked out of the room, closing the door behind him.

My Angel.

Rubbing my hands over the back of my neck, I tried to relieve the tense muscles there. I spent hours thinking about what Lyov and Viktor said. I paced, frustration building inside of me with each passing minute.

The next time I checked the clock, it was almost ten. Ayla would be waiting for me in the piano room. Closing my eyes, I sighed. Ayla's smiling face flashed behind my closed eyelids. After many frustrating hours, I came to only one conclusion.

I *needed* Ayla.

Remembering my father's words from twenty years ago, I stood up.

An angel is the person you can't see yourself living without. Don't ever let her go. Because if you lose her, then you will forever be incomplete.

He was right. I would be incomplete without Ayla. I thought about her sweet voice, gentle touch and kisses, and her loving eyes. She was *mine*.

As I walked out of my office, I prayed that Ayla could forgive me. I had to tell her the truth about Sasha. I didn't fuck her, but I still touched her. I wasn't going to lie. Ayla didn't deserve anything less.

I also prayed that she accepted me. I wasn't going to change. I was still the Boss and would be until my last breath. I prayed she was ready for this fucked-up life.

I stopped in front of the piano room and took a deep breath, trying to calm myself. All I wanted was to hold her in my arms and forget everything.

Opening the door, I stopped when I saw the room empty and dark.

What the fuck?

Quickly walking out of the piano room, I made my way to our room. I opened the door and saw it was only gently illuminated with the lamp on the nightstand.

Ayla was sitting on the edge of the bed, facing the wall. The soft glow danced over her beautiful face as she sat stoically.

"Ayla?" I questioned, walking further into the room and closing the door behind me.

"Cold. Ruthless. Heartless. Arrogant. Killer. Unlovable. Alessio Ivanshov can't love or be loved. Those are all the words that you are known as, right?"

Ayla's words stopped me dead in my tracks, my heart stuttering at her bleak, distant tone. She let out a small laugh, shaking her head.

"Ayla, what are you talking about?" I asked, panic welling inside of me. I didn't like her tone or the way she avoided looking at me. She didn't sound like my Ayla.

"I wanted to believe you were different," she

whispered, this time her voice breaking over the words.

I lurched forward, desperately wanting to wrap her in my arms and erase all her sorrow. Ayla's head snapped toward me, and I sucked in a painful breath at her expression.

Her eyes were filled with tears, her face red and filled with pain and grief. She looked at me as if I betrayed her.

The look in her eyes was enough to tell me what I needed to know.

No. No. No. I panicked.

"I thought you were different." She wiped her tears away. "But I was wrong."

Chapter 10

Ayla

"Ayla, what are you talking about?" Alessio asked. He was panicking, scared about what my words meant, while I was breaking inside.

"I wanted to believe you were different," I whispered hoarsely, hating how my voice broke over those words. I hated how much power Alessio had over me. He was my peace, my strength, but he was also my weakness. He had the power to break me.

And that was exactly what he did.

After putting my heart together, after giving me hope, he took it all away, leaving me empty and broken again.

"I thought you were different," I continued in the same small voice. It was true I knew what type of man he was, but with me, he was different.

The Alessio I knew was sweet and gentle. Out there he was a killer and heartless, but with me, he was everything I needed.

But it was all a lie.

Swiping my tears away, I finally turned toward Alessio. Even in the darkness, I could see his tensed body and rigid shoulders. His face was twisted with panic and dread.

"But I was wrong." I choked on the words.

I didn't have to say anything else. Realization flashed in his blue eyes. He understood that I knew the truth.

"Why?" I asked, my voice dropping to a mere whisper. He took a step forward but stopped when I shook my head. A sudden surge of anger coursed through my body, prompting me to quickly stand up and face him.

"Ayla…" he breathed, his voice shaky. I didn't know why, but his voice made me angrier. It reminded me of when my world fell apart around me, crushing me mercilessly.

"Where are you going?" Maddie asked as I walked up the stairs.

Without stopping, I said over my shoulder, "I'm going to see Alessio." Since the morning, after Lyov and Isaak made their appearance, I hadn't seen Alessio. His missing presence had left an aching hole in my chest, and I just wanted to be near him again, even if it was just for a few minutes.

Smiling, I made my way to his office. I was only a few feet away when I saw the door open, and Sasha ran out, her face panicked. My eyebrows pulled up in a frown at the sight of her.

"What's wrong?" I asked, walking closer. She gasped at the sight of me, her hands going up to her

chest. My eyes widened when I saw what she was holding. A ripped red thong.

My eyes snapped to hers, and she looked away guiltily, biting on her lips nervously.

No. Please.

"Why are you holding your underwear?" I asked curtly after a moment of silence. Before she could answer, Viktor's loud booming voice came through from Alessio's office.

Confused, I looked back at Sasha, but she avoided eye contact with me. Without answering to my question, she walked around me. I was left dumbfounded, as I stood frozen in my spot.

My hands were shaking, and I trembled slightly as Viktor continued yelling. When I heard Alessio's voice, I finally snapped out of my daze and walked forward until I was standing in front of the door.

I didn't know what to expect, my mind still lost on what I just saw. But then my heart stuttered to a stop, my chest contracting painfully when I heard his words...Alessio's words. My legs weakened, and my stomach twisted. I suddenly felt nauseous.

"My plan was to get close to Ayla to make her reveal her truth. We had to know if she was a traitor. That was the fucking plan."

I choked back a sob when I understood his meaning. They still thought I was a spy. It was all a lie. They never believed me.

Having heard enough, I pushed away from the door.

Alessio and I...whatever he said, his sweet words, his kisses, his gentle caresses, were they all a lie? Was it just a ploy to get closer to me?

I was paralyzed by just the thought of it. Bringing a shaky hand to my mouth, I tried to control my breathing. But it felt like my world had just ended around me. I could feel myself spiraling down toward the darkness again.

I heard yelling, but none of the words made sense to me. I could only think about what I heard. The same words repeated over and over in my head. My ears were ringing from their painful betrayal.

Giving the door a final glance, I turned around and blindly ran to my room. I needed to escape this harsh reality. I didn't want to believe it. Not Alessio. Not my Alessio.

The door closed behind me, and I sank down to the floor, holding my knees to my chest as I sobbed.

He wouldn't do that. He cared...I saw it in his eyes.

But Alessio Ivanshov was known to be deceitful. If he thought I was a traitor, he would stop at nothing to find the truth.

Even if it meant breaking me until I had nothing left to give.

When I saw Alessio take another step toward me, I snapped out of the painful memories and took a step back. His eyes flashed with hurt, and he placed a hand out as if to comfort me.

"What did you do with Sasha?" I asked, my voice almost emotionless, hiding the true turmoil inside of me. Alessio's face contorted in guilt, and he swallowed nervously. His eyes shifted away for a few seconds, his hands tightening in fists.

At his reaction, I felt my already fragile heart

crack further, deepening the holes in it. He didn't have to say anything. I already got my answer.

"Ayla, it's not what you think—" he started, but I quickly cut him off.

"Did you touch her?" He paused at my question, his eyes closing tightly for a second. Alessio paced in front of me, his fingers going to his hair in frustration.

"Did you touch her, Alessio?" I asked again.

"Ayla..." he growled.

"Did you?" This time my voice was louder.

Turning toward me, he glared. "Damn it, Ayla. It's not what you think."

I let out a small harsh laugh, leaning back into the wall. "So you did."

Alessio lost his glare, and he shook his head. He moved toward me, but I raised a hand, stopping him again. "Don't come near me."

"I heard you talking to Viktor," I admitted, my voice strangely soft. Alessio flinched, if possible his whole body growing tenser. "Is it true? Do you think I'm a traitor?"

Deep inside, I prayed he would say *no* and that it was all a misunderstanding. "I'm not the spy," I continued softly, desperately hoping he would believe me.

I saw Alessio visibly swallow hard, and he slightly shook his head. "I know, Ayla."

He accepted my plea, but I still couldn't forget those words. It still hurt. I still felt like I was breaking. Under the layers of hurt, deep anger was raging. Never had I felt this way. Not even when I was tortured.

I loathed that Alessio could make me feel this way.

My body vibrated with the force of my anger, and as I stared at Alessio's guilty face, I snapped. I was holding on tight to the string, desperate not to lose control, but right at the moment, I lost it.

Lurching forward, I slammed into Alessio's body, holding onto his collar tight. "Why? Why did you do it? Was it all a lie? Tell me!"

His arms wrapped around my waist, but I pushed him away, hard. He stumbled over his feet before quickly straightening up, his face a mask of complete bewilderment.

"You want to know the truth, right? Fine. I'll tell you," I yelled, my chest heaving with exertion. My harsh breathing filled the room, and Alessio looked in pain.

"I believe y—" he started to say, but I talked over him.

"I was sixteen when I was raped." Alessio's mouth snapped shut, his jaw clenching as his eyes glittered with a sudden rage. But I continued, pushing forward in my own anger.

"The man who I was supposed to marry raped me on my sixteenth birthday, and he continued to do so every single night for seven years." I choked on the last words.

Tears blinded my vision as the memories assaulted me. They flashed in front of my eyes, and my body shook as if I was experiencing all the nights of torture again.

"My father never did anything. He never even paid attention to me. I was alone, never allowed to leave the house. And then he handed me over to *him*. A cruel man who destroyed me."

As I revealed my truth, I saw Alessio's face changing. So much fury. I could feel it from where I was standing. The air around us grew rigid as my words echoed around us.

"Who hurt you?" he growled, his body prowling forward to me. His voice was deadly, his words so sharp it felt like a whip had sliced through the air. And his eyes…the look he gave me was completely ferocious.

I could see the monster there. The one everyone feared.

I felt my chest start to burn with the pressure building there. I didn't know how to feel. He looked in pain for me…but he was also the cause of my pain.

"He used to beat me. He would chain me to our bed and then whip me if I did something wrong or what he perceived wrong."

His face was already a mask of rage, but it darkened more ominously as I admitted another truth. I held my breath when I saw him clenching and then unclenching his fists. Alessio did that a few times, and each time he clenched his fist, my heart squeezed.

"I was running away from home when I found you and hid in your car. That's how we met. I'm not a spy, Alessio. I'm just someone running away from her nightmare, desperately seeking peace," I murmured as my shoulders sagged, the anger leaving my body until I felt empty.

My mind was lost somewhere I didn't want to

go.

"I'm not your enemy. I'm just another victim," I whispered brokenly, hoping he could hear the truth in my words. I might have been an Abandonato, but I wasn't Alessio's enemy. My real enemy was my own family.

Alessio's face was thunderous as he moved into my space. Even when I placed my hands out to ward him off, he didn't stop. He kept moving until he was in front of me, my shoulders held tightly in his hands. I flinched when his fingers dug into my skin.

"Who?" One simple word but it spoke volume. The raw brutal energy coming off Alessio wrapped around us. He exuded danger, his eyes filled with murderous intent.

When I didn't answer, he shook me, his beautiful bluish eyes darkening even further. "Who the fuck hurt you, Ayla?" Alessio roared.

"You!" I screamed, pushing him away from me. A sudden surge of anger coursed through my body again. "You hurt me. You are hurting me."

He flinched at my words, his body tensing fiercely. Hurt flashed over his face, his eyebrows pulling together tensely.

"I never had hopes for my father or the man he handed me to. I grew numb in their hands, learning to block away the pain. But you." I pointed at Alessio. "You hurt me because I trusted you. I gave you everything. I let you touch me—" I broke off on the last words. *I gave you my heart.*

Deep regret was written over his face as he stayed rooted on the spot. "Ayla, please let me…"

"When I ran away, I didn't expect to find peace. I didn't even know what I wanted until I found you. You brought me peace. I was basking in this light until you took it away," I snapped, my voice rising.

I felt something wet on my cheeks and brought my hand up. I didn't even realize I was crying. Alessio made an agonized sound at the sight of my tears, and he moved forward again, wrapping his arms around me before I could say anything else.

My head was right over his loudly racing heart. His arms tightened around me at my next words. "You were my savior. My own guardian angel."

At the word Angel, I felt him suck in a harsh breath, his arms growing impossibly tight around me. "But it feels like my heart is splintering into pieces right now, Alessio."

Pulling away from me, he palmed my cheeks. "I'm sorry, Ayla. So sorry. Just let me explain," he pleaded.

"What do you want to explain, Alessio? I heard it loud and clear. The truth was right there. Sasha came out of your office. You touched her. And then you admitted getting close to me because you thought I was a traitor. What is there left to say?" I muttered softly, losing all the battle in me.

"You didn't—"

"I need you to leave."

We both spoke at the same time, our words clashing together. Alessio flinched, and my heart clenched.

"No. I'm not leaving until you listen to me," he stated firmly.

"I can't do this right now. Just leave, Alessio."

"No."

"Leave!" I screamed, pushing him away. God, why couldn't he understand? If he didn't leave, I was going to break down right there in front of him. My thoughts and feelings were in turmoil.

I saw Viktor appear in the doorway. He walked inside and stopped behind Alessio. "Alessio, let's go. Give her some time," he said softly.

"No. Stay the fuck out of this, Viktor," he snapped, his voice hard. His gaze was still glued on mine, and I looked away.

"I want you to leave," I bit out.

He shook his head stubbornly. "I'm not leaving until you listen to me."

"I don't want to listen to you! Just leave," I snapped back. He moved toward me, but Viktor held him back.

"Let's go, Alessio."

Turning away from them, I faced the wall, tuning them out. I heard them arguing, and the door closed after a few minutes.

Then complete and utter silence. I stood in the darkness as the silence surrounded me. The tears fell down my cheeks, and I made no effort to swipe them away.

With a resigned sigh, I got into our bed and pulled the covers over me. The bed felt big and empty without Alessio. It was the first time I would be sleeping without him since he brought me to his room.

My tears soaked his pillow as I laid on his side of the bed. His scent enveloped me, and my heart ached, knowing he wasn't here with me. I had pushed him away, but I was now missing his presence.

I told him the truth about my past. Part of it. I still left out the part where I was an Abandonato. During our fight, the truth was at the tip of my tongue. I wished I could have told him, but the fear of his reaction always stopped me.

The irony of this situation was almost laughable.

I accused him of betraying me. But I was betraying him too. By keeping this truth from him, I was betraying his trust.

I was angry at Alessio, but some of that anger was directed to me too. And that was exactly why I needed him to leave. With Alessio, I was weak. My emotions were uncontrollable when he was around.

Closing my burning eyes, I hugged his pillow to my chest. I prayed that sleep would come fast.

But it didn't. My chest was still unbearably tight.

Chapter 11

The next morning was filled with tension and anxiety. My stomach twisted dangerously, and my heart was constantly aching. Stepping out of our bedroom, I saw Viktor walking around the corner. His steps faltered at the sight of me.

Giving me a nod, he walked closer. "You should have let Alessio explain," he stated curtly without any greeting.

"I heard what I needed to know. Nothing he would say can change the truth," I replied, holding his cold eyes, and they burned into mine.

He shook his head. "And that's where you are wrong. Let him explain, and you'll understand."

"He hurt me," I whispered.

Viktor's eyes softened, and he took a step closer until we were only inches apart. "He is a confused man, but he cares about you deeply."

"If he cared, he wouldn't have touched Sasha." My voice was barely a whisper as Viktor's words registered in my mind. I wanted so badly to believe him.

Alessio cared. I knew that. I saw it in his eyes. But his betrayal still left a gaping hole in me.

Viktor's hand came up to my face, and he pressed his thumb lightly over my cheek, brushing away the single drop of tear that had escaped. I looked up and saw him glancing briefly over my head. Something flashed in his eyes. It was so quick I didn't have a chance to catch it.

And then everything happened so fast.

One minute, Viktor was standing in front of me, comforting me in some way, and then his lips were on mine.

I blinked rapidly and let out a gasp, my hands going to his chest. He didn't kiss me. His lips were just there, pressing into mine gently and almost feather light.

When I heard a roar from behind me, I flinched and quickly pulled away, Viktor releasing me without any struggle.

It was almost a blur. Viktor was ripped away and slammed against the wall; Alessio held him tight against the wall as he landed a few furious punches into his face.

"Oh my God," I squeaked, my hands going to my mouth in shock. "Stop!" I yelled.

Alessio's face was filled with murderous intent. Viktor punched him back, but it only pissed him off. "If you fucking touch her again, I will kill you," he hissed into Viktor's face.

Running to them, I tried to pull Alessio off Viktor. But he was unmovable. Holding his arm, I pulled hard, finally bringing his attention to me. Alessio glanced up, his glare intense and fierce.

"Stop! Let him go, Alessio."

I felt his tense muscles relax under my fingers. That was when I noticed my hand on his back, and without thinking, I was rubbing his shoulders, almost soothingly. Quickly removing my hand, I took a step back, and he pushed himself away from Viktor.

Alessio tried to wrap his arms around me, but I skirted around him, moving away from his touch. "What is wrong with you?" Without waiting for his answer, I turned to Viktor. "And you? Don't ever do that again." Glancing at Alessio, I continued. "Don't lower yourself to his level. You are better than that," I said, my words meant for Viktor.

I watched Alessio flinch at my words, hurt flashing in his eyes. I wanted him to hurt. I wanted him to feel what I was feeling.

Giving the man who held my heart in the palm of his hands a final glance, I walked away. I heard him call my name, but I kept walking.

I needed Maddie.

Making my way to the kitchen, I found it empty. It was still early in the morning. She probably wasn't even awake yet. I walked back upstairs, where I knew her room was.

I heard a sleepy reply, and a few seconds later, the door opened to reveal a half-asleep Maddie. "Ayla?" she questioned. "Is everything okay? I heard yelling."

"No. Nothing is okay," I replied, walking inside and closing the door behind me. Her eyes widened, and she quickly grabbed my hand, pulling me to the bed.

"What's wrong? Did Alessio do something?" she asked, her voice rising with alarm.

Taking a deep breath, I let everything out. Her eyes glittered with anger at my words, and finally she let out a tired sigh when I finished. She placed a comforting hand over my knee.

"This is a mess." I agreed. "Why didn't you let him explain?" she questioned.

"I don't know, Maddie. I was just so angry and hurt. If I had let him explain, I would have probably not believed anything he would have said," I murmured, looking down at my lap.

"I can't believe he would do something like that," Maddie grumbled under her breath. "What are you going to do now?"

I closed my eyes with a sigh. "I don't know."

I didn't know how to feel. So I was just going to retreat back and lick my wounds, needing time to think and understand.

I needed to be away from Alessio. Until this pain disappeared and I could breathe normally again, without it feeling like my chest was being squeezed tightly.

***

I was sitting on my bed when I heard a knock on the door. "Come in," I called out, placing my book down.

The door opened, and Viktor walked in, holding a tray of food. I winced at the sight of him. His face was multiple shades of red and purple. When I raised an eyebrow at him in question, he grumbled something under his breath.

"What is this?" I asked as he placed the tray on the nightstand and sat down on the bed beside me.

"I brought you dinner. I heard from Maddie that you didn't eat anything since this morning," he replied briskly.

"Oh." I looked at the tray and then back at him again. "Thank you."

"Did you talk to Alessio?"

My shoulders went rigid at his name. We hadn't seen each other since this morning, when he fought with Viktor. It wasn't because of his lack of effort. Alessio had tried to talk to me on numerous occasions, but I walked away every time.

"No. I haven't talked to him," I replied before taking the book in my hands again. I stared at the pages but couldn't bring myself to read. My concentration was elsewhere.

Viktor and I were both silent for a few minutes. "About this morning, I apologize."

Glancing up at him, I waited for him to continue. He was staring at the wall, and I saw his lips lift up in a small smirk. "Scratch that. I'm not apologizing for kissing you." He turned toward me before continuing. "I never apologize for kissing a pretty lady."

I mentally scoffed and looked down at the book again. "But I had my reasons for doing what I did. I needed to get my point across."

Curious to where he was going with this, I glanced up again, this time giving him my full attention. "To you, I needed you to see his reaction. If he didn't care, he wouldn't have reacted the way he did. He doesn't give a shit if I fuck around with the other women he slept with. But you…only you can get that type of reaction out of him."

My stomach warmed at his words.

"And it was barely even a kiss. He cares deeply, Ayla."

My fingers tightened around the edge of my book as he continued. "And to him. He is a stubborn son of a bitch. He needed to come to his senses, and that was the perfect way to do it."

I felt my heart wrench, and my eyes stung with unshed tears. Blinking them away, I refused to cry again.

When I didn't answer, he got up and gave me a nod before walking away. As he neared the door, I called out, halting his movement.

My gaze moved to the tray on my nightstand. Keeping my eyes on it, I asked the question that I already knew the answer to.

"It was Alessio who sent you here, right?"

From the corner of my eyes, I saw Viktor turning around to face me. "He knew you didn't eat. Alessio was bringing the tray to you but realized he wouldn't be welcomed. He didn't want to cause you anymore pain."

His words made my heart ache. Not in a good way. A sense of guilt overcame me, but I quickly pushed it away. One thing I knew for sure was Alessio didn't eat, either.

"Can you please make sure he eats?" I asked softly. Viktor sighed and then nodded before leaving the room.

As soon as the door was closed, I pushed my

book away and laid down on my back, staring at the ceiling thoughtfully.

Maybe I was being too stubborn, but it had come to a point where I didn't know how to face him.

All my life I never had a choice. Whatever was done to me, I had to accept it without any complaints. I didn't want Alessio to think that everything was acceptable, because it wasn't. I had a choice now.

I didn't know how long I laid there, lost in my thoughts, but when I check the time, it was almost ten p.m. This was *our* time. Just *us*. Alessio would be waiting for me in the piano room.

My fingers were itching to play. I wanted to be there, but a small nagging part stopped me.

Chapter 12

Alessio

My heart raced as I made my way to the piano room. Sweat broke on my forehead and the back of my neck. Stopping in front of the room, I laid my hand on the knob. I sucked in a shaky breath, feeling my throat constrict.

I felt so uncertain. Worried. Scared. Panic rose like bile in my body, and my nerves were tingling.

Every minute spent without Ayla, it felt like I was going insane. My heart ached without her. I needed her. *My Angel.*

I wished she'd give me a chance to explain. From how it ended this morning, I wasn't even sure she would be in the piano room. But I still hoped.

Blood rushed in my ears, and my pulse skyrocketed as I opened the door. A sea of anxiety curled in my stomach when I found the room dark and empty.

My Angel wasn't here.

A wave of pain went through me as I stumbled

back outside. How did I mess up so bad? I should have just accepted my feelings instead of trying to fight it.

Now…now I may have lost my Angel.

My heart stuttered, my eyes going wide. *No.* She was mine. My everything. I would have her listen to me, even if I had to fucking tie her to the bed. But she would listen to me.

At the thought of tying her to the bed, Ayla's words resonated in my ears.

He used to beat me. He would chain me to our bed and then whip me if I did something wrong or what he perceived wrong.

I went still, my chest growing tight. Closing my eyes, a fresh wave of pain hit me with a ferocious intensity. Each of Ayla's words felt like a serrated edge over my heart.

I never thought that Ayla had been through all of this. The thought of her going through so much pain made my blood boil, until the monster inside of me was raging to spill blood. His blood.

When I get my hands on the bastard, he is going down.

Opening my eyes again, I stared at the empty hall. Ayla needed to know what she meant to me, how important she was to me.

Stalking to our bedroom with a newfound confidence, I opened the door but frowned when I found the room empty.

She must be in her room. Last night was pure torture. I found that I couldn't sleep without her. But tonight, that was going to change. Moving to her bedroom, I knocked on the door, but got no response. My fist moved over the door a few times, but there was only silence.

Confused, I opened the door but found this room empty and dark too.

What the fuck? Where was she?

Walking out, panic welled inside of me. My heart thumped harder as my stomach rolled with tension. I quickly walked down the hall, my hands going up to my hair in frustration, my fingers digging in my scalp.

"Ayla?" I called out.

I saw Viktor coming out of his room, and he looked at me confused. "Where's Ayla?" I asked.

"She was in her room the last time I saw her," he replied, alarm flashing in his eyes.

"She's not there!"

My feet quickly took me down the stairs as I looked around the house in panic. My body trembled at the thought of losing Ayla.

Stopping at the last step, I saw Maddie coming toward me. Her stares were hard, and she scowled before turning her face away, ignoring me.

"Where's Ayla?" I growled low, glaring at the stubborn woman in front of me. If there was someone who could answer this question, then it was Maddie.

Her chin went down in a defiant movement, and she huffed, crossing her arms over her chest. Fuck! Anger coursed through my body, and I roared, not caring that I would be waking everyone up.

"Where is she?"

Maddie's eyes turned cold, and she stared at me blankly before stepping forward. Looking up at me, she hissed, "Fuck you."

With that, she walked around me and went up the stairs. My whole body was vibrating with fury. And dread. Raking my fingers through my hair, I clenched them tightly as the muscle in my jaw ticked from the way I was gritting my teeth.

"I saw her going into Maddie's room."

Nikolay's voice snapped me out of my dreadful thoughts, and I swiveled around to see him standing beside Viktor on the top of the stairs. He nodded, and I released a shaky breath, relief filling my body.

Without sparing them a glance, I quickly walked back upstairs and knocked on Maddie's door. I heard quiet footsteps approaching from the opposite side, and my shoulder sagged in relief. She was in there. I could feel it.

The door opened a few seconds later, and there she stood, wearing her light pink nightdress. My heart squeezed at the sight of Ayla, and I just wanted to wrap my arms around her. I just wanted to hold her, feel her.

Her eyes widened at the sight of me, and she made a move to close the door, but I stopped her movement with my foot. "Ayla. Stop," I growled.

Her lips twisted ruefully, and fire sparkled in her angry eyes. "Alessio, I told you—"

"I know what you said, but this time you are going to listen to me," I continued, talking over her.

"No," she snapped, her shoulders pushed back stubbornly.

"Why are you doing this?" I said with a sigh, a sense of defeat taking over me.

Ayla stared at me for a few seconds. I saw the

hurt in there. Pain, guilt, anger, sadness. My Angel was hurting, and she wouldn't even let me comfort her.

"You taught me how to be strong," she started, her voice soft.

I blinked up at her, confused. But her next words were like a knife stabbing at my heart.

"This is me being strong."

With that, she shut the door in my face. I didn't have a chance to stop her. I was overwhelmed with shock as I stared at the door.

Placing my forehead on the door, I closed my eyes.

How am I going to fix this?

Chapter 13

Ayla

I was dreading opening my eyes. Falling asleep last night without Alessio was painful. I had to take my sleeping pills, just in case my nightmares came back.

In the back of my mind, I had this annoying voice whispering to me that it was my fault. But the other voice fought back, telling me I needed time to think.

Holding the other pillow to my chest, I burrowed deeper under the comforter with a sigh before opening my eyes. But I quickly covered my mouth with my hand to stifle the gasp that threatened to escape at the sight in front of me.

"Alessio," I breathed, my eyes fixated on his sleeping form.

Shoving the purple comforter from my body, I got off the bed and walked to him. He was sleeping on the chair beside the bed, his legs stretched out in front of him, his head rolled to the side in what looked like an uncomfortable position.

His suit jacket was thrown carelessly on the floor while his black shirt was unbuttoned on the top, his sleeves rolled up to his elbows, showing just a little of his tattoos that ended there.

I came to a stop in front of him, my heart thumping at the sight of his face. His eyebrows were furrowed, his forehead pinched with tension even in his sleep. He looked tired, his lips turned down in a frown. Leaning forward, my fingers brushed lightly over his forehead, softly easing the tense lines.

Alessio shifted slightly under my touch, and I quickly moved my hands away. He always looked peaceful in his sleep...but this time, he looked almost in pain. And I hated it.

I hated it even more knowing that I could be the cause of his pain.

Closing my eyes, I could still see his tormented expression from last night when I had closed the door in his face.

I opened my eyes again and slowly moved my fingers over Alessio's face, caressing him but without touching him. I traced his lips, his eyes, his nose, his eyebrows, my fingers just an inch away from his skin.

"I don't know what to do, Alessio. I don't know what to feel. I'm so confused," I whispered before pulling my hand away.

When I saw his forehead furrow at the sound of my voice, I quickly stepped back. Giving Alessio's sleeping form a final glance, I turned around and walked to the bathroom. As soon as the door was closed behind me, I leaned against it and shut my eyes.

Alessio was both my strength and my weakness. With him, my heart soared with happiness. Without him, I felt empty.

Opening my eyes again, I shook my head. "Stop thinking about it, Ayla," I said to myself, facing the mirror. My reflection stared back at me, my face looking just as haggard as I felt.

After freshening up and getting dressed, I walked out to the door but hesitated.

Was he still there? Did he wake up yet?

I didn't think I had the courage to see him again. If I saw him again, I knew I would forgive him in an instant and beg him to hold me.

Finally, my fingers wrapped around the knob, and I opened the door. I took a deep breath and stepped out.

The room was empty.

Alessio was gone.

My shoulder drooped low as I stared at the chair he had been sleeping in before. I didn't know if I was sad or relieved. As my eyes stayed glued to the chair, I realized that I was secretly hoping he would still be here.

These feelings were confusing. Frustrating and definitely annoying.

I glared at the chair, my lips twisting ruefully. Shaking my head, I walked out of the room without a final glance.

Maddie was waiting for me in the kitchen, and as soon as I walked inside, she raised an eyebrow in my direction. "I saw Alessio walking out of my room," she commented, crossing her arms over her chest.

"Yes," I sighed. "He probably spent the night there. I woke up to see him sleeping in the chair."

"Did you talk to him?" Lena asked. I glanced at her from the corner of my eyes, and I saw her staring at me expectantly. When I shook my head mutely, her shoulders dropped sadly.

"How long are you going to avoid him? I'm not telling you to forgive him, because he doesn't deserve to be forgiven so easily after that stupid act, but I think you need to let him explain. Not for his sake, but for your own," Maddie explained, her expression a little hopeful.

I knew she was right, but I just had to find the courage to confront Alessio now.

***

I had successfully avoided Alessio all morning and at lunch. It pained me to do so, but I had spent most of the day thinking. About him, us, and what had happened.

But every single time, I came to the same conclusion.

I was scared.

I was scared that what he felt for me was a lie. I was scared that he could move on so easily, forgetting me. After all, he had so many women lining up for him.

I was always second...even with Alberto. Even though he claimed that I was *his*, he was never mine. I had to share him with other women. He would fuck them in front of me, forcing me to watch. And then he would fuck me right after.

Closing my eyes against the painful memories, my fingers tightened around the comforter. Behind my closed lids, all I saw was Sasha coming out of Alessio's office, holding her ripped panties. It was painful to think that Alessio had touched her so easily.

I lost track of how long I sat there lost in my thoughts, but when I finally looked at the time, it was time to prepare dinner. Getting off the bed, I walked out of my old bedroom.

I was making my way downstairs when my steps faltered at the sight of Alessio coming up. His head was cast down as he stared intently at his phone. My throat was suddenly dry, and my hand clenched the banister.

He continued upstairs, completely oblivious that I was standing in his way. But when he was a few steps below me, he froze, his head slowly coming up to stare at me.

I sucked in a harsh breath at the sight of his beautiful, tired face. His face softened, and he slowly walked up the stairs until he was one step below me. In this position, we were almost the same height.

His blue eyes, filled with pain and longing, raked over my face as he took me in with a sorrowful expression. His eyes spoke volumes.

For the first time, he was letting me see what he was feeling. It was right there in the open, his eyes shining with vulnerability, something I was sure he had never shown anyone before.

THE MAFIA AND HIS ANGEL PART 2

But here he was, giving me yet another part of himself.

His hand slowly came up until his finger was tracing a line down my cheek. His touch was gentle, almost feather light.

"Ayla," he whispered, my name sliding past his lips as if he was whispering a prayer. His thumb brushed over my lips as his eyes stayed on mine.

With Alessio so close, I was lost in his captivating, pain-filled eyes. My body was instinctively drawn to him before I could think.

"Alessio," I breathed, moving just a little closer. At the sound of my voice, he cupped my cheek, holding my face gently.

But then the connection was broken. The spell that had bound us together in that moment vanished in thin air, leaving us both stunned and completely dejected.

"Boss."

I felt Alessio's warm touch disappear from my face as he pulled away and turned toward the voice that had called him. Phoenix looked between us and then fixated his eyes on Alessio.

Quickly looking down, I released the breath that I hadn't even realized I was holding. Phoenix was saying something, but I tuned him out.

Feeling disappointed that my moment with Alessio was interrupted, I avoided eye contact with him and Phoenix and continued my way down.

I felt Alessio's eyes on me the whole time, his stares burning holes in my back. My body was strung tight with tension, and I rubbed my sweaty hands over my dress, trying hard to control my breathing and racing heart.

Stepping into the kitchen, I sent Maddie a quick smile, acting as if everything was fine when I was feeling anything *but* fine.

I couldn't keep doing this any longer. It was only hurting me. But in the process, it was hurting Alessio too. And the thought of him being hurt felt like a knife stabbing in my chest.

He was a confident man. Arrogant and so sure of himself, but the Alessio standing on those stairs, he was a completely different man.

For both our sakes, I willed myself to be strong.

A hand on my arm snapped me out of my thoughts. Maddie stared at me, an eyebrow raised in question.

Swallowing nervously, I looked down at my feet and looked back up again, finally speaking my thought.

"I need your help."

Chapter 14

My legs bounced up and down almost frantically. In their nervous movement, a random rhythm was found. It matched the beating of my pounding and wildly racing heart.

If the bouncing of my knees were not enough to show my anxiety, then my hands showed it clearly. My trembling hands rested on my lap, my fingers clenching tight, and then unclenching around the fabric of my dress.

It wasn't a surprise that I was slowly going crazy with tension.

After all, I was sitting at the piano, waiting for Alessio to make his appearance.

It had been two nights since I last played the piano. The last two nights, it was Alessio hoping that I would come to the piano room and play for him. And now, it was *me* waiting for *him*.

Was he going to come? Or was he angry at me? Was he going to make me wait, like I did to him?

With each passing second, I was growing more alarmed at the thought that Alessio wasn't going to come.

What was he doing right now?

Did he receive my note?

The flower?

Did he smile while reading it? Was he happy about them?

Or did he ignore them?

My lips turned down in a frown at the thought of him refusing my gifts. But then I shook my head. "Stop it, Ayla," I muttered.

As soon as the words were out of my mouth, I heard a sound at the door, and my head snapped toward it.

There he was. *Alessio.*

He was standing tall, his hands resting on the door as he struggled with his breathing. It appeared as if he had run all the way here. There were beads of sweat dotting his forehead, a few strands of hair clinging on his skin as his eyes fixated on mine. His breathing was almost frantic, his eyes presenting a wild look as he walked further inside.

I saw him swallow nervously several times, his throat bobbing up and down with the movement. Alessio walked to his sofa chair, which was directly in front of the piano.

Taking a seat in his usual spot, he extended his legs forward in the exact same position he would take every single night while I played the piano.

We didn't say anything. There was only silence.

But the silence between us was enough. It was *always* enough. We only needed each other's presence, our eyes on each other. Words were never needed to express what we were feeling.

THE MAFIA AND HIS ANGEL PART 2

So I kept my eyes on him, and he did the same.

Blue to green.

Taking another deep breath, I tried to relax my tense shoulders, and I placed my trembling hands on the piano keys. My touch was light, barely even touching. My fingers softly moved over the keys, and my mouth curved up in a small smile.

I missed this.

Not just the piano, but this moment between just Alessio and I.

I missed him. His presence, his smile, his twinkling bluish steel-colored eyes. I missed everything about us.

So I played.

While we never took our eyes off each other, I played to him like I did every night. I played for *us*.

The music flowed, cocooning us in its warmth. A sweet, gentle melody. Something I had learned while I was trying to escape the darkness that Alberto would always throw me in.

It always brought me peace, but in this moment, I wasn't doing it for me.

I was doing it for Alessio, hoping it would bring him peace and ease the pain I had caused him.

I didn't have much to give him, so I gave him the only thing I had. The only thing I knew I had. Something I had treasured close to me for years.

After playing the song once, I played it a second time. My eyes caught Alessio's shoulders dropping as he started to relax in his sofa chair. A breathy sigh escaped past his lips, and the pained expression on his face slowly started to fade away, until he was staring at me with soft eyes.

I melted into his stares, my heart accelerating as I took him in.

As the song came to an end for a second time, I paused, my fingers laid gently over the keys as I breathed. Alessio stayed still, and he waited for my next move.

Slowly pushing the bench away, I stood up and walked around the piano until I was standing in front of it, facing Alessio. There was nothing between us. I just had to walk a few steps and I would be in his arms.

And that was exactly what I did.

One second I was standing away from Alessio and the next, I was right in front of him, standing between his spread legs. My knees touched his sofa chair as I looked down at him.

My eyes moved over his hard, muscled chest and then down the length of his arms until they landed on his right hand.

He was still holding the flower I had given him.

A single white peony.

His fingers were wrapped around the stem like he never wanted to let go. But even then, his hold looked almost gentle, as if he was scared to ruin the delicate flower.

I choked back a sob as my eyes moved to his other hand.

He was holding the note I had sent him before coming to the piano room. I knew what it said. I had stared at it for hours before finally having the courage to send it to him.

Please come to the piano room. I want to

play for you.

That was what it said. Simple words, yet it meant a lot to both of us.

Glancing away from his hands, I looked into his eyes again. Without giving it another thought, I sat down on his lap, settling myself sideways and leaning against his chest.

I felt Alessio's shocked breath, and then his arms were around me, so quick that it took me by surprise. He crushed me to him and buried his face in my neck.

My name was barely a whisper against his lips, but I heard it. I felt it. Placing my head on his shoulder, I wrapped an arm around his waist.

We were both silent for a few moments. Alessio kept his face buried in my neck, and I felt him place a soft kiss there before tightening his arms around me.

"Ayla," he started, but I squeezed his waist, stopping him.

"Just let me talk, okay? I need to say something," I replied.

"Okay," he readily agreed. "Whatever you want, Ayla."

Moving my head from his shoulder, it forced him to shift away from my neck too. I sat up straight on his lap, our faces a few inches apart. My hands came up to cup his cheeks, my fingers rubbing gently over the slight stubble.

"I'm sorry," I whispered.

Alessio's eyes widened, and he quickly shook his head. "No. Don't—" But his flowing words were stopped by my finger pressed over his lips.

"No, listen to me, Alessio. Please, just let me get this out, okay?"

He sighed and gave me a sharp nod, his fingers digging into my hips. "I'm sorry for hurting you. I was angry and hurt, and I wanted you to hurt. I'm still angry and hurt from what you did, but I can't hurt you. It torments me to think that you were in pain because of me."

Alessio made a strangling sound. He brought his hand up his face and placed it over mine. I looked at his stunning face, my heart thumping at how beautiful he was, even when he looked so tired and forlorn.

"I get why you did it," I continued. "I get why you thought I was the spy. It makes sense, so I don't blame for you not trusting me before. These last two days, I kept thinking if it were possible that whatever we had was a lie. I was and still am scared."

Rubbing my fingers over his lips and then tracing his nose, my fingers continued their way up under his eyes. "I can forgive you for that."

I paused and then swallowed hard before uttering the next words. "But I don't think I can forgive you so easily for what happened with Sasha."

Alessio opened his mouth, but I shushed him again. "Even if you didn't have sex with her, you still touched her." I choked on the last words.

The thought of Alessio touching another woman was gut-wrenching. I might have been lying too. I was keeping a big secret from Alessio, I was just as guilty, but I couldn't accept the fact that Alessio had touched another woman.

"The thought of you touching another woman—the thought of you being with someone else so easily, it's painful, Alessio. I don't think I'll get over that soon. I might forgive you for the rest, but it'll take me time to forgive you for touching Sasha."

"Ayla," he whispered brokenly, his eyes filled with guilt. "I'm so sorry."

"I don't know the whole story. The only thing I know is that you touched her. I have my reasons why I don't want you to explain," I murmured, my fingers brushed over his eyebrows, my whole body tingling like it always did when I was touching him.

"Because if you explain now, I will doubt you and your intentions. My judgments will be clouded by my anger and hurt. And I don't want to ever doubt you."

I cupped his jaw again, and he leaned into my palm, nuzzling into my touch. I felt my heart crack and then slowly piece together at the show of affection.

Leaning forward, I placed a sweet kiss on the tip of his nose. I felt Alessio sighing almost contentedly.

"I have thought about this for so long. You have showed me so many times that you care, Alessio. You helped me, stood by me, and made me strong. You never gave up on me and never left me in the darkness, even when I was so stupidly stubborn. When I think about everything we've been through and everything you have done for me, I think I can forgive you. I will eventually forgive you."

"And that's all I need. I just need your forgiveness, Ayla." The words were spoken low and almost fiercely.

Giving him a tentative smile, I continued. "When it's time for you to explain, I want to be ready to believe you. And for that I just need some time to get over this anger and stupid hurt that's filling my heart right now."

"How much time? How long do you need, Ayla?" he asked, his eyes wide with caution, layers of desperation clouding his expression.

"Just a few days. That's all I'm asking."

After those words were spoken, we fell silent. I leaned my forehead against his, and we breathed. My hands went to the back of his neck, my nails softly dragging up and down the skin, just the way I knew he loved. He slowly started to relax, his tensed muscles loosening under my touch.

"Being away from you hurts, Ayla. It's painful."

My eyes snapped open at his words, and I quickly blinked away my unshed tears. "I'm sorry."

"But I don't want you to be sorry," he interrupted quickly. "You have every right to be angry and hurt. I fucked up bad. This mess we are in right now is my fault. So I understand. If I saw another man touching you, I would probably kill him without a second thought."

At his words, I remembered the scene that took place yesterday, when Viktor had kissed me. Alessio had snapped and went ballistic at the sight of Viktor touching me.

"So I don't blame you, Ayla," he said. "I'll give you however much time you want. Just *please* don't

THE MAFIA AND HIS ANGEL PART 2

take too long. I don't think I can wait for a long time."

Alessio paused before confessing softly, his next words taking my breath away. "I need you."

I need you too, I wanted to say.

"Okay," I agreed before placing my head on his shoulder again. Alessio wrapped his arms around me, holding me close.

"Where will you sleep?" he suddenly broke the silence that we were both basking in.

"In my room. I don't think I can sleep in our room without touching you. I can't bear having any kind of distance between us," I replied dejectedly, hating the thought of sleeping without him.

"I don't think I can sleep in our room without you, either," he confessed, his fingers tracing random patterns on the length of my bare arms.

Pushing my head up, I looked at Alessio, my gaze searching his in question. "Our room will stay empty until you are ready for me to explain. When you are ready, we'll meet in our bedroom," he explained, his bluish eyes holding me captive.

That sounded perfect. "Okay," I agreed again. Alessio sent me a small smile and quickly gave me a peck on the lips.

I pressed my forehead against his and closed my eyes again, letting myself feel his arms around me. I let this moment make its way into my heart, holding it closely there. I absorbed his warmth for one last time, knowing that it was almost time for me to go.

After a few minutes, I leaned back and Alessio's eyes turned sorrowful. "I have to go now," I whispered.

Alessio nodded, and I slowly got off his lap. His arms fell to his lap, and a shuddered breath left his body, an agonizing expression passing over his face.

Giving him a final glance, I turned to walk away, but a hold on my wrist stopped me. Looking down, I saw that Alessio's hand banded my wrist, refusing to let me go. I faced him again, and he stared up at him, his eyes glistening in the light.

"Don't take too long," he ordered gruffly in an authoritative way that made my toes curl. His voice was hard, demanding, and held a clear warning.

I couldn't help but smile before nodding.

He still didn't let go of me. So, this time, I answered verbally. "Okay."

When he was satisfied with my spoken answer, his fingers unwrapped around my wrist as he let me go.

I walked backward a couple of steps before turning around and leaving.

Entering my room, I closed the door and got straight in bed. After taking my sleeping pill, I burrowed deep under the soft comforter and closed my eyes.

But sleep didn't come as fast as I expected.

Instead, all I could think about was Alessio.

My body was tingling and warm under the comforter. Even though Alessio wasn't holding me any longer, I still felt him on my skin. It was as if he branded me, letting me know that I was *his*.

And there was no denying it.

I was *his*.

Chapter 15

"Are you serious?" Maddie growled as she walked into her room, slamming the door behind her. My head snapped up at her tone, and I placed my book down, giving her a questioning look.

"Huh?" I asked.

"Three fucking days. No, scratch that—five days, Ayla! How long is this going to last?" She glared at me. I knew exactly what she was talking about, and as she voiced out her frustration, I looked down guiltily.

"I don't know what to do with you, and it can't go on like this anymore," she cried, her unconcealed impatience evident in her tone and expression.

Sighing, I nodded my head. "I know—"

But she interrupted me, not giving me chance to talk. "Alessio is practically going insane. He isn't eating and barely even sleeping. Have you seen him? He looks horrible! And let's not forget the anger. Oh God, I'm shuddering with just the thought of it. He's snapping at everyone and is threatening to shoot people left and right. I'm going to admit this only once, but even I am scared of him right now." She paused and sucked in a quick breath before continuing with her rant.

"I have never seen him like this. He's like this dragon breathing fire, and everyone is scared of going close to him. Every single member of his household is keeping their distance from him, even Viktor and Nikolay. And Mom, too. We are so done with this shit and want it fixed, right now! And only *you* can fix this," Maddie snapped, stabbing a finger at me.

In the last three days, the only time I saw him was at night when I would play the piano. But that was it. After playing, I would get up and walk away.

It was torturous and left a deep ache inside of me. Even worse, I knew it was hurting Alessio too.

Maddie was right. I had kept this on for too long. The problem was that I had already forgiven him, but I just didn't know how to say it. Or maybe I didn't have the courage to say it. Either way, now everything rested on my shoulders, and I had to ask for *his* forgiveness too.

Before I could open my mouth to say something, Maddie kept going as she crossed her arms over her chest, trying to look very intimidating. But with the way her glare was centered on me, she didn't have to try too hard.

She was frightening when she was angry.

"You're hurting yourself too, Ayla. This is hurting both of you. You aren't eating properly either, and I can see you lack sleep. Those dark circles don't look pretty on you. Can you please, for everyone's sake, let him off the hook and just let the poor man explain!"

Yup. She was definitely scary.

Crossing my arms over my chest too, I leveled her with a look. "I know."

Maddie scoffed, but then her expression softened. "I know he hurt you."

Shaking her head, she mumbled something under her breath before speaking loudly. "And that's why you need to let him explain so you both can figure this out together. You need each other. I also know that you have forgiven him already but are too scared to say it. Just let him fucking explain!"

"Whose side are you on, anyway?" I fired back.

Maddie paused, her mouth opened, but then she closed it again. She huffed and twisted her lips in a pout. "Aylessio's side."

Aylessio? What?

She stared at me expectantly, wiggling her eyebrows teasingly.

Ayla and Alessio. *Aylessio*. Her ship name for us.

I let out a laugh when realization dawned to me. She really wasn't giving up.

"Don't laugh. This ship is not sinking, you hear me? It has sailed and will keep sailing! It's not sinking under my watch." She narrowed her eyes at me, but her tone had taken a teasing lilt now.

"I messed up, didn't I?" I asked, thinking of Alessio.

"Not really. You just need to talk to him and fix this misunderstanding," she replied, coming to sit beside me. "I understand why you reacted the way you did. I would have done the same thing. But it's now time to fix the hurt both of you caused each other."

"I know. I'll talk to him tonight," I replied. It was time to mend this broken relationship. I had to let Alessio know that I had forgiven him, and I had to ask for his forgiveness in return.

Maddie breathed a sigh of relief beside me. "Oh, thank God. Make sure Alessio is back to his normal self, please. He scares the shit out of us at the moment. Although I'm glad he is taking it out on everyone else but you."

I didn't think I would be able to bear it if his anger was directed at me.

Maddie shrugged and then encouraged me in a sweet voice, "Go get your man. He needs you. Just don't give up on him."

She was right. Alessio was always fighting for everyone, even for me. He fought to keep me. He fought to get rid of my darkness and never gave up on me. And now it was my turn to fight for him.

Maddie got off the bed and smiled. "In the meantime, I'm going to get my man." She sent me a wink and then walked out of the room.

As soon as the door closed behind her, I quickly went to the bathroom. After washing my face, I combed my hair and decided to leave it down. It flowed beautifully down my back, just the way Alessio loved it.

I walked out of the bathroom but stopped dead in my tracks when I saw Alessio standing in the middle on the room. He was turned sideways, facing the wall.

He looked even worse than last night. His rough stubble had grown another inch, and it was obvious he hadn't shaved for days. His suit was wrinkled, as if he'd slept in them. The side of his lips were cast down in a frown.

Even though he appeared completely worn, Alessio was still the most handsome man to me.

My thoughts were interrupted when he turned to face me. My eyes widened when I saw the change in his expression. Alessio crossed his arms over his chest; his legs were shoulder-width apart as he glowered at me.

He was glaring at me so fiercely I almost took a step back.

"Alessio—" I started, but he cut me off.

"I'm not doing this anymore."

Oh no. Please no. Did I break us beyond repair?

Alessio started toward me, his steps slow. *No*, he *prowled* toward me, looking dangerously like a predator hunting his prey.

I lifted a hand up to explain, but my mouth snapped shut when a deep, angry growl vibrated from his chest.

Maddie was wrong about one thing.

This time, Alessio was definitely taking out his anger on me.

"I told you I won't wait for long. I am not a patient man, Ayla," Alessio said in a low, deadly voice.

"Alessio, please—" I muttered shakily.

As he walked forward, I retreated backward, but then bumped into the wall. Damn it, the wall always got in my way. Every single time.

Alessio tilted his chin up as he regarded me with angry blue eyes. My chest squeezed painfully tight, and I swallowed nervously under his penetrating, intense gaze.

"I was just about to come up and talk to you," I tried to explain, hoping this would calm him just a little bit.

But it didn't.

"Oh really?" he spat.

I nodded mutely, begging him with my eyes.

Alessio stopped inches from my body as he cornered me against the wall.

"Really," I mumbled.

"I thought you said you weren't going to take too long," he hissed in my ears. My heart thumped faster at his words, and I placed a trembling hand over his chest, trying to push him away from me.

Bad move. It only pissed him off more.

His finger wrapped around my wrist and squeezed in warning. "Don't test me, Ayla," he growled low.

"You hurt me, and I needed time," I suddenly snapped.

Another bad move. This time he was furious.

Alessio cocked his head to the side and stared at me, his eyes sizing me up.

He stepped forward until his body was plastered against mine. His hands wrapped around my waist, his fingers digging into my hips. "This was so much easier when you were scared of me," he snapped back.

My eyes widened, and I gasped. Struggling against his hold, I saw his blue eyes crackling with

THE MAFIA AND HIS ANGEL PART 2

fierce intensity.

Alessio pulled me away from the wall, and I saw the corner of his lips lift up in a small smirk. That should have been warning enough.

"We are doing this my way now, kitten," he said gruffly, his voice deep and low.

But I didn't have time to think.

Within a second, I found myself over his shoulders, dangling upside down.

"Alessio, let go of me," I demanded, struggling against his hold. Alessio didn't listen. Instead, he stalked out of the room and walked down the hall that led to the staircase.

"Alessio! Stop it!" I snapped. "Let me down."

When I felt a slap over my butt, my eyes widened, and my mouth snapped shut. Did he just spank me?

From my position on Alessio's shoulder, I saw Viktor, Nikolay, Maddie, and Lena standing in the living room, staring at us with big smiles on their faces.

Well, Nikolay wasn't smiling big. His lips were just turned up in a tiny barely there smile. Viktor was smirking while Maddie and Lena both had big smiles on their faces. Maddie looked extremely proud of herself, and she wiggled her eyebrows at me.

I couldn't believe they were seeing this.

I pinched Alessio's butt in return, and that earned me another slap on the ass. The spot he slapped burned a little, although it didn't hurt. I twitched and struggled against his hold.

That earned me another spank. And another.

Four actually. Two on each butt cheek. They came down hard and fast and rendered me speechless.

"Wiggling that pretty ass of yours in my face isn't helping your case, kitten. So I suggest you stop moving. Or not. You can keep struggling. It's making me really hard at this moment."

Feeling completely mortified and shocked that he would say that in front of everyone, I closed my eyes and stopped moving, lying limply on Alessio's shoulders.

I was dangling upside down a lot longer than I wanted, and my head started feeling heavy while he walked up the stairs. He made his way to our room and walked inside, kicking the door closed behind him and stalking to our bed.

He threw me on it, and I bounced on the mattress. Opening my eyes, I gaped in shock when Alessio climbed on top of me. With his knees on either side of my hips, he held me immobile.

My heart stuttered to a stop for a second before thumping faster again.

"Alessio—listen—"

"Shut up."

His lips found mine, successfully shutting me up. He took my lips possessively and kissed me breathlessly.

Oh yeah, he definitely shut me up. He knew exactly how to shut me up.

As he pulled away, I tried to move my hands and realized they were trapped. While kissing me, Alessio had brought my arms up above my head, and now he was holding me captive.

I was completely immobile and at Alessio's

mercy under his body.

His lips were only inches apart from mine when he spoke the next time.

"This time I'll be doing the talking and you will listen. Not a word, kitten. Not until I'm done talking."

Chapter 16

Alessio had left me breathless and completely in a daze with his kiss, and now his words made my heart jump. My body melted under his, and I stared up into his furious yet painful eyes. I should have been scared, but I wasn't. Not of Alessio.

He might have been angry with me, but he was still gentle. Even as he gazed down furiously, his fingers were gently and softly caressing my cheek. Alessio was doing it almost unknowingly, as if he needed to touch me, feel me.

We stared at each other for a few seconds, Alessio looking suddenly lost for words. Slowly the rage in his eyes disappeared until they were soft with unspoken emotions. Still holding my hands captive above my head and my body under his, he slowly bent down until our foreheads were softly touching.

"I'm going to tell you a story," he said.

Confused, I only blinked up at him. A story? Is that why he dragged me here…for a story?

"Alessio—" I started, struggling under him,

twisting my body with hopes that he would let me go.

But he didn't. Instead, his hold on me tightened, and the glare was back.

"Stop moving and listen. Not a word, Ayla."

With a sigh, I laid limply and waited for him to start his story. In fact, I was curious what he had to say. So I was going to listen to his story.

And then I would let him know I forgave him.

Alessio lost his glare again, and his lips touched the tip of my nose in a small feather light kiss. "There was once a woman with blue eyes and beautiful long black hair. She was so beautiful and the kindest person ever. Her smiles and laughter were infectious. A man saw her, and she saw him. It was love at first sight, they said. They fell irrevocably in love with each other."

A love story? More confused than ever, I listened silently, my heart accelerating just a little bit.

"They had a boy." Alessio paused and took a deep breath before continuing. "He was her sweet gentle boy." His voice cracked at the last words, his fingers tightening around my wrists. "They were a happy family."

My body prickled with nervousness. I had a feeling that this wouldn't end happily.

"The man would always call his wife *Angel*. The little boy was curious to why. So they told him what Angels were and why she was an Angel."

Angel.

Sleep, Angel. I will watch over you.

A sudden memory flashed in my head. It was blurry, the voice barely a whisper in my head, but I heard it. Alessio's voice, whispering to my ears once.

Sleep, Angel. I will watch over you.

I didn't even have a chance to react because Alessio continued speaking. "The father replied that an Angel is someone who is sweet, kind, caring, calm, and mellow. The most beautiful woman on the planet. Someone who is amazing in every way. An Angel is the girl who makes your heart beat faster when she walks into the room. The girl you will need wherever you go. The girl who makes you want to be better. Angel is someone who is your rock. The person who you love with your entire heart. The person you can't see yourself living without."

His answer was almost monotone, like he practiced it. Like this had been running in his head for a long time and he knew it by heart.

And I had a feeling that this story, the definition of Angel, Alessio did know it by heart.

The way his voice had cracked slightly over the words and the way his muscles were locked tight with tension, I knew this story wasn't just any story.

"They also said that if you find your angel, don't ever let her go. Because you would forever be incomplete without her." His voice had softened a little, just above a whisper now. His fingers on my wrist were not tight anymore, so I twisted my hands a little, to see his reaction.

Instead of struggling to get free from his grasp, my hands went to his shoulders. My fingers tightened around them as I held him. When Alessio shuddered with relief, I didn't regret holding onto him.

My body was calling to his; the need to hold and be held was a need impossible to refuse. So I didn't fight. I gave in and held onto this broken man as he continued to tell me his story.

"The little boy was happy with the explanation, and he couldn't wait to meet his Angel one day, although he was hell bent on believing that his mother was his Angel." A small smile played on his lips when he said that last few words.

When he lost the smile and his face twisted with a wave of pain, my heart slammed to a stop before restarting with a painfully racing beat. My hold tightened on Alessio, my fingers softly caressing his shoulders. I wanted to offer him any type of comfort.

"But then the mother died. A slow, painful death. A cruel death that left everyone heartbroken, especially the little boy."

I sucked in a harsh breath, and I knew...I just knew...this wasn't a story. It was reality.

"All he felt was darkness and pain. He was blinded by it, but over the years, he learned to be numb. Not to feel. He became darkness. He became a monster." Alessio paused and then gave me a small sad smile.

"Cold. Ruthless. Heartless. Arrogant. Killer. Unlovable. These are all the words that little boy goes by now. He's respected and feared by all. He can't love or be loved."

I flinched, my eyes squeezing shut for a second with sorrow. Those words were the same words I had hurled at Alessio in my attempt to hurt him.

"The boy long ago lost hope to find to his *Angel*. He thought it was a stupid idea. He refused to believe in Angels, for he believed that a monster can never have an Angel. And he was a monster." His voice was low and gruff, almost pained.

Never once did he stop touching me while talking. And I never let go of him.

"Alessio, no." I shook my head, trying to stop his agonizing story.

But it was impossible to stop him once he had started. He softly continued to caress my cheeks.

"But then everything changed when he found a broken girl hiding under his bed. She was dirty and so damn scared of him. But he was instantly taken by her. There was something about her that called to him and made him…feel. He hated it. He loathed the idea of feeling. He pushed until he couldn't push anymore. He couldn't deny the truth anymore."

While speaking, he placed another kiss on the tip of my nose and then continued with his tale, this time taking away my breath yet again. Tears sprung in my eyes, and one single drop slid down the corner and disappeared into my hair, leaving a wet trail.

"She was the sweetest, the kindest, and so gentle. So beautiful that he couldn't take his eyes off her. She was the true definition of beauty—inside and out. She was love, while he was hatred. She was kind while he was unlovable. She was sweet and gentle while he killed in cold blood and felt no remorse. She was light while he was darkness. He realized that he'd found his *Angel*. He couldn't deny it any longer. Because he needed her. He couldn't live without her. He didn't want to imagine a world where she wasn't in it."

Alessio paused for what felt like the longest time, leaving the words hanging around us, our eyes connected together. We breathed together, our heart racing in unison.

Another tear spilled from my eye and ran down my cheek. Alessio caught it quickly with his lips, kissing it away. When another fell down my face, he did the same thing. Closing my eyes, I hiccupped back a sob.

"That little boy was me, Ayla," Alessio whispered in my ear, his breath tickling me there. "And the broken girl he found under his bed, his Angel, she is you. You are my Angel."

"I—" I started but then quickly snapped my mouth shut. I didn't know what to say. His confession had truly left me with a mix of emotions.

I felt light, almost as if I was floating. My heart was beating as fast as the wings of a hummingbird, and it hummed just like a hummingbird. It sang with happiness and so much…love. I was filled with pure elation.

Alessio's lips lingered on my cheeks before he slightly pulled away, looking down at me with his beautiful blue eyes. His expression was soft yet determined. "You are right. I did touch Sasha."

I blinked away tears, my fingers digging into his shoulders painfully. He didn't wince, not that I expected him to.

He instantly noticed my change in demeanor. He soothed me, caressing my cheeks yet again. "I touched her, but I didn't kiss her. I touched her, but

I didn't fuck her. I didn't do anything with Sasha."

I only blinked up at him, confused and feeling slightly bewildered. "I'll be blunt and honest. Yes, I was so close to fucking her. Yes, I had ripped her panties and had her bent over my desk, but no, I didn't fuck her. I couldn't, Ayla. You were all I could think about. You. Every single minute. All I could see were your eyes, beautiful smiles, serene expression as you played the piano and walked to the creek. All I could hear were your laughter and sweet voice."

Alessio dragged in a harsh, deep breath before releasing it with a tired sigh. His expression was haggard, his voice filled with uncertainty and so much grief that my heart ached. It ached for his pain. "I was mad. At my father and at everything. My feelings. My weakness for you. And I was so scared. My mother died because my father loved her. An angel living in the world of the devils, and in the end, she got killed because of it. I am so fucking scared that I'll lose you too. The mere thought of losing you drives me insane."

"I didn't do anything with Sasha," he said again, his voice almost filled with ferocity as he willed me to believe him with his eyes. They begged me to see the truth. "Tell me you believe me, Ayla."

My hands left his shoulders, but instead of pulling away, I palmed his cheeks. "I believe you," I whispered.

I truly did. His words and face spoke honesty. It was right there for me to believe. Not once was I filled with doubt when he said he didn't touch Sasha. If I had doubts before, it was now erased.

"I believe you, Alessio," I said again, my fingers pressing gently into his cheeks. Alessio shuddered in relief atop of me, his eyes closing as he finally relaxed in my hold.

We stayed like that for a few seconds, with me soothing him. When he opened his eyes again, this time the blueish orbs were glistening with intensity. "The plan was to get close to you to find out if you were a traitor," he started.

Flinching, I started to let go, but he quickly grasped my hands, holding them firmly to his cheeks.

"But it was just an excuse," he quickly added. "I was using it as an excuse to get close to you. From the very first time I saw you, I had this urge to be close to you. To hold you. But it was a show of weakness. So I tried to find every excuse to get close to you. The plan ended the same day it was made, because no matter what, I couldn't lie to myself. I kept telling myself it was what I had to do for the safety of everyone, but deep inside, I knew I was doing it for myself. I needed you, since the very beginning." He looked in her eyes.

"I messed up," Alessio breathed sadly. "I know I did, but I'm asking you to forgive me. To give me another chance to prove myself. Please let me in your heart again. Give me this chance and I'll never let you go again. I'll never break you again."

He paused and took a deep breath before continuing in the same soft voice. "I'll never be the man you deserve, but I'll be the man you need. I'll be the man who makes you laugh and smile, the one who drives away all your nightmares, the one who kisses you good morning and good night and so many kisses in between. I'll be your savior. Now and for the rest of my life."

Tears sprung in my eyes at his confession, and I gave him a wobbly smile. "You definitely do have a way with words," I replied.

Alessio let out a small laugh and shook his head, his lips lifting up in a small smile. "Only for you, Angel."

My eyes widened as he called me *Angel*, the tears falling before I could stop them. "You are making me cry," I muttered as Alessio swiped the tears away.

"Are they happy tears?" he asked, looking a bit uncertain.

I nodded, speechless, and he gifted me with one of his breathtaking smiles. "Good. From now on, the only tears you will cry will be happy tears."

"You're sweet."

Alessio looked affronted by my admission and sent me a mock glare. I couldn't help but laugh. It looked like the Mafia Boss didn't like being called *sweet*, although he really was…sweet.

"I'm a killer, Ayla. Definitely not sweet," he said, looking deep into my eyes.

Smiling, I leaned up and placed a kiss on his nose like he had done to me. "You might be a killer out there, a monster, as you said, but in here," I pressed my hand over his heart, "in here, you are sweet. To me, you are sweet."

Another breathtaking smile from Alessio. This time the smile lit up his face and eyes with such happiness that it made my heart ache…in a good way. It fluttered, and I melted into his embrace.

Finally, the pain that I had seen before was no longer there. He looked hopeful.

Taking a deep breath, Alessio continued. "When I'm with you, it feels as if I can finally breathe. I have been living in the darkness for so long, but you bring me light and peace. You make me laugh and smile, something I haven't done in so damn long. When I'm away from you, I feel empty, like I'm missing a piece of myself. I don't ever want to be without you, Angel. I don't think I'll survive it. When I'm with you, it feels like I'm the king of the world. I can accomplish anything with you by my side. I used to believe that you are my weakness. You are. You will always be my weakness, but you are also my strength."

Oh wow. Wow. My throat tightened up at his confession until it felt impossible to breathe. "Alessio," I murmured, a constant smile on my lips.

"I don't know what love is," Alessio mumbled, brushing his lips against mine in the lightest kiss. "But if what I feel for you is love, then so be it."

"I don't know what love is either," I admitted, my fingers softly moving over his cheeks and then his lips.

Kissing me again on the lips with the slightest pressure, as if he was scared to break me, Alessio smiled. "We'll learn it together then, Angel."

Angel. I didn't think I would ever get tired of Alessio calling me that.

"You called me *Angel* once. When I had my breakdown," I murmured.

Alessio smiled. "Yes. I always knew you were

my Angel, but I was too stubborn to admit it."

It didn't matter anymore if he was stubborn or not.

"You are my Angel."

Yes, I was. I was *his*. I was his Angel.

And he was mine. My Made Man. My monster. Whoever he was, whether he was the killer or the sweet man he was with me, I accepted him.

I breathed him in. Closing my eyes, I let my senses take over, feeling Alessio, savoring his touch and voice. I couldn't live without him. This beautiful broken man had given me his heart, and in return, I had laid mine in his palms.

We were two broken hearts. Two broken halves making a whole.

"I can't promise you everything will be perfect." My eyes snapped open at Alessio's voice, and I waited for him to continue. "My life is not perfect. The world is fucked up and dangerous. Life is not going to be rosy. But I can promise to make it as perfect as I can. All I know is that I need you. This makes me a selfish man, Ayla. I should let you go. You would be better off without me, but I'm selfish when it comes to you."

My fingers went to his lips to silence him. "It's okay. That's all I needed to hear, Alessio. I can't live without you, either. This is enough for me. It's more than enough. I don't need or want anything else. I just want *you*."

Before I could say anything else, Alessio had me crushed to his chest, hugging me so tight. My ribs felt like they were about to break. "Can't breathe," I squeaked, but I still wrapped my arms around him,

THE MAFIA AND HIS ANGEL PART 2

returning the hug just as fiercely.

He kissed the top of my forehead, his lips lingering there. "You are my Angel."

There it was. Those words again.

I sighed in contentment. *I love you* was needed. We were more than that. The words that Alessio had whispered to me meant more than those common three words.

You are my Angel. These held more power.

"And you are the man who brings me peace." I whispered the words ever so softly. "The man who makes my heart flutter and fills my stomach with butterflies. Just one look from you, a simple word, just one sweet kiss, or one soft caress, it is enough to make me the happiest woman. You are my strength, Alessio."

His arms tightened around me, and I smiled. Oh yes, my words had the same effect on him as his words had on me.

Alessio was a man of few words, yet he was able to say so much to me. I wished I had more to say. I wished I had more words to show what my heart…what I truly felt. But I didn't.

I'd rather just show him. Bringing his lips to mine, I kissed him. Softly and gently. The kiss wasn't fast or hard. It was sweet and slow. We took our time, our lips moving in sync, and we savored each other. Alessio let me lead the kiss. He didn't push for more. He let *me* kiss *him*. So I did, for the longest time.

Our tongues mated together in a slow, sweet loving. We kissed until we were breathless. And when we pulled apart, my heart felt like it had been restored. By the look Alessio was giving me, I could tell he felt the same.

My lips still tingled from the kiss. I could still feel him there, and a dreamy smile spread across my lips.

"I dreamed of you before you came into my life. When I was still a little boy, I dreamed of you. Black hair and green eyes, with a beautiful smile," Alessio said gruffly, his voice tight with emotions.

I stuttered, and he smiled. "You were always meant for me, Ayla."

"I was." I nodded in agreement. "I just wished I had found you sooner, Alessio. Then you wouldn't have needed to wait for me for so long."

"It doesn't matter. You found me now, and I'm never letting you go."

"I don't want you to ever let me go. Even if you tried, I'll just come back," I teased, although the words spoken rang with the truth.

"Good." This time, it was Alessio who took my lips.

The kiss wasn't sweet as before. He devoured me. He kissed me a like a madman. Like an animal craving for his mate. He took my lips deeply and possessively. Alessio kissed me with all he had.

His tongue shoved past my lips, kissing me with a frenzied desperation. I moaned against his lips, my hands going to his hair, my fingers tightening. He nipped at my bottom lip, and I leaned more into his kiss, demanding more.

When he pulled away, I could feel his pounding heart against mine. Alessio stared down at me with soft eyes, although the lust was blazing there with ferocious intensity. I trembled in anticipation for him.

"Do you forgive me?" he asked, his voice rough with desire.

Smiling, I combed my fingers through his hair, gently grazing my nails on the back of his neck, just the way he loved it. "I do. I had already forgiven you before you even dragged me here. Actually, I was coming up to talk to you but you beat me to it."

"Yeah?" he asked, his eyes roaming over my face and then staring into mine deeply, looking for confirmation.

"Yes, Alessio," I nodded. "I forgive you."

And then his lips crashed to mine again. Giving me a hard, bruising kiss, he left me breathless. When he pulled away, I groaned a little. I could feel his hard on between my parted thighs.

I was turned on. I needed him. I forgave him.

"I forgive you, but I'm still a little mad that you touched Sasha," I mumbled as his lips started to descend toward mine again.

Alessio froze, his lips mere inches from mine. "I know," he mumbled back.

And then there it was. That smirk I loved so much. The corner of his lips tilted up just a little, and I had to suppress my moan.

Before I could say anything else, he rolled us over quickly, eliciting a shocked gasp from me. Alessio laid on his back, his head on his pillow as I straddled him, my knees on either side of his hips.

Alessio gifted me with his perfect smirk before slightly pushing upward and rolling his hips against mine. This time a moan escaped past my lips unashamedly when his hard cock pressed into me.

"I know," he said again.

And then another roll of his hips.

He teased me, his rigid length rubbing deliciously against my covered crotch. Even through his slacks and my panties, I felt him. Hard, warm and ready.

"You can give me any punishment you want," Alessio replied gruffly. I stared down at him through hazy eyes, and he sent me a wink, raising an eyebrow in suggestion.

Alessio slowly moved the hem of my dress upward, his fingers moving over my bare thighs. He drove me crazy with his teasing touch. When I finally got what he meant, I let out a small laugh.

He was impossible. Insatiable.

I hummed, giving my hips a tentative roll. Alessio groaned, slightly bucking upward. My hands went between us, and I cupped him through his slacks.

"Fuck," he hissed.

I gave him a small squeeze, teasing him in return. I almost let out another moan at the feel of him, the hardness of him, pressing into my palm. I rubbed him over his pants, my hazy eyes on his lustful ones.

"Any punishment? Anything I want?" I asked, continuing my slow teasing touch.

"Yeah," he groaned. "Anything."

Leaning forward until my face was inches above his, our lips almost touching, I whispered, my voice coming out huskily. "Anything?"

"Anything, kitten," he readily agreed, rolling his

hips upward again, pressing into my palm.

Smiling, I gave him a quick kiss on the lips and then leaned back. Letting go of his cock, I raised an eyebrow of my own.

"Fine. You can't touch me for three days."

Alessio's eyes widened as he froze, his mouth falling open in shock. "What?" he sputtered. Before he could stop me, I rolled off him and quickly got out of the bed.

He sat up, still staring at me in complete bafflement. "You heard me. You can't touch me for three days."

"No," Alessio snapped. "We are not doing this. One fucking week of being away from you, not touching you. And now another three days? No. Fucking. Way."

"Yes," I replied back calmly. "That's your punishment."

Rubbing a hand over his face in frustration, he growled. "I had another type of punishment in mind."

Oh yeah, he definitely did. I wouldn't have minded either, but this time, it was my turn to tease him. I was going to enjoy it.

Alessio stared blankly at me for a few seconds before he smirked, his eyes turning dark with lust again. "Kitten," he said huskily.

Oh no. No. I knew what he was doing.

I took a step away from the bed as he got off, stalking toward me. "No, Alessio."

"I know you want me," he continued, his hand going down to cup himself. He was still hard.

I was in trouble. I couldn't deny him, especially

when he was like this.

Placing a hand out, I tried to glare, although I could already feel myself growing wet. *Ah! Get yourself together, Ayla.*

"No. Stay," I ordered.

He paused, cocking his head to the side. "I'm not a dog, Ayla."

"Your sexy voice and sinfully delicious, beautiful body is not going to work on me this time," I muttered. I meant it to be low, but he heard the words.

Wanting to smack myself, I only glared at Alessio when he chuckled low. "Hmm…so you like my sinfully delicious, beautiful body?"

Rolling my eyes, I crossed my arms. "Stop it."

Alessio stalked toward me until he was standing in front of me, our bodies almost touching. "There is nothing wrong with that. You're my woman. You have every right to appreciate my body and call it whatever you like," he muttered in my ear, his breath tickling me there.

"And if you stop being stubborn, you can do anything you like with it too." He placed a kiss on my ear, his tongue moving downward to my neck, leaving a wet trail. He kissed, licked, and sucked until it was almost impossible to refuse him.

"Alessio," I breathed.

"You want my cock inside of you, don't you? I know you're wet right now, dripping for me."

He was right. This infuriating man.

"Alessio." Placing my hand over his chest, I pushed him away. "Behave. It's only three days."

"Exactly! Three fucking days of torture!" he

growled, crossing his arms over his chest. "One day," he tried to bargain.

Not happening.

"Nope. Three days."

"One day, kitten. That's all you're getting."

"No."

"Fine! One day and a half."

"No. Three days."

"Ayla, stop being stubborn," Alessio glared.

"You stop being stubborn. You said any punishment." I glared back.

"Two days! That's it. No more," Alessio snapped.

"No."

"Two days, Ayla. Whether you like it or not, I'm coming for you in two days," he said, the promise clear in his eyes and voice.

Throwing my hands in the air, I huffed. "Fine! Two days of no touching."

"Can you wait for that long?" he asked, coming closer again.

No. It was going to be torture.

"No," I replied honestly. "You're right. It's going to be torture."

Alessio sighed before wrapping his arms around me. "Then why?"

"Maybe I am still a little mad?" Returning his hug, I placed a kiss over his chest. "I forgave you. But that doesn't mean I'm not still slightly hurt."

"Okay. Two days," he mumbled in my ear.

Alessio pulled back, and I leaned on my tip-toes, kissing him soundly on the lips. Pulling away, I pressed my palm over his chest. "I need to get back to work."

He brought his hand up and trailed a finger down my cheek. "I'll see you down for dinner."

Chapter 17

I left Alessio in our room and joined Maddie in the kitchen. Without giving her any warning, I pulled her away from the oven and twirled us around. She looked surprised at first but quickly let out a laugh.

Coming to a stop, I hugged her tight before letting go. "I see everything went well," she remarked.

"Yes. It was perfect. Maddie, he is simply amazing," I gushed in utter contentment. "Sometimes I feel like I don't deserve him. But I'm selfish. I don't want to be without him."

Maddie smiled, her face glowing with happiness. "I'm so happy for both of you. Don't give up on him, okay?"

Shaking my head, I promised, "Never."

It was a promise I was going to hold close to my heart. He was mine, and I was going to fight for him every day.

"I'm surprised you came down so fast." Maddie raised an eyebrow at me before going back to the oven to remove the roasted chicken.

"Umm…yeah about that. *Itoldhimhecan'ttouchmeforthreedays*." I said the words so fast they ran together before snapping my mouth shut in embarrassment.

"Huh?" Maddie asked, confused.

Sitting on the stool, I cleared my throat before speaking again. "I told him he can't touch me for three days because I was still mad."

Maddie stared at me for a second before busting in laughter. "You're withholding sex? Oh my God, this is priceless."

I shrugged. "But it's two days now. He tried to bargain with me."

"Of course. This is Alessio we're talking about. I'm surprised he even accepted two days."

"It was a hard bargain," I agreed.

"I'm proud of you, girl," Maddie said, her chest puffing out proudly. "Alessio needs to know what he did was wrong and won't easily be forgotten."

I nodded and helped her out. Maddie and I switched to small talk about anything and everything when I heard a very familiar voice.

My back straightened, and I saw Maddie freeze.

The voice came closer, and I held my knife tighter.

Nina.

What was she doing here?

I saw Maddie glaring at the doorway, and I took a deep breath. And then I heard her.

"Maddie," she greeted. "I just need a glass of water."

Maddie didn't reply. Turning around on my

THE MAFIA AND HIS ANGEL PART 2

stool, I faced her. She was wearing a pretty tight black dress that barely came to mid-thigh. Her red heels were pretty but so tall I wondered how she walked in them. Her blonde hair curled beautifully around her shoulders. Her face was glowing, her lips red with lipstick. In other words, she looked absolutely gorgeous.

Nina looked at me up and down, sizing me up before scoffing, rolling her eyes. "I'm surprised you're still here," she mumbled.

"What?" I asked, placing the knife down on the counter.

"After what you saw, I thought you would be all butt hurt and poor you would be running away in embarrassment," she replied frankly.

"I'm still here," I said.

"I can see that. But for how long? None of his fuck buddies last very long," she shot back. "Except me." Nina flipped her hair over her shoulder and leveled with a look.

Was she serious?

I saw Maddie glaring holes into Nina from the corner of my eyes. *Oh, she is definitely scary when angry.*

"Oh well, it's not like he'll still be interested in you after a few weeks." She shrugged.

"Why do you say that?" I asked as calmly as I could. Deep inside, I felt slightly embarrassed, but that wasn't what I was trying to control. It was the anger boiling inside of me that I was trying to keep at bay.

Giving her my best smile, I waited for her answer.

She scoffed, shaking her head. "Have you seen yourself?"

Confused, I looked down at myself. "I see myself every day in the mirror," I mumbled.

"You are so…stiff," she said through gritted teeth. "Do you really think you can keep Alessio interested for long?"

"That's enough, bitch!" Maddie growled on the side.

"Oh please. I'm just speaking the truth. Truth hurts, doesn't it?" Nina snapped back. Turning toward me again, she continued to hurl her insults.

"You are so plain. Stiff. Looking at you, I can already say you are probably a shit lay. Alessio needs someone adventurous. Someone who can keep him on his toes. Someone who isn't as frigid as you."

Calm down, Ayla. Take a deep breath. It's okay. She's just trying to hurt you. Don't let her win.

"You little—" Maddie started saying, but Nina talked over her.

Walking closer to me, she continued. "Do you really think he would leave me for you, someone he had just met?"

My hands tightened into fists, and I stared blankly at her.

"I'm more like him. We have always been compatible. In bed and outside the bed. Whether he is fucking me or if we're just working."

Jealousy was a red haze in front of my eyes. And so much anger.

She licked her red lips and then smiled. The smile wasn't friendly at all. It was mocking me, daring me to prove her wrong. "I've known him for years, and he always comes back to me. Alessio always comes back for more. And when he's done with you, he will be back in *my* bed. You will be long forgotten, like every other stupid woman in his life."

That's it. I have had enough!

Quickly standing up, I caught Nina by surprise, and she took a step back, her eyebrows pulling together in confusion. Without thinking, I reached across the counter, my hand blindly reaching for something. Anything.

Too bad, my hand caught the cake Lena had baked this morning.

Everything happened so fast then.

One second I was standing in front of Nina while she glared at me, and the next, the cake was planted in her face.

She squealed and took several steps back, the cake falling from her face to the floor. Nina swiped her hands over her face furiously. "You fucking bitch. You're going to pay for this."

I didn't give her a chance to react. Bending down, I grabbed the leftover cake and smashed it in her face again, smearing it all over her beautiful blonde hair and perfect face.

"You stupid ugly bitch!" I growled.

Chapter 18

My loud voice resonated in my ears and rang around the room. I never swore. Ever. And I had never been this mad before. I was seething, my heart pumping fiercely with the need to extract revenge on the woman standing in front of me.

How dare she?

She not only insulted me, but Alessio also. She insulted what Alessio and I had. Our relationship was not perfect, but our feelings for each other were pure. I wasn't going to stand there and watch someone else taint it.

Nina's face was covered in chocolate cake…my favorite cake, actually. Lena had baked it for me, and for a moment, I felt a pang of sadness that it got spoiled, but the anger—my body was shaking with it. I was blinded.

All I could hear were Nina's horrendous words.

She tried to reach for me, but I quickly stepped out of the way and reached for her hair, wrapping my fingers around the strands that weren't spoiled by the cake.

THE MAFIA AND HIS ANGEL PART 2

"Let go of me!" she yelled. My fingers only clenched tighter.

"Don't you *ever* speak about my relationship with Alessio like that," I hissed in her face. "You are so wrong and so blinded by your hatred to see what Alessio and I have. Maybe if you open your heart just a little, maybe then you will understand what love is and how pure it is."

"Love is stupid. And you're stupid to think Alessio loves you. He can't love. He doesn't know how to love," she snapped back.

"You are wrong again." My fingers fisted in her hair, and I pulled her face closer to mine. "Everyone says he's heartless, but I have seen the man behind the cruel monster. He might be hard and ruthless…" I paused, thinking about Alessio and his confessions. I thought about all his sweet words, kisses, and gentle caresses. Looking back into Nina's furious eyes, I continued, "But he can love. I believe in him."

"And that will be your first and last mistake," she replied, her harsh laughter ringing in my ears cruelly.

My patience had been hanging on the end of a small thread, but it just snapped. I was blinded by a sudden rage that tasted bitter but surprisingly satisfying.

"My mistake would be listening to your hateful words." Before she could say anything else, I was dragging her out of the kitchen, pulling her by her hair.

"Let go of me!" Nina screamed, her voice loud in the estate.

Nina's fingers wrapped around my wrist, her nails digging almost painfully into my skin. I winced but didn't let her go. She scratched me, and when a stinging feeling spread across my wrist and arm, I knew she had drawn blood.

Ignoring the burning sensation, I finally reached the main doors, which were thankfully already open. I dragged and pushed Nina out, releasing my grip on her hair.

She tripped and fell down on her knees before quickly standing up again. Turning to face me, she was seething with anger. Her body was shaking with it.

"Don't come back again, and stop sprouting your hate and insecurities on others. You have not only insulted Alessio and me, but you have also insulted yourself in the process. Be with a man who can love you and make love to you. Not with someone who will only fuck you and then leave you to sleep with other women. That's nothing to be proud about."

At my words, I saw Nina somber up a little, just a little. It was for but a fleeting moment. Her lips twisted ruefully, and even though her face was covered in cake, I still saw the glare she was sending me.

"Oh please, I don't need your lectures. What are you? A saint?"

Shaking my head sadly, I let out a small, remorseful laugh. She was hopeless.

"No, I'm not a saint." I paused, my own words catching me by surprise. It was true. I was no saint. I was a liar, betraying the trust of the only man who made me feel something. I was betraying the trust of the family, who in many ways adopted me.

The guilt was almost unbearable, my heart aching with it. I almost ran inside to go and tell Alessio everything, but my feet stayed rooted in the same spot.

The fear of the unknown was something bitter and scary.

"No, I'm not a saint," I repeated, looking at Nina. "But I do know the difference between love and hatred. Pain and love. Kindness and cruelty. But you don't understand. You chose hate above love and kindness."

Giving her a final look, I took a step back so that I was inside the house again. "Don't come back. And Stay. Away. From. Alessio." I punctuated each word, trying to make her understand that I was serious.

"What are you going to do if I don't?" she taunted.

Sending her a glare of my own, I crossed my arms over my chest. "I will do worse than throwing a cake in your face and dragging you out. Don't test me. I don't know my own anger and what I can do. You don't want to be an experiment."

"You are useless. Mark my words. Alessio will come back to me," Nina growled, hoping her words would be a slap in my face.

But they didn't hurt. I knew the truth. I trusted Alessio.

"Alessio doesn't want you. He chose me." Taking a deep breath, my lips tilted up in a small smile at the thought of him.

Without seeing her reaction, I closed the door in

her face. A sigh escaped my lips as I turned around but stopped at the sight of everyone standing there.

Viktor, Nikolay, and Maddie were standing in the living room, staring at me in absolute shock. Maddie had a huge smile on her face, and she was practically bouncing on her toes.

Viktor shook his head, a smirk in place, and it was obvious he was trying hard not to laugh. "Remind me to never piss her off," he said with a fake cough. "Damn, the kitten has claws."

Nikolay simply nodded, his face expressionless as always.

"That was epic!" Maddie squealed. "Oh my God. Yes! I feel like a proud momma. My girl has grown so much."

As Maddie squealed proudly, I stared at my hands in astonishment when realization finally dawned at what I had done.

I was still reeling from my encounter with Nina when Maddie came over and hugged me. "You were amazing and definitely showed Nina her place."

What was I supposed to say? "Umm…thank you?"

Maddie laughed, shaking her head at my obvious bewilderment. Viktor sent me a nod before walking away, Nikolay following closely behind him.

Maddie started to pull me toward the kitchen, and that was when I noticed Lyov and Isaak standing on the stairs. Lyov's eyes were focused intently on me, following my every move.

I shivered under his intense gaze. Lyov and Isaak weren't staying in the estate, and I barely saw them.

But whenever they *were* here and we came across each other, I always felt their eyes on me, watching me. Sometimes, it felt like they could see the real me, like they knew who I really was.

I could see and feel the distaste in Lyov's gaze. He hated me, although I didn't understand why.

Quickly looking down, I avoided looking into their eyes and hurried into the kitchen. Whenever they were in the house, I stayed far away. As far as I could, without drawing attention to myself.

"Poor cake, though. It got spoiled on her ugly face. The cake didn't deserve it." Maddie's voice snapped me out of my thoughts, and I looked down at the mess.

"Do you think Lena will be mad?" I asked, pushing the thought of Lyov to the back of my mind.

"Oh, I don't think. I *know* Mom will be mad."

Uh oh.

Chapter 19

My eyes were locked on the bathroom's door. Alessio was in there, taking his shower.

A few minutes later, I heard the shower turn off. And then there was silence.

The silence only made my palms started to sweat, and I rubbed them over my nightdress. The door opened a few seconds later, and Alessio walked out, wearing only black sweatpants.

His eyes were instantly on me, and when he noticed me looking, they twinkled almost teasingly. Walking closer, he stopped next to the bed, his big body looming over me.

My gaze followed a path down his chest, his ripped abs and then slightly below, but my head quickly snapped up when I saw the noticeable bulge.

Alessio chuckled while I glared at his chest, refusing to look into his eyes when my cheeks heated in embarrassment.

"So how is this going to work?" His voice was low and deep. I gripped the comforter to stop myself from reaching out to him.

"What?" I looked up to see him nodding toward the bed.

"We are not supposed to touch. How are we going to sleep?" he asked, raising an eyebrow in question.

Oh. Right.

I glanced at the couch in the corner of the room and smiled. "You can sleep on the couch."

Alessio glanced at it, then back at me again, his expression filled with surprise. "You are seriously kicking me out of my own bed?"

"You said it's *our* bed. So I get to decide too, right?" I batted my eyelashes up at him innocently, trying to put up the most innocent face I could muster.

Alessio simply glared as he walked over to the couch, throwing his towel on the coffee table in agitation. I watched his shoulders tense, and the smile on my face slipped.

I was being unfair. It didn't matter if we called it *our* room; this was still *his* room. Making him sleep on the couch wasn't reasonable. Or nice, either.

With a sigh, I started to get out of the bed. "I should go to my room," I suggested quietly.

Alessio's eyes widened, and he snapped, "No."

He pointed at the bed, glaring at me in the process. "Get back in there," he ordered. "I'd rather have you in the same room and not touch you than have you in the other room, so far away from me."

"Alessio—" I started but never got a chance to explain before he cut me off.

"No. There is no *my* room or *yours*. This bed is

as much yours as it is mine. It's ours. This is your room now. Got it?" he replied, his words punctuated as if he wanted me to understand and never doubt what he was saying. "So get that pretty ass of yours back in bed and go to sleep."

I lost the fight and sat on the edge of the bed, still feeling a little guilty. My eyes were cast down, but I heard Alessio's audible sigh, and he quickly approached the bed. He stopped in front of me, and I stared at his feet.

When his hands came to rest on the mattress, on either side of my hips, caging me in, I had no choice but to look up in his eyes. "Stop thinking so hard, Angel," he soothed quietly.

Angel. My heart melted at the word, and I smiled. Alessio leaned forward, his forehead just mere inches from mine, but we didn't touch. We were so close, yet not touching. All I had to do was lean the slightest bit forward and we would be touching.

But neither of us moved.

"Good night," he whispered.

"Good night," I replied just as softly.

He still didn't move, and neither did I. And when he finally did, I could see the disappointment in his eyes, and I felt my own, my chest aching as he stepped away.

That small moment between us had lasted shorter than we wanted.

"I want to kiss you so bad right now, Ayla," he confessed. His words sent a shiver down my body. I wanted that, too. But we both knew we couldn't just *simply* kiss. It would lead to more, and we wouldn't be able to stop ourselves.

"But I'll wait. For you, I will wait."

He was perfect and said the sweetest words. It was hard to resist him.

I could feel myself slipping, forgetting about his punishment. I could feel myself reaching for him, but he was already stepping away. "Go to sleep, Angel."

Nodding, I laid down under the covers as he turned off the lights, only the lamp beside me casting a soft glow around the room. I faced the couch and saw Alessio lying down, crossing his arms over his chest. In the dark, I couldn't see if his eyes were closed or not.

Maybe he was too big for the couch. He really was. The couch appeared dainty with Alessio laid down on it.

I burrowed deeper under the comforter and pressed myself into the soft mattress, willing myself to stop worrying and just sleep.

Hours later, I was still not asleep. I glanced at Alessio and wondered if he was already asleep. Without thinking much about it, I quietly got out of bed, making my way to Alessio.

My feet stopped in front of him to see his eyes closed, his face calm with sleep. He was so beautiful like this. When I looked at Alessio, I didn't see the cruel man, the killer or the monster. All I saw was *him*, the man who called me Angel. I saw the real him.

I pulled the bed sheet over his body, my heart accelerating just a little bit. I hoped he wouldn't wake up. When he didn't, my hands moved to his head, my fingers lightly brushing his forehead as I pushed the strands of hair away.

I caressed him, almost soothingly, wishing he was awake to feel my touch.

"I thought we weren't supposed to touch."

At his voice, I snatched my hand away. Alessio cracked one eye open, sending me a smirk of his own. Scoffing at his teasing look, I crossed my arms over my chest. "You were awake this whole time?"

"Yes," he replied, looking down at the bed sheet covering his body.

"Why didn't you say anything?" I mumbled under my breath.

"And miss the opportunity of you touching me?" he shot back.

"Well, that's cheating," I replied.

"You are the one who touched me." He raised an eyebrow before shutting his eyes again.

"Go to sleep." This time it was me ordering him around. His chest rumbled with a low laughter, and I smiled back. Two days. We could do this.

With renewed confidence, I got back in bed. As soon as my head hit the pillow, I closed my eyes and waited for sleep to come.

It was dark. Raining and foggy. My body quaked with each harsh shudder. The wind blew violently around me. It was dark. So dark. Why was it dark? Where was I?

I couldn't see anything. Just darkness. Were my eyes closed? I tried to open them...but they were already open.

Help. I tried to shout, but no words came out.

THE MAFIA AND HIS ANGEL PART 2

And then I heard his voice. His sinister voice. My skin crawled, my back stiffened, and a shiver ran down my spine.

No. No. I wanted to scream.

I now understood why it was only darkness. I was back in hell. He got me. The devil had me and wouldn't let me go this time.

I wanted to scream again, but my voice was gone.

"Did you really think you could escape?"

His voice was right next to my ear, but I couldn't see anything. I only felt him. A small part of me died as I felt his breath on my neck.

"I will always find you."

I recoiled from him, but his hand clamped down painfully on my arms, and I screamed. This time, I heard it. My voice came out hoarse, and my scream rang through my ears.

"Scream. Scream all you want. Nobody will save you this time. Not even him."

Not even him.

Alessio. No. Alessio, where are you? I wanted to scream, but my voice was gone again.

And then I saw him. Even through the darkness, I saw him. He was walking toward me. My savior. My peace. He was here. He would save me. He would save me from the devil and this nightmare.

But all I saw was rage in his eyes. They glowed with it. So much anger. So much hatred.

I gasped when I realized it was all directed at me. I tried to shake my head, tried to explain, but I was numb.

He stopped in front of me, his big body looming

dangerously over mine. Instead of feeling safe, all I felt was fear. I could feel all his fury and hatred for me. They were vibrating off his body, letting me know exactly how he felt.

I betrayed him. And now I had to pay the price.

"I hate you." He hissed the words, shattering my heart in a thousand pieces. "You deserve what you got. Your soul belongs to the devil."

No. No. No. Please. Believe me.

He was walking away. Away from me, leaving me behind with the devil.

No, come back. Please come back. Don't leave me.

He started to fade away. I screamed and screamed, but no sound was made. Only the laughter of the devil could be heard.

"I hate you." Those words resonated in my ears.

"She is yours," he said to the devil. No! I'm yours! Only yours. Please come back.

"Never show your face to me again. You are dead to me."

I'm sorry. Please forgive me. Please. Please.

Then he was gone, fading away into the dark, leaving me behind with the devil who tortured my mind, body, and soul. I shattered as I lost sight of my savior.

"NO!"

I shot up in bed, my body drenched in sweat. My ears rung with my screams. The light was instantly on, and Alessio was by my side in a matter of seconds, but I flinched away.

All I could see was him walking away from me,

THE MAFIA AND HIS ANGEL PART 2

fading in the darkness and leaving me behind. *No.*

Lurching forward in bed, I wrapped my arms around his neck, holding him tight to me. My hold was unyielding. I refused to let him go. He quickly wrapped his arms around my waist, pulling me onto his lap, holding me just as tight.

"Don't leave me. Please don't leave me. Don't ever leave me. I can't. Please. Don't leave me, Alessio," I mumbled in his chest, my heart racing at the thought of being without him. My body was shaking with silent tremors, and I trembled in his arms.

Tears ran down my cheeks in an endless flow. I continued to beg him.

"Shhh...I'm here. I'm not leaving. I'm right here, Angel."

His words were soothing, but the fear inside me wouldn't subdue. Alessio continued to soothe me as I cried in his chest. He never let go of me, his arms remaining tight around me. I felt his fingers softly caressing my hips.

"I'm not leaving. I will never leave you. Don't cry, Angel. I can't bear your tears. I'm right here. I got you," Alessio continued sweetly in my ears, willing me to believe him.

I wished I could. I wanted to believe him. It was just a dream, just a nightmare I tried to convince myself.

But was it really? Maybe it was just showing the truth, my reality when Alessio learned the truth.

After all, he hated me. The real me. He hated the Abandonatos, and no matter how much I wished it wasn't my reality, it was...and I was his enemy.

My fingers tightened around his neck at the thought of losing him. My guilt tasted bitter. My heart ached, and my mind felt numb. I wanted to forget. I just wanted to live in this happy bubble with Alessio, but for how long?

My tears eventually stopped, my sobbing turning into small hiccups. Alessio's soothing words finally penetrated through my foggy mind, and I went limp against him. We were still holding each other, refusing to let go.

I couldn't even if I tried. It felt like if I let him go, I would crumble to pieces.

"Please don't leave me," I whispered one final time.

"I won't," he vowed.

"Promise me."

"I promise you, Angel."

"You said you don't break your promises." My voice was muffled as I buried my face in his hard chest.

"And I don't. I will never break my promise to you, Ayla. I'm yours as much as you are mine. I'm never letting you go," he soothed in my hair, placing a kiss on the top of my head.

His words were what I wanted to hear. They were more than I wanted. Except whatever promises he made to me, they would mean nothing if he learned my truth.

But I still made him promise. It was selfish of me. Maybe…just maybe, if he made this promise, he wouldn't leave me?

Alessio was the type of man who would never break his vow, no matter what. So I tried to bind him to me in any way possible.

My hands went to his chest, one place right over his heart. I felt its beat against my palm. It was racing just as hard as mine.

He was worried. Scared even.

My fingers softly caressed his chest as I took a deep breath and confessed one thing.

"My name is not Ayla Blinov."

They were the hardest words ever spoken by me. It broke a little piece of my heart. In that moment, I wished I was Ayla Blinov. Not an Abandonato.

I wasn't ready to lose him yet. But I could confess something. Anything. One step at a time.

But his next words took me by surprise.

"I know."

My head snapped up, and I stared at him, fear slithering down my spine. His face was almost unreadable, but his eyes were soft, regarding me as if I was someone precious.

"You know?" I sputtered.

"I made a background check the very first day you came here," he simply replied. "And got nothing. We searched up every single Ayla in the country. Even did some background checks on names that sounded similar to yours. But still got nothing. It was like you never existed. So I knew you were lying about your name."

"You knew I was lying this whole time?" I asked, completely astonished at this new revelation.

"Yes." A simple word, one syllable, but it was enough to tilt my world upside down.

"But why? Why did you let me stay?"

"I was curious at first but then realized that I

couldn't let you go. It didn't matter that you were lying to me anymore. Sometimes, I forget that you are even lying," he explained quietly.

"But what if I had turned out to be the spy? Or the enemy?" I choked on the words, my throat closing up as I suddenly felt nauseous. "What would you have done?"

Alessio stared at me for a second, his bluish eyes penetrating into my soul. "I would have had to kill you."

Bringing my hand to my mouth to stop the sudden cry, I buried my face into his chest again. "I'm not your enemy," I whispered.

"I know," he replied just as softly. His hands were caressing my arms, and I melted into his embrace.

"Why are you lying, Ayla? Is Ayla even your name?" Alessio asked suddenly.

"Yes, Ayla is my name. I didn't lie about that."

"Then why did you lie about your last name? What are you trying to hide?" He pushed for more. "Are you in danger? Is someone after you?"

I gave him a stiff nod. Just one simple nod, and then we fell silent. Alessio didn't ask anything else. I knew he was waiting for me to reply.

"The man I am to be married to."

I whispered them, and Alessio froze, his body tensing, his arms tightening around me like bands of steel. "What?" he asked, his voice calm and low, but I knew he was feeling anything but calm.

I knew when he spoke in this tone he was at his angriest.

"He wants me, Alessio. It doesn't matter that I

ran away; he will never rest until he finds me, dead or alive." Taking a deep breath, I sniffled, trying to keep my tears at bay. "I'm his obsession, his prize possession, and he will not stop looking for me until I'm in his bed again."

Alessio's fingers dug into my hips, and I winced. "Who is he?"

I shook my head. "Ayla, who is he?" he asked, his voice deadly.

"No."

"Damn it!" he growled. "Why are you protecting him?"

My head snapped up, and I shook my head wildly. "No! I'm protecting *you*! And me. He is a dangerous man, Alessio. A mad man."

His eyes turned into slits. "More dangerous than me?"

"I don't know," I answered honestly. I knew Alberto was obsessed with me, but to what extent he would go, I didn't know.

"He is a dead man, Ayla," he vowed. "Tell me his name."

The fury in his eyes was unmistakable. But it wasn't at me. It was *for* me. It was directed at the man who had hurt me.

I stayed quiet. I thought he would snap, but he didn't. Instead, he leaned his forehead on mine. "Why are you so stubborn?"

"Because I want to stay alive. I want to live with you. And I don't want to lose you."

"Angel," he murmured. "You are not going to lose me."

"I might be lying about my name, about who I

am, but that is the only thing I am lying about. What I feel for you is the truth," I confessed, hoping that when the time came, he would remember those words.

"Will you ever tell me the truth?" Alessio questioned.

I wish I never have to tell you the truth, Alessio. For the truth will break you. And I can't bear to break your heart. But I have to. One day, I will have to tell you. And that day might be the day I lose everything.

"I will. When I'm ready. Right now, I want to forget. I don't want to live in the past."

Understanding flashed in his eyes, and he sighed. "I will protect you, Angel." There it was. Another vow.

I didn't say anything else. Laying my head on his shoulder, I breathed out a sigh, letting my body relax in his embrace. Alessio laid us down on the bed and pulled the cover on top of our bodies. Not once did he let me go.

"I know I'm not supposed to touch you, but we both know we can't sleep without each other. I will hold you tonight, and tomorrow, I will keep my promise," Alessio said in my ear before placing a kiss there.

One of his arms was wrapped around my stomach, my back to his front. He held me tightly, cocooning me into his body. I placed my hand over his and closed my eyes. "I know you will keep your promise."

"Sleep, Angel. I will watch over you."

Holding his promise to my heart, I let sleep take

over me. This time I was filled with peace. After all, I was in the arms of my savior.

Chapter 20

I glided around the room, moving to the rhythm of the song as I folded Alessio's clothes. I hummed along, my body light.

It had been two days since my nightmare. Alessio and I didn't talk about it again. He never pushed for more or asked more questions. He was giving me the time I needed, and I was forever thankful for that.

I should be counting my days. I should tell the truth. But soon, I would.

I just wanted to live this moment for a little while longer before I left my life in the hands of fate.

Once I gave Alessio my truth, he would be the judge, jury, and the executioner. I would have no choice but to accept his decision, even if it meant my death.

I just wanted to bask in this happiness for a little while longer. Maybe I was a horrible person for that.

I didn't know…but I didn't care, either. I just

wanted to continue being happy.

After folding the last of Alessio's clothes, I quickly tied my hair in a ponytail. Smiling, I thought about Alessio pulling it down again.

It had been two days. Alessio's punishment was over. He would be coming for me soon. Anticipation and desire licked its way through my body, and I quivered, pressing my thighs together.

I was about to step away from the bed when I noticed my book on the floor. Shaking my head, I bent down, my fingers grasping the book.

I went to stand up. My back was almost straightened, but I never got a chance.

A hard body wrapped around me. I let out a scream, and a hand covered my mouth, muffling me. I struggled as tears stung my eyes, but the strong body kept me in place.

Fear slithered its way into my body, and my mind started to race, my heart pounding. I was pushed forward, and I fell onto the bed, my eyes closing on the impact.

My body was flipped around so that I was on my back, and the body settled over mine. I squeezed my eyes shut, refusing to look at the man.

What if the devil had found me?

Chapter 21

My thoughts ran wild. The man settled on top of my body, and I froze, fearing what would come next. Taking a shuddering breath, I willed myself to relax and think. My mind refused to cooperate. All I could think about was Alberto's sinister laughs.

A second passed and then another. He didn't move, and neither did I. As the seconds ticked, the fear that was suffocating me slowly started to slither its way out. Even through my messed-up thoughts and alarm, it felt like I knew the person.

The way his body pressed into mine, every inch of it, I knew it. I had spent nights exploring it, feeling it. His scent wrapped around me, and I felt my muscles start to loosen.

My body knew him, and it reacted accordingly.

I knew *him*. And he wasn't the devil.

My hands instinctively went to his shoulders, and I held on almost desperately. My eyes snapped open to meet bluish-steel colored ones. I stared into his molten eyes. They were hard but filled with so much desire and lust.

Another second ticked, and my body melted under his, the fear evaporating, my muscles unlocking as I gave him control.

And then he smirked, looking so sinfully handsome and devilishly sexy.

"Alessio," I snapped, my fingers digging into his shoulders in warning. "You scared me!"

He hummed, his eyes growing more heated if possible. Alessio leaned down until his face was in my neck, his body pressing mine into the bed. He ran his nose along the length of my neck, placing small kisses as he went.

"You've been a very bad kitten," he muttered, his voice husky and deeper. Oh God. "Flirting with my men."

Oh, that! I squeezed my eyes shut in realization. I was in deep trouble. In my attempt to tease Alessio, I played a minx. Maddie was right. I had been playing with fire.

Alessio placed another kiss, and then he gently bit down in warning. "Trying to get me jealous. Such a bad kitten."

He kissed along my collarbone and then up again, leaving wet trails from his kisses, licking, sucking, and nibbling on the skin until I was putty in his arms. "Oh," I moaned unashamedly.

His teeth grazed on the sensitive skin just above my collarbone, and my back arched off the bed as I pressed against him. I felt his hard length between my legs, and he groaned.

"Alessio," I breathed. The fear was now replaced by desire and anticipation. No longer was I scared. All I needed was him.

He pulled back slightly to look down at me. "I'm hanging on a thin thread right now, Ayla. I won't be gentle."

Alessio leaned down again until his lips were next to my ear, his next words causing me to tremble in excitement. "I'm going to fuck you. This is going to be hard and fast."

I tried to squeeze my legs together when I felt a tingle between them from his words, mixed with the roughness in his voice. But Alessio's hips settled in between them, stopping my movement.

Through hazy and lustful eyes, Alessio stared at me. "Tell me if it gets too much, because I am about to push your limits." His voice held a warning, but also desperation, almost as if he couldn't hold himself in check any longer.

I could only nod, my body hyper-aware of his every movement. As soon as he saw my nod, I didn't have a chance to blink or think before he pulled away abruptly. Then I heard a rip sound, echoing loud in the silent room.

My eyes widened, and I looked down at myself to see the top of my dress ripped. And then Alessio was on me again, not giving me a chance to react. His lips slammed into mine, kissing me possessively. My mind and body spun out of control from his bruising kiss.

It was clear his control had snapped.

Instead of being scared, all I felt was pleasure. I surrendered myself to him, trusting him to give me the pleasure I needed—we both needed.

His lips never left mine, even as he shifted slightly to pull my dress down. I struggled to help him, both of us refusing to break the kiss. When my dress was finally down to my waist, his hands came back up, and he pulled my bra cups down.

I moaned into his lips when his fingers found my nipples. They strained into perfect buds toward him, begging for his touch and attention. His tongue slid into my mouth, and the kiss deepened, his mouth devouring mine, tasting and nipping at my lips.

His fingers stroked over my nipples, and I trembled in his embrace, pushing into his touch, wanting more. And he gave me more.

His lips left mine, but they didn't leave my skin. Alessio trailed kisses down my neck until he reached my nipples. I was already wet and dripping between my legs. I ached, wanting to be filled. Alessio swirled his tongue over the tip, my back arching for more. "Uhh…"

"You like that?" he teased.

I didn't answer. But he gave me what I wanted. He licked, sucked, and played with my nipples, leaving me both hot and cold at the same time. My skin tingled, yet I felt strangely empty.

My fingers wrapped into his hair, pushing him into me, begging him for more without words. His lips left my skin, and I moaned in regret. "No."

Alessio pulled back and gave me a heated look. "Are you begging, kitten?"

I glared up at him, and he chuckled. "No? Okay, don't worry. You'll be begging soon."

His body left mine. Alessio quickly removed his clothes in haste. He tugged at his tie almost angrily and then threw it on the floor with his suit jacket and discarded shirt.

"Are you taking the birth-control pills Maddie gave you?" he asked. I could only nod, giving him the answer he wanted. His pants and boxers were next.

And then he was standing in front of me in all his naked glory. His hardness bumped upward toward his stomach, and I moaned at the sight.

Another chuckle came from him, and he wrapped his fingers along his hard length. "Remove your dress," he ordered gruffly as he rubbed himself.

I stared at his hand, biting on my lips in anticipation. "Ayla," he growled. I sat up at his tone and quickly removed my shredded dress and threw it on the floor, next to Alessio's discarded clothes.

My body tightened as the cold air kissed my bare skin. I removed my bra, my eyes still on Alessio's thick, hard, and long inches.

"Remove everything. I want you naked to my eyes," he demanded. Swallowing hard and suddenly nervous, I slowly pulled my lacy panties down my legs and threw them on the floor.

I knelt, staring at Alessio, waiting for his next command. His eyes flared, and he bit his lips, giving me another sexy smirk.

"Your body is made to be worshiped."

I wanted to be worshiped by him. The look in his eyes, I wanted it only for myself. And in return, I wanted to give him everything he needed or wanted. I wanted to be his, wholeheartedly.

"Spread your legs," Alessio said.

I did, almost instantly. His eyes stayed glued between my legs, and he let out a string of curses.

Before I could blink, he was on me again. Alessio flipped me over until I was on my knees and hands, my back to him.

I gasped in surprise but didn't complain. His body molded over mine, and with his knees, he spread my thighs wider to accommodate him.

I couldn't see him this way. I was forced to focus on my hearing and his every touch. With my cheek pressed against the pillow, I waited with anticipation. I thought he would take me quickly, but instead, his cock laid between my legs, not pushing forward.

Instead he rubbed against me, coating his tip with my wetness, and I moaned at the sensation. I moved my hips with him, wanting more friction, but his fingers tightened around my waist, keeping me still.

"Are you wet for *me*?" he asked, his voice deep and warm against my neck.

"Yes," I moaned as I felt the head of his hard length at my entrance.

"Then show me."

I licked my lips nervously, not knowing what to do.

"I—" I started but Alessio cut me off.

"Place your hand between your legs, play with yourself," he ordered.

I reached between my legs with tentative fingers, and as soon as I touched my wetness, I froze.

"Show me, Ayla."

Pulling my hand away, I showed him, my cheeks heating as he grabbed my fingers and brought it to his lips, tasting me, licking my wetness from my fingers. He hummed in appreciation at my taste, his hips rocking against mine.

"Alessio…" I moaned again.

"What do you want, kitten?"

"You."

He chuckled low, his chest vibrating behind my back.

"You need to be more specific."

Ah! Why was he doing this?

"Please," I begged.

His lips were next to my ear, his breath tickling the skin there. "Do you want my fingers? My lips?" he paused for a second as my hips pushed back, begging him wordlessly. "Hmm…or do you want my cock? Fucking you deep and hard until you are breathless and begging for more?"

"Yes. Alessio, please!"

"Yes to what? My fingers? My mouth?"

"No!" I cried out.

"What?" he taunted shamelessly. "Say it. I'm waiting."

"I want—" I gasped and broke off when he pushed just an inch inside of me. But then he pulled out again, leaving me empty again. "I'm waiting, kitten."

He reached forward and teased my nipples with his fingers.

"Damn it! I want you! I want you to fuck me!" I said, his touch and my desire for him driving me crazy.

That was enough for him. As soon as the words were past my lips, Alessio slammed inside of me in one unforgiving stroke. The air left my lungs in a harsh cry, and I bucked underneath him.

His hard thickness filled me almost painfully. Without the condom, I felt every inch of him, pulsing inside of my wet heat. Pressing my face into the pillow, I moaned loudly.

Alessio pulled back almost all the way, only to drive back into me with such force that I struggled to breathe. He fucked me relentlessly, and I met each thrust with raw need.

"Shit," he swore into my neck. "You feel so fucking good."

I clenched around him every time he slammed back into me. Harder. Faster. Deeper. His controlled strokes losing their control.

"You're *mine!*" he growled into my ear, his breathing harsh.

"Yes!" I was achingly aware of his need because I felt the same way.

The sensation was too much. My body was tingling and out of control. Only Alessio could rid me of that feeling, but he wasn't giving me what I wanted.

Desire pooled in my stomach, and I clenched, the need to come filling my body, driving me over the edge.

Alessio pulled out of me, leaving me empty and hanging. "Alessio," I protested.

"No, you cannot come. I'm nowhere near done with you yet, kitten," he growled before pushing inside me again. "Tomorrow, when you are sore, throbbing, and aching, you'll remember that I made you feel this way. You'll remember that I was the one fucking you."

He filled me to the brim with his hard cock. "I'm going to ruin you for every other man."

Alessio slammed into me repeatedly in furious strokes, showing me that he meant every word he said. His fingers dug into my hips, and I knew they would leave bruises tomorrow.

My fingers tightened around the pillow as I held my moans and screams in. He was driving me crazy, but I couldn't do anything except surrender to his deep thrusts and submit beneath his hard body.

My hips bucked against him, wanting more, demanding more, but he held back. He held my pleasure and drove me over the edge every time before pulling away, leaving me empty over and over again.

My wetness pooled between my thighs, and I bit on my lips to keep from screaming in frustration. My muscles were coiled tight with the need to come. I heard his groans each time he thrust into me, and I heard my desperate moans every time he pulled out.

So close. So close. I could feel myself climbing over the edge, almost falling. "Alessio…" I screamed into the pillow when he pulled out again.

Alessio's fingers wrapped around my hair and pulled my head back almost harshly. "Scream my name. I want to hear your screams. I want everyone to know that I'm fucking you, that my cock is deep inside you right now."

The possessive growl and when he shoved fully into me, buried to the root, sent me over the edge. The air left my lungs at the brutal impact as he hit home, deep inside of me. My screams filled the room, his name echoing around the wall.

"Alessio!"

I lost it. I sobbed, begged, and pleaded for more. I needed him with such fervor, and only he could give it to me. Finally, he did. Alessio rammed back into me, pulling at my hair, forcing me to meet each of his hard thrusts.

And just like he said, I didn't stop begging. He took me like an animal starving for his mate. He fucked me brutally. Harder. Faster. Deeper.

I begged, his name always on my lips, until finally I burst. My orgasm assaulted me with such ferocity that my knees gave out, but Alessio's hands supported me, continuing to lift me to meet his thrusts. I broke into a million pieces, my body trembling with the force of my orgasm.

As I floated, I felt Alessio pump into me two more times before planting himself deep. He came with a roar, my name on his lips.

I felt him…inside of me. Everywhere. In my mind and in my heart. He felt so right. Inside of me, on top of me, his body molded over mine. I was his, and he was mine.

Our harsh breathing filled the room, and I could feel his pounding heart at my back. Alessio let go of my hips, and I fell on the bed with him collapsing over me, his body covering mine like a warm blanket.

As soon as my head hit the pillow, I closed my eyes and felt Alessio rolling off me. I moaned in protest and heard his deep chuckle.

I felt a smack on my ass, and my eyes snapped

open. Turning my head to face him, I stared into this beautiful, rugged face.

"Woah," I whispered. He smiled, showing me his dimples, and my heart squeezed.

"Did I hurt you?" he asked, suddenly serious.

I shook my head. I was definitely sore and aching everywhere, but he didn't hurt me. Instead, he gave me pleasure that I had never experienced before.

"Good, because I'm not done with you."

My eyes widened. Alessio rolled me onto my back and settled between my spread legs. "That little stunt you pulled…trying to make me jealous. Let me tell you, I'm very pissed. I'm going to be taking you all night…to teach you a lesson."

I moaned at his promise.

And he did keep his promise. He took me again and again. Sometimes fast, sometimes slow. He fucked me until I was completely worn out and sore.

I lost count how many times we came, but by the time he collapsed on top of me, I wrapped my arms around his shoulders, caressing his neck. "I think I've learned my lesson," I breathed through my panting.

Chapter 22

I could barely keep my eyes open. Alessio laughed before placing a kiss on my neck, where his face was currently buried.

"Are you sore?"

"Yes."

"Good." Alessio pulled away and fell on his stomach beside me, presenting me with his back. I rolled onto my side to face him.

Alessio smiled almost sleepily, his eyes drawn to my neck. He reached forward and gently caressed a finger down the skin. "I marked you," he whispered, looking extremely proud of himself. His eyes shone with a possessive glint.

Shaking my head, I smiled. I had never seen Alessio lose control like that. For the first time, I'd seen the extent of his possessiveness. I should have been scared, but I wasn't. Instead, I felt wanted and desired. And lastly, I felt loved.

I scooted closer to Alessio and saw his back bunch. Lying my head on his arm, I sighed dreamily. I knew he would never hurt me. Alessio would only ever give me pleasure.

My hand moved to his back, and my fingers traced the bird tattoo that covered half of his back and around his shoulder blades. The bird looked like it was rising from fire, but the design was beautifully executed. Every time I looked at it, I was completely mesmerized.

Alessio's muscles flexed under my wandering and exploring touch. "What type of bird is this?" I asked curiously, my fingers tracing his spread wings.

"It's a Phoenix," he muttered in reply. "I got it the day I took over as Boss."

"Oh." My fingers continued to touch the bird as I asked my next question. "Is that fire it's rising from?"

I felt him nodding. "Fire and ash."

"Ash?" I questioned.

"When I took over, the Families were almost destroyed. After my mother's death, Lyov completely lost it. He was drunk all the time and barely took care of the Families. We were almost ruined and were so close to losing everything. He was not fit to be Boss anymore. He wasn't strong enough. When I turned nineteen, he handed the title over to me, and I became the Boss," Alessio explained. At the mention of his mother's death and father's name, my wandering hand froze and the air left my body.

Alessio didn't seem to notice at first as he continued with his tale. "The ash represents the Families when I took over. Everything and everyone was destroyed. We lost so much, and I had to start over, building our empire again. I had built a stronger and bigger Army, my empire from the ash."

Sometimes I forgot who he was. He controlled and ruled New York City and every other part that belonged to him with an iron fist. He was a Boss. One of the most powerful. Even more than the Italians. "The Phoenix is you," I choked on my words.

I felt his nod again. "Why did you stop touching me?" he asked, flexing his muscles as if demanding my touch.

"Sorry," I mumbled and continued with my gentle caress, even though I was shaking with sudden dread. "What about the fire?"

"The fire is what I own now. I rise above everything and everyone. I'm the master, the judge, the jury, and the executioner. Everyone else bows in front of me." His voice was strong and filled with power.

Swallowing hard against my nervousness, I closed my eyes. How was I going to tell him my truth? I trusted him, yet in many ways, I still feared him…his reaction.

"You stopped again."

My eyes opened again, and I mumbled another quick apology. As my hand moved over his back, I heard Alessio sigh in relief and contentment. "I love your hands on me."

"I love touching you," I admitted softly.

"You calm me, Ayla. You calm the fire raging inside of me," he confessed.

I placed a kiss on his shoulder as my fingers

started to trace the chain tattoo on his arm. It started from his neck and curved around the Phoenix before continuing down the length of his arm, stopping right above his elbow.

"What about this one? What does it mean?" I asked, soothing my hand over the heavy, black chains.

Alessio froze underneath my touch.

I froze too. I started to divert the conversation when he answered, his voice low and deep.

"It means I am chained to my past."

I sucked in a deep breath, trying to calm my racing heart. I didn't like where this conversation was going, but that didn't stop me. "What do you mean?"

"It represents my vengeance."

His words were a blow to my chest, and I felt a crack in my heart. It was almost as painful as the thought of losing everything I had just found. I looked at the chain that marked Alessio's body, and tears filled my eyes, but I quickly blinked them away.

"Every time I catch a glimpse of it in the mirror, it serves as a reminder. It is a reminder that I need to take my revenge against the Italians. Every time I look at the chain, it fuels my anger and hatred."

Oh, his voice, it was filled with so much loathing and disgust. His words were laced with years of fury. His body was tense, muscles coiled tight as his words filled the room, his confession weighing heavily around us.

He hated the Italians—the Abandonatos—so much that he had marked his body as a reminder.

"Every time I look at the chain, I see my mother's lifeless eyes, her blood around me." Alessio's voice broke over the last few words, but then I felt him taking a deep breath. He shuddered under my touch, and I pressed my lips together to stop an agonizing cry from escaping.

"I'm consumed by it. It is what keeps me going, all these years and even now. My need for revenge has kept me alive," Alessio continued in the same tight voice.

I was distraught at the thought of him being in pain for so long. I wished I could take it all away, erase all his pain and the years of suffering.

I didn't dare lift my head from his arm. I kept my face hidden from Alessio as I soothed him with my gentle touch. "Alfredo is already dead. What will you do? To the Italians?" I asked softly.

"Alberto is still alive. He is their so-called Boss. Alfredo may be dead, but that little fucker has taken over, and he needs to die." Alessio paused for a moment as my heart accelerated, sweat forming on my forehead in tension.

When he continued, I had to stop myself from shifting away from him. "Every single one of them. I will kill anyone who comes into my path. I will slaughter until I'm their fucking Boss. I will not stop until I have them under my feet."

Alessio laughed humorlessly, his body shaking under my hand. "That's the ultimate payback. Making his empire, his army bow down to me, worshiping me as their God."

I had seen sweet and gentle Alessio. I had seen angry Alessio. But this one…the one who was filled with so much hatred and vengeance, that was the first time I had seen or heard him speak.

And out of all the different shades of Alessio, this was the one who scared me the most.

But even through my fear, I felt sudden relief. And safe in Alessio's arms.

During his confession, I didn't miss the one promise he made.

Alessio had vowed to kill Alberto, my tormentor. He didn't know how much that meant to me, to know that one day, I'd be rid of this man—the devil in my life.

"Alessio," I whispered.

"Yes?"

My fingers traced the chain and then the Phoenix. "You said you'd kill anyone in your path. But what about the innocent?"

Alessio tensed. "What?" he said slowly. Oh no, I knew that tone. But I continued to push. I needed to know.

My voice trembled as I spoke. "What about those who are innocent? Will they perish, too? Just because they were doomed to be an Italian—an Abandonato?"

Like me. The words were at the tip of my tongue, but I stopped them just in time.

He didn't speak for what felt like the longest time in my life. Then he spoke. And when he did, I knew that no matter what…my ending would always be the same.

"There is no fucking innocence in that family. They are all the spawn of the devil. They are tainted with my mother's and sister's blood."

Bringing a hand to my mouth, I choked back a sob. It didn't matter that I was a victim and innocent, because at the end of the day, I was an Abandonato.

"Tell me something, Alessio," I said hoarsely. "You said there is no innocence in that family. You hate them. But…" I paused and took a deep breath. "What would you have done if I was one of them? What if I tell you I'm an Abandonato?"

My question was met with silence. I quickly swiped my tears away and waited. And waited. And waited. Seconds passed by…and then minutes. I still waited as silence enveloped us.

Alessio suddenly shifted from under me, and then I was on my back, and he was looming over me, his gaze intense, his eyebrows furrowed in question.

"What are you talking about?" he growled.

Palming his cheeks, I whispered, "It's just a question, Alessio. I'm just wondering."

"Ayla, that's a stupid question. Why would you even ask that?" He glared down at me. "Don't say that ever again."

He leaned down and placed a kiss on my nose. "I don't ever want you to associate yourself with those fuckers again. Not even as a fucking *joke*. Do you hear me?"

My heart stuttered at his words, and before I could stop myself, I pulled him down until our lips met each other. I kissed him with everything I had. I kissed him until I was breathless. I kissed him with such fervor as if it were my last kiss.

Alessio growled into my lips and slowly pulled

away, both of us breathing hard, our heart pounding, singing to each other with the same rhythm.

"You're too innocent, sweet, and gentle to ever be an Abandonato. Your heart is pure. An angel can't belong to the Abandonato," he whispered against my lips.

My breath hitched, and my fingers tightened in his hair.

"Alessio…" I said softly. He gazed down at me with loving eyes. And I knew he could see the same thing in my eyes, for I had given myself to him. My heart, my body, my soul, and my love.

Even through the searing pain my chest, I smiled.

And then he did, too.

Our smiles had lightened each other's hearts. I could see the pain fading from his eyes until they were soft.

"Enough with this now. We should sleep. It's late," he admonished quietly. Getting off the bed, he turned off the lights, leaving only the night lamp on before joining me in bed again.

Alessio rolled us over until he was on his back and I was half lying on top of him. I wrapped my arms around his waist and laid my head on his chest, right over his beating heart. He wrapped an arm around my hips, holding me close to him, and he pulled the comforter over us.

I closed my eyes with a sigh.

Alessio's vengeance was weighing heavily on his shoulders. I knew he would kill Alberto soon. It was coming. His death had been signed the moment he took over.

For the first time in my life, I prayed that someone's death would come faster. I prayed for the day that Alessio would end the life of my tormentor and release us from the chains of our pasts.

The moment Alessio refused to believe that I was an Abandonato was the very same moment I had made a decision.

It was a naïve thought. Stupid even. Maybe my naivety would get me killed me in the end.

But in that moment, I had decided that I was no longer Ayla Abandonato.

I was just Ayla.

Alessio's Ayla.

Alessio's Angel.

With that as my final thought, Alessio's heartbeat lulled me into a peaceful sleep. I dreamed of us at the creek, kissing and making love as happiness radiated around us.

Chapter 23

2 months later

I groaned while looking at the mirror. Alessio had left hickeys—love bites, all over my body *again*. He left his mark on my neck in plain visible sight for everyone to see. So they knew who I belonged to. Those were his words.

Over the weeks, I finally got a glimpse of the real possessive man behind the sweet gentle Alessio. He was a jealous man, and I purposely drove him mad with jealousy. Sometimes, just a quick innocent kiss on his men's cheeks, just to rile him up.

I admit that I only did it for the sex afterward.

Like last night. At the thought, I squeezed my legs together as the tingling sensation intensified. He took me over and over again. On the bed, against the wall, on the floor, on the nightstand and the sofa. We had consummated our love on every surface in the room.

He was a beast, I thought with a shake of my

head, although I couldn't stop the smile that appeared on my swollen red lips.

Quickly getting dressed, I combed my hair so that the marks were hidden. Well, I tried to hide them as best I could.

When I was ready, I went downstairs to join Maddie. "Good morning, Lena. Maddie."

"Good morning, babe."

"Good morning, dear."

I tied the apron around my waist and started to help them with breakfast. I had finally learned how to cook, and I found that I enjoyed it.

After setting the table for breakfast, Lena went to rest while Maddie and I cleaned up. "You know, I'm thinking we need soundproof walls," she said casually.

I choked on my apple, my eyes tearing up. Feeling completely mortified, I looked down at my apple. "I was loud? Again?"

"Yup." She laughed.

"Well, you were loud the night before!" I shot back.

Her laughter died. "You heard that?"

"Yes." This time, it was my turn to laugh.

"No way!" she gasped, but then paused. Maddie looked at me curiously, leaning a hip against the counter. "Why does this feel like the guys are making a contest out of this? Like who can make their woman scream the loudest."

My eyes widened, and I shook my head vigorously. "No!"

She only nodded. "Trust me, they would do something like that. They go all caveman when it comes to us."

"Wow."

We stared at each for a second before busting out in laughter. "They are impossible."

"And insatiable," she added. That was true. Alessio had a stamina like no other. Sometimes, I couldn't keep up with him. The last few nights, I would fall asleep almost instantly the moment he would slip out of me.

My body was almost always sore and aching. But Alessio was a gentleman through and through. He made sure I was always taken care off. Warm and relaxing baths after our frenzied sex sessions. Sometimes he would give me a massage. Just little things to show he cared.

There was never a day that went by I didn't feel cherished and completely loved by him.

"I'm going to nap. Artur barely let me sleep last night," she mumbled behind a yawn. I snapped out of my thoughts and waved at her.

***

I was so completely lost in reading that I didn't hear the door open.

"Angel," Alessio called. My head snapped up, and I closed the book with a smile.

"Alessio," I replied, placing my hands out for him, silently calling him to me. He walked further inside and closed the door behind me. Coming to me, he grabbed my hands and placed a kiss on my forehead before straightening up.

"I have to go," he announced abruptly.

My heart slammed to a stop before racing again. "You have to leave?"

Alessio made a regretful sound, his eyes sorrowful when he nodded. "I have to take care of some business. Outside the state. So I will be gone for a few days."

"When?" I asked, my fingers moving nervously over the comforter. I hated the idea of being without him.

"We are leaving tonight," he said softly, looking into my eyes.

My shoulders drooped low, and a resigned sigh escaped my lips.

"I want you to come with me."

My mouth fell open in shock, and I looked up in surprise. Alessio's blue eyes were glimmering from the rays of sunlight showering in the room, and a small smile played across his lips, showing the small indentation in his cheek.

"What?" I sputtered.

"Have you ever been to the beach?" he asked, cocking his head to the side in question.

I shook my head silently.

"We're going to Florida. There are some beautiful beaches there," he murmured.

I couldn't leave. Alberto was still out there. The thought sent chills down my spine, and I shook my head.

"But—"

Alessio didn't give me a chance to utter any excuses. "You'll be safe."

I didn't answer. I desperately wanted to go with him, to see the beach. To be with Alessio.

Alessio made the decision for me. He leaned forward and kissed me soundly on the lips, leaving me breathless. "I want you with me. I *need* my Angel."

I had only one answer. "Okay," I whispered against his lips.

Alessio sent me one of his beautiful smiles before straightening up to his full height. He pulled me off the bed until I was standing in front of him. "Good. You don't have to pack a bag."

Confused, I started to protest, but he placed a finger over my lips. "It's okay, Angel. Everything will be taken care off."

After giving me another kiss, he left the room, leaving me alone with my wandering thoughts. I was going out of the estate for the first time since I had escaped Alberto.

Fear slithered its way into my body, and I struggled to breathe.

Alessio's words resonated in my head, loud and clear, calming me just a little.

You'll be safe.

I need my Angel.

It was dangerous, yet I was willing to take such a big risk. Only because I trusted Alessio…only because I couldn't bear to be without him. And I knew he felt the same way.

Throughout the day, I willed myself to be strong. I told myself repeatedly that everything was going to be fine. I was safe.

Maddie came to my room, and I told her. She was excited, deliriously happy for me. She talked animatedly about the beach and how much I was going to love it, but still the panic never left me.

And then, finally night had fallen, and it was time for us to leave. Alessio came into the room, and I jumped off the bed, swallowing nervously.

He made his way to me, his eyebrows furrowed at my tense expression. "Hey." He cupped my face, tilting my face up so my eyes were on his. "What's wrong, Angel?"

"I—" Words failed me, and I broke off with a shuddering breath.

Alessio quickly wrapped me into his arms, holding me tight against his body. I took a deep breath, and my muscles slowly started to relax. I held on to him for dear life and pressed my ear to his chest, listening to his beating heart.

"Ayla, if you don't want to go, then you don't have to. I don't want to force you," he whispered gently in my ear, his hand rubbing my back soothingly.

My fingers tightened around his suit jacket, and I shook my head. "No."

"What is it? Talk to me, Angel."

"I want to go," I muttered.

"Are you sure?" he questioned, his voice slightly hoarse.

I nodded. "Yes. Take me with you, Alessio." This time, it was my choice, not Alessio's demand.

Alessio pulled away and looked down at me with prideful eyes. "That's my girl. You always leave me in awe with your strength."

I closed my eyes, feeling slightly relieved. His lips feathered over my lids. He kissed each one and then laid a kiss on the tip of my nose. His lips touched my cheeks in the softest kisses, and then they were on mine, kissing me slowly and deeply.

Pulling away, he wrapped his fingers at the back of my neck, caressing softly, and then gave me a reassuring squeeze. "Ready?"

I simply nodded. We walked down the stairs, my hand clasped in his tightly. He was my strength.

But when we reached the main door, my steps faltered. I saw Nikolay, Viktor, Phoenix, Artur, and two other men standing there, waiting for Alessio and me.

As we neared the doors, I started to sweat heavily, panic clawing at my throat. I was frightened that this would end in tearful hyperventilation. I cast a fearful look at the door, and my hands tightened around Alessio's.

He gave me a squeeze and slowed his steps to match mine, giving me the time I needed.

My stomach rolled and twisted. My head was pounding, the blood rushing in my ears until it felt deafening.

I wanted this…yet I was still scared.

Alessio gave my hand another squeeze. There it was. His silent support as he sent me his strength. I could do this. I had to do this. I had to overcome this fear.

As soon as we stepped out of the door and into the night, my breath stuttered and my legs almost gave out, but Alessio quickly wrapped his arm around my waist, supporting me.

"I got you, Angel."

I can do this. I can do this. I can do this. I have to do this. For Alessio. For me. I can't live with fear anymore. I have to be strong. I have to be fearless.

We walked to the car, and Viktor opened the door. I slid in the backseat first, and Alessio joined me seconds after. The door closed, and darkness enveloped us. Alessio pulled me onto his lap and placed a kiss on my forehead.

"I got you," he repeated again.

Placing my head over his shoulders, I breathed out a sigh of relief. "Thank you."

"Never thank me for taking care of you," he muttered in my ear. Alessio slid a hand around the back of my neck, beneath my hair, and squeezed gently.

I heard the door slam close, and then Viktor's voice filled the car. "Ready?"

Alessio didn't answer. Realization slowly dawned to me that they were waiting for *my* answer.

I can do this. Taking a deep breath, I gave them the words they needed. "Ready."

The car started moving, and I opened my eyes, looking out of the window. I saw us leaving the estate, and the gate closed behind us.

I was out. Panic started to make its way into my body again, but Alessio's firm hand around my neck calmed me. I buried my face into his neck and closed my eyes.

This was going to be a long drive.

"Sleep, Angel," Alessio whispered.

And I did. I slept soundly for hours, and the next time I woke up, it was morning already, the sunlight brightening the inside of the car.

"How much longer until we reach there?" I asked in Alessio's chest. I was no longer on his lap;

instead I was seated beside him. Still, I was wrapped around him like a vise. I was using his chest as a pillow, and my arms were around his waist.

"Eight hours or so," he replied, his chest rumbling with his voice. "We have to make a few stops along the way." I must have slept for some time.

He chuckled low. "You must have been tired, and the stress you put yourself through last night has weighed heavily on your mind and body."

"Alessio?"

"Yes?"

"I need the bathroom," I said as quietly as I could.

"Nikolay, take the next exit. We need to rest for breakfast," he ordered.

"Boss," Nikolay acknowledged Alessio's demand.

When the car came to a stop, Viktor and Nikolay stepped out first. They guarded our door, and then Alessio stepped out, pulling me behind him. We walked into a coffee shop, and after Alessio handed me a small bag, I quickly went to the bathroom to freshen up.

After I deemed myself presentable again, I walked out and almost bumped into Nikolay's back. He turned around. "Boss is waiting for you there." He nodded toward the entrance. We joined Alessio and Viktor and walked back to the car.

"Viktor got you donuts and muffins," Alessio said, handing me a brown bag.

"Thank you, Viktor."

THE MAFIA AND HIS ANGEL PART 2

"You are welcome, baby girl."

I giggled at the name while Alessio growled beside me. "Don't call her that."

It had been a few weeks since Viktor gave me the new nickname. After several attempts at flirting with him, he also joined in the fun to make the brooding man sitting beside me jealous. Viktor found the best way to push Alessio's button.

His new nickname for me: *baby girl*. Alessio hated it and looked like he was murdering Viktor multiple ways in his head every time the name was uttered.

"What type of name is *baby girl*, anyway?" he snapped.

Viktor laughed and winked at me. "Look who's talking. The one who calls his woman *Kitten*."

"Fuck you! She loves it," Alessio said, raising an eyebrow at me.

"Ayla, you like when I call you *baby girl*, right?" Viktor asked, just to taunt Alessio.

"I love it," I said, hiding my giggle behind my hand.

Alessio's hand came to rest on my thigh, his fingers pressing into my skin in warning. He leaned into me and whispered in my ear, his voice taking a huskier tone. "You are going to pay for that, kitten."

Oh, I know.

Smiling innocently at him, I gave him a quick peck on the lips. Alessio's eyes turned molten with desire, and I bit down on my lips. I shook my head, giving him a warning look.

I must have fallen asleep on Alessio's shoulder, because the next thing I knew, someone was shaking me to wake up.

My eyes opened to meet Alessio's smiling blue ones. "We are here."

My head snapped up, and I looked outside the window. We were here. I made it without a nervous breakdown or panic attack.

Alessio opened the door and stepped out first. He took my hand and pulled me out of the car. The first thing I heard was the sound of the waves. And then I felt the wind on my skin. Everything was quiet except the ocean waves. The smell of the ocean filled my nose, and I smiled.

Peace. It felt like peace.

I looked up at Alessio to see that he was already staring down at me, his gaze filled with adoration.

"Where are we?" I asked.

"I bought this beach house yesterday. This place is ours. And the beach is ours, too. It's a private beach. Nobody is allowed here except us," he explained.

"We are the only ones here?" I asked in astonishment.

He nodded and started to pull me away from the car. But instead of walking us toward the house, we walked the opposite way.

The sound of the ocean grew closer, and the smell of it hit me harder. Excitement and anticipation filled my chest.

As soon as I saw the first glimpse of the ocean, my breath came out in a whoosh. The beauty of it stole of my breath. It looked unreal.

Alessio let go of my hand. "Go," he urged. "Feel the sand under your bare feet."

I quickly took off my flats and took my first step on the sand. The softness tickled my feet a little, and I wiggled my toes, my feet sinking deeper into the sand. I looked back at Alessio, and he smiled encouragingly.

I took another step…and then another. Each step, my heart grew fuller with love for the man who gave me this.

I bent down and scooped a handful of sand before letting it slip free between my fingers. A tidal wave of emotions crashed through me, and my eyes stung. Was it possible to be this happy?

I lifted my head to the sky and closed my eyes, letting the sun kiss my face. After the longest time, I stood up and walked toward the water. I felt Alessio at my back. He wasn't far, but he also wasn't stopping me.

Alessio was letting me explore…on my own. He was giving me freedom to do what I wanted as he kept watchful eyes on me.

The sand was wet as I drew closer to the tide. The first step I took and the water passed over my feet, I let out a small gasp. I stood there, letting the water wash over my feet.

When I felt an arm wrap around my waist, I smiled. Alessio pulled me into his body, and I placed a hand over the arm that rested possessively and protectively over my stomach.

As the tides crashed gently around us and a smile spread across my lips, I could only think of one thing.

The words ran through my mind, but I didn't say them.

The words were a mere whisper in my thoughts. Words that were meant for only Alessio.

I love you.

Chapter 24

Alessio

I watched her wander toward the ocean, watched her experience the feel of the sand for the first time. Ayla's steps were almost feather light, as if she was floating toward peacefulness. As she grew closer and the water rushed around her feet, I saw her shoulders relax further, and she tilted her head toward the sky.

I've been to many places with beaches but never cared about it. Never thought of taking the time to feel the sand or the ocean. But watching Ayla experience this, it showed me that sometimes we needed to be grateful for what we have.

And I was grateful for her. My Angel.

Rolling my slacks up above my ankles, I walked over to Ayla. When I was close behind her, my arms instinctively went around her waist, pulling her small body to mine until her back was pressed against my front. She rested a hand over my arm, and I smiled.

This…this was what I needed. Her. Us.

As the tides crashed gently around us, I could only think of one thing.

I was never letting her go. Now that I had had the taste of true happiness, I didn't think I could live without Ayla. She was everything and more.

Placing a kiss next to her ear, I let my lips linger there. Ayla sighed and then turned around in my arms. Her hands went to my waist, and she tilted her head up.

Ayla beamed up at me, her smile so big, her green eyes lighting up…actually her whole face lighting up. It was enough to make me catch my breath as I stared back in awe at her beauty.

"Thank you for bringing me here," she said, her eyes trained on mine.

"Do you like it here?" I asked, my fingers brushing against her cheek lightly.

"Yes. And you still have to show me the house," she murmured. Leaning forward, she placed a kiss in the middle of my chest and then laid her head there. Seconds turned into minutes, and I had no desire to move.

Finally, I gently pulled away. "Let's go. I'll show you around the house. And then I have to take care of some business."

"Okay!" She stepped back and grabbed my hand, pulling me toward the house excitedly. We walked up to the porch that overlooked the ocean, but instead of going inside, I froze on the steps.

"Right. I need to do something first," I muttered, looking down at Ayla's confused face. Without giving her a chance, I bent down and swept her off her feet, cradling her to my chest.

"Woah. What are you doing?" Her arms went around my neck, but I just smiled, walking inside the house with her in my arms.

"Carrying you over the threshold," I announced, almost too proudly. Thank fuck the guys weren't present or I would never hear the end of this.

"Why?"

"Maddie said I had to do it. Don't know why. She said it's important." I rolled my eyes, remembering her order and murderous intent if I didn't do as I was told.

"That's weird."

Agreed. I didn't know why we had to do this either, although I wasn't complaining. I would carry Ayla anywhere, and having her in my arms was enough to make me a happy man.

Damn, I really was pussy whipped.

Putting Ayla back down, we walked around the house, showing her everywhere. Ayla loved it. If I wasn't mistaken, she loved it more than the estate. It was a simple beach house.

Our final stop was our bedroom. Ayla pushed open the door. "Wow. We can see the beach from here." She ran toward the balcony and laughed. "Alessio, this is gorgeous. I love it!"

"Glad you love it." I watched Ayla bounce on her tip-toes as I made my way to the closet. "Ayla," I called out, bringing her attention back to me.

She swiveled around, and her eyes went wide. "How?" She walked toward me in astonishment.

"I hired a maid when I bought the house. She made sure it was clean, and I told her to buy some clothes for you."

"That's not just some clothes. That's a lot!" Ayla mumbled, looking at the closet and then back at me.

I shrugged, suddenly finding myself fidgeting under her intense gaze. Ayla stepped forward and slipped her hand into mine. A breathtaking smile appeared on her face. "You are so sweet."

Great. I was now sweet.

"We've been over this before, kitten."

She nodded furiously. "And I'm sure we came to the conclusion that you are sweet."

"No. *You* came to the conclusion that I was sweet."

"And what's so wrong about being sweet?" she argued, her smile now a frown as she glared up at me.

I felt my lips turn up in a small smirk. Grabbing her waist, I pulled her to me, her body molding mine. Soft against hard. She bit on her lips nervously. "Do you want me to show you why I'm not sweet?"

"You're teasing me now," she muttered. "I take it back. You are a beast."

"Oh, kitten, I'll show how much of a beast I am when I get back home," I promised before pulling away. After kissing her soundly on the lips, I sauntered out of our room.

As I made my way outside, I saw Nikolay, Viktor, Artur, and Phoenix standing next to the car. "Viktor, I want you to stay with Ayla. I don't want to leave her alone."

Viktor nodded and went inside. Without a word to the others, I got into the car. I didn't have to say anything. They already knew the routine.

I had several underground fighting rings operating in several states. Several checkups were made through the year, and this month it was Florida.

It was time to recruit more members. Only the best fighters—killers—have the honor to work for me.

Now that Ayla was in my life, more protection was needed. I didn't want to risk anything. I was going to protect her with everything I had.

As the car lurched to a stop, I was already pumped. I walked toward the door, Nikolay, Artur, and Phoenix closely behind me.

The men bowed their head as I entered. Walking further inside, I heard the screams from the crowd. People were cheering, pushing for more, chanting for death.

I walked upstairs to the VIP lounge, where we had the best view of the fight. My gaze stayed on the glass window when I sat down.

My blood roared as I watched the fight. The ring looked more like a dungeon. It was a cage, and only one person walked out after the fight. Only the winner. The fighters sliced, stabbed, bled, and fought to live. They were brutal, almost animalistic in their attacks.

After watching for several minutes, I already had my favorite, and I knew he was the one to win. He was, after all, ruthless. I watched him play with his opponent, turning him into a puppet with his moves.

"What's his name?" I asked.

"He's known as KILLER. He's twenty-three

years old and has been fighting since he was thirteen. He's one of the best and never loses a fight. Makes about five million dollars for every fight," Nikolay quickly reported.

"Hmm…hire him."

"Boss, he also does Alberto's dirty work. I guess you could say he's a mercenary."

"Hire him. I will give him thrice what Alberto is giving him."

"And if he betrays you?" Phoenix asked behind me. "He can't be trusted."

"He won't betray me. If he does, then simple—I'll put a bullet between his eyes. If he is Alberto's man, then having him on our side is important. He will lead us to the fucker. And also, he won't refuse the money I'm giving him."

In this world, when it came to business—it was only about the money. Whatever worked in your advantage, you went for it.

I didn't have to go far to know that KILLER wasn't a loyal man. He might have been working for Alberto, but there was no way he was loyal. Men like him didn't bow down to others. Everyone feared killers like him.

I didn't watch the rest of the fight. I didn't have to. It was obvious who won. Getting up, the crowd exploded, the volume deafening as the winner was announced.

The screams still rang through my ears as I walked to the car. Alberto's end was coming soon. I could taste my need for revenge. The Italians would bow to me. Every single one of them. I was going to make sure of it.

Chapter 25

When I arrived at the beach house, the sun was already disappearing behind the horizon. I went inside to see Viktor sitting on the couch, polishing his guns and knives. The bastard loved to keep his toys shiny.

"Ayla is upstairs," he mumbled without taking his eyes off the dagger he was holding.

Our room was empty, but I could hear soft singing from the room next to ours. Of course, she was there. I should have known better.

Walking closer, I quietly pushed the door open, only to have my heart squeeze at the sight in front of me.

Ayla was moving around the room. A slow song played in the background as she twirled around, a smile present on her beautiful face.

She was oblivious to my presence, and I took the opportunity to admire her. Leaning against the door, I didn't take my eyes off my Angel.

Ayla was wearing a light pink dress that came down to her knees. Her black hair hung loose at her back as she danced around barefooted. She looked angelic. Impossibly beautiful.

When she swiveled around and saw me, a small gasp escaped her plump red lips. Ayla froze and stared at me for a second.

I walked toward her until we were standing a foot away. She stared at me, her head tilted to the side, waiting for my next move, which surprised us both.

Extending my hand out to her, I uttered the words I never thought I would. "May I have this dance, Angel?"

Her mouth fell open and then snapped shut. I saw a hint of color rise in her cheeks as she ducked her head shyly, a small smile playing on her lips.

I found it absolutely endearing that after all the time we had been together and all the things we had done, she was still shy around me.

Oh, she was also definitely bold and had turned into a little minx under Maddie's influence, but there were times when she was shy and nervous—the sweetness in her actions almost making my chest tight.

"I don't know how to dance," Ayla whispered.

Grabbing her waist, I placed a kiss on her forehead. "Neither do I."

Ayla beamed, and when I chuckled low, she ducked her head again, hiding her face in my chest. My arms tightened around her hips as she placed hers around my waist.

And then we moved. Slowly, matching the rhythm on the song.

Ayla sighed in contentment as we held each

THE MAFIA AND HIS ANGEL PART 2

other. I wouldn't say we danced. We only moved in small circles, but it was enough for us. That silent moment spoke hundreds of words between us.

As our dance came to an end, I lifted Ayla up by the waist and twirled her around. Her laughter echoed around us. My heart squeezed as her face glowed with complete happiness. Ayla was precious.

The need to protect her was so overwhelming. I couldn't imagine ever losing her.

Placing her down, we stared into each other's eyes. "You are so beautiful," I whispered.

Again. There it was. That shy and sweet smile.

When our lips made contact with each other, it was a sweet kiss. Light, soft, and so very sweet. We kissed until we were breathless.

We pulled apart only to catch our breath, and then our lips were on each other again. This time, our lips were firm and demanding, both of us slowly losing control. I had her against the wall in a matter of the seconds with her legs wrapped around my waist.

"What do you...like?" Ayla asked, her voice a little husky.

"Hmm...you," I said against her neck, kissing my way down.

"No...I mean...eat. What do you like to eat?"

"You. I'm going to eat you." I nipped on the skin at her collarbone and heard her moan.

"Food," she gasped.

What the fuck? Why was she talking about food at a moment like this?

Ayla's fingers wrapped around my hair and she

pulled my head away. "What's your favorite food? Like dessert?"

"Why?" I asked, completely confused at the sudden turn of events.

She shrugged. "I want to take care of you. Cook your favorite food and all. You do so much for me, Alessio, yet I give so little in return."

Her smile was lost, her happiness replaced with sadness.

I placed a kiss on her lips before answering. "You already do take care of me, Angel. You do more than you think."

"But…" she started to argue.

"No." I cut her off.

"I still want to, though. What's your favorite cake?" she asked again. Over the last few weeks, I had also found out that Ayla was very stubborn. There was no point arguing because she always won in the end. Although only because I let her win.

"Chocolate," I answered. Actually, I didn't care. I didn't eat cake, but if she wanted to bake for me…if this brought back her sweet smile, then I wasn't going to stop her.

And there it was. Her sweet breathtaking smile.

"Okay!" she announced excitedly. Her legs unwrapped around me, and she pushed at my chest. I didn't have a choice but to let her go.

Ayla leaned up on her toes and gave me a kiss. "I'm going to make the best chocolate cake for you."

Before I could say anything else, she was already running out of the room.

Shaking my head, I couldn't help but chuckle. I

walked out behind her, but not before catching a glimpse of the piano in the corner of the room. I made sure to have one in before we arrived.

The piano was a part of us. I knew how much it meant to Ayla. Even though we weren't at the estate, she was still going to play for us.

I walked into the kitchen to see Ayla talking animatedly on the phone as she placed the ingredients on the counter. "I have everything. Maddie, stop it. It's not funny."

She listened to Maddie talk for a second and then growled in frustration. "I'll get it right this time. I'm going to make the best cake…you're so mean."

I didn't know how long I stood there and watched Ayla talk while she tried to bake. I listened and watched and smiled.

And then her angelic voice snapped me out of the moment. "Alessio, can you taste it for me?"

Ayla showed me the spoon filled with chocolate batter. She dipped her finger in it and waved at me. Walking closer, I took her hand in mine and sucked on the finger. I heard Ayla gasp, and then she licked her lips.

"Hmm…sweet," I mumbled, licking her finger clean. "Like you."

"Umm…okay," she replied in a daze.

"Oh hi, Alessio!" I heard Maddie's voice from the speaker. Fucking cockblocker.

"Hi," I mumbled, glaring at the stupid phone.

Ayla let out a small laugh before turning around again. I stepped up to her back and wrapped my arm around her waist, holding her to me as she continued baking.

Ayla looked over her shoulder, her green eyes meeting mine as they twinkled merrily.

I was right. She was too precious.

Chapter 26

Ayla

"Where are we going?" I asked for probably the tenth time as Alessio and I got into the car.

"Somewhere," he muttered in reply.

"That's not an answer." I glared at him, but he just smirked, giving me that devilishly sexy look that I couldn't resist.

"It's a surprise, kitten. Retract your claws."

"But I want to know."

"It's a surprise, woman. Give the lovesick puppy a break, baby girl," Viktor said from the front. Phoenix let out a laugh.

I had to stop my own giggle from escaping when Alessio gave him a death glare.

"Fuck you," Alessio snapped. "Drive."

"Oh, he is snappy this morning. Did he not get some loving last night?"

Viktor really had a death wish.

"I will shoot you. Don't test me," Alessio warned in a deathly tone.

"Give Boss a break. If he shoots you, I will have to clean up the mess afterward," Phoenix mumbled.

"Whatever. I'm only stopping for my baby girl. We don't want to taint her innocent eyes." Viktor winked at me through the rear-view mirror.

I saw Alessio's hands tighten in fists, and I quickly placed my hands over his. Releasing my seat belt, I moved forward until I was sitting sideways on his lap.

With my lips next to his ear, I whispered my next words so only he could hear. "You have nothing to be jealous of, Alessio. I'm yours. Wholeheartedly. You have me. Mind, body, and soul. Nothing and no one is ever going to change that."

His body instantly relaxed. "You always know when to say the right thing," he mumbled back.

"It's the truth, Alessio."

"I know, Angel." He placed a kiss on my forehead, and I laid my head on his shoulder. We stayed like that until the car came to a full stop.

"We're here," Alessio announced. "Close your eyes."

I did as I was told, trusting him. The door opened, and then I was being pulled out. I was swept off my feet as Alessio held me to his chest.

"Can I open my eyes now?" I asked, feeling suddenly giddy, my heart jumping in excitement.

"No. I'll tell you when," he replied gruffly.

We walked for a few minutes, and then Alessio placed me down until I was standing next to him again. "Last night, you said you were going to miss the creek. Open your eyes, Angel."

I did, and then my heart stuttered. Oh my God.

The beauty in front of me took my breath away.

THE MAFIA AND HIS ANGEL PART 2

A field full with flowers. So many of them and all different colors.

"It's not the creek. But close."

"This is beautiful," I breathed in complete astonishment. "I have no words, Alessio."

Tears stung my eyes as I stared at the landscape in front of me. I was standing in the middle of a field, where thousands of colorful flowers bloomed.

The light breeze touched my face, and I smiled. So peaceful.

Turning around, I faced Alessio and ran into his arms, hugging him as tightly as I could. I covered his face with kisses before pulling away and laughed happily.

"Thank you for this. I love—" *you*. My lips snapped shut before I could utter the last word. The words were always on my lips, begging to be released.

But I still couldn't bring myself to tell Alessio how I truly felt. Something in my heart was stopping me. Every time I wanted to tell him, my chest would feel tight and my heart would ache. So those three words stayed unsaid.

Swallowing nervously as Alessio stared at me, almost in anticipation, I mustered up the best smile I could.

"I love it," I said instead.

He wrapped his arms around my waist, pulling me into his body again. We stared into each other's eyes when he spoke. "I know, Angel. I know. I love it too."

There it was. His affirmation. We didn't need the words between us. It was there without it even being said. From our actions and through our eyes. I knew how he felt, and he knew where my heart belonged. That was enough for us.

He didn't smile, but his soft eyes said it all. Oh, how I loved him. He was everything I needed and wanted. He was perfect…for me.

But I wasn't…for him.

At the thought, my chest grew tight.

I couldn't lie anymore.

This had gone on for too long, and I couldn't betray him anymore. Every single day, I had to live with the knowledge that I was betraying the man I love. Not only him, but my newfound family.

Every single night, I prayed that I could find the courage to tell him, while every single day, I tortured myself with the knowledge that I was weak and a traitor. To him and his heart. I was a traitor to us. To our love.

I hurt…my heart and my soul. I felt empty. I was hollow inside.

I had to tell him the truth.

Even if it meant my death. I was ready to take any punishment Alessio had to give me. I would bear his wrath and let him take his revenge, but I was not going to lie any longer.

I saw Alessio frowning and I knew why. I had lost my smile. I palmed his cheek and said softly, "Can we go back to the beach house?"

I couldn't tell him here. Not in the place filled with serenity. I wasn't going to taint it with our harsh reality.

"I have to tell you something."

Alessio's face grew worried. "Ayla, what's

wrong?"

"Please, Alessio," I murmured. I could even hear the defeat in my words. My bottom lip quivered as I tried to keep my tears at bay, and my stomach tightened in knots.

"It's something important. But I don't want to say it here," I finally managed to get out through my labored breathing.

Don't have a panic attack. Not now, Ayla. You have to do this.

Alessio's gaze moved over my face, and as he saw the distress there, his body went tight in panic and fear flashed in his eyes, but it was quickly gone.

He wrapped his arms around me and pulled me to his chest. "Whatever it is, it's going to be okay," he whispered shakily.

I slightly stepped out of his embrace so I could see his face. My fingers traced his lips and nose until they laid softly on his cheeks. "My feelings for you are real, Alessio. Whatever is between us is real. Please don't forget that."

Alessio swallowed hard, his arms clenching around me. He looked confused, worried, but he still nodded.

Pressing against his body, I brushed my lips against his. "You are my everything, Alessio. The reason why I'm still alive. The reason why I smile every day."

"Ayla, why…" he started to ask but I cut him off with a bruising kiss. He growled and returned my kiss just as fiercely, possessively taking over.

"When I tell you my truth, please remember those words," I whispered.

Alessio didn't say anything, but he kissed me again. He kissed me until we were both gasping for breath. And I kissed him in return, as if it was my last kiss. Maybe it was. And I wanted to remember this.

We walked back to the car hand in hand, and the ride was wrapped with silence. No one said a word. My head was laid on Alessio's shoulder as he played with my hair. The silence between us was always filled with peace. We loved the silence, and maybe this was the last time I would get to experience this.

My eyes filled with tears, and I quickly blinked them away.

I can't—shouldn't cry.

After all, for once I was about to do the right thing. Something I should have done way before, but now I was ready. After getting the little piece of happiness and being loved wholeheartedly by Alessio, I was ready to face whatever I had to.

My heart ached at the thought of breaking him, breaking us.

Alessio had given me everything. He gave me himself, a part of him that nobody else knew but me. He loved me, even though the words were never uttered.

He gave me peace and happiness. He was my happiness.

And now…I was about to take away *his* happiness.

I could take the pain, anything he would unleash on me, but I couldn't watch Alessio in pain, knowing that I would be the cause of it. It would

THE MAFIA AND HIS ANGEL PART 2

kill me...slowly and painfully.

But even when I was preparing to face his wrath, I still had hope. Maybe—just maybe, Alessio would forgive me. Maybe he would understand why I did it, why I lied to him.

Maybe he would still accept me as his Angel. Maybe we would live happily ever after. They were childish thoughts.

But I still hoped that his love was stronger than his anger and need for revenge.

I was snapped out of my thoughts when the car stopped. I dreaded this moment, but it was here and now I had to face it.

"Fuck," Viktor swore loudly at the front and punched the steering wheel.

"What the fuck is he doing here?" Phoenix growled.

Alessio froze beside me, his body locking tight, his tensed muscles bunching underneath my head. I stilled too, my heart jumping in my throat.

I saw Alessio's hands tighten in fists on his thighs, and the air around us grew cold. When he moved, I lifted my head from his shoulders. I suddenly felt nausea, and the dizziness took over. My vision swam in front of me like waves as my throat closed.

Alessio stared straight ahead, his lips thinned into a straight line. He had lost the soft look in his eyes. Now, he just looked like a cold-blooded killer. Emotionless, vicious, and murderous.

"Alessio," I breathed, my heart stuttering as I watched Alessio change from a loving man to the monster he was known as, right in front of my eyes.

Viktor got out of the car first, and then Phoenix. I saw their hands going to the back of their waistbands, right over their guns. Alessio grabbed my arm, almost too roughly, and I winced as he pulled me out of the car.

I was hidden behind his large back, Alessio covering my body with his own as Viktor, Phoenix, and Artur came to stand beside us, forming a circle, while I stood in the middle.

Having four large muscled men standing around me, their stance protective, I couldn't see anything from where I was standing. I didn't understand what they were protecting me from.

My throat was suddenly dry, and I quivered in fear. The air around us was tense and cold…so cold. I could sense the hatred and anger rolling off the men protecting me like waves.

Viktor drew closer to my side, and I saw his jaw ticked, his face just as emotionless and cold as Alessio's.

"What are you doing here? On my property?" Alessio growled low, his back tensed, his voice filled with anger.

"I'm just here to take back what's mine, what belongs to me."

Chapter 27

I froze, my whole body going numb.

That voice. The same voice that haunted not just my sleep every night—but my whole life.

That voice broke me—until I thought I was beyond repair.

That voice belonged to the devil.

Alberto, my mind screamed. *No. No. No. Please no. Not now.*

I wanted to cry and scream at this unfairness. I wanted to fall down and crumble into dust until I had nothing left. That way Alberto wouldn't get to me.

My head ran wild until I could feel myself almost fainting. *Breathe. Breathe, Ayla.*

I sucked in a harsh breath and took a step forward, peeking past Alessio's shoulders. I was still hidden behind him; only the top of my head was visible as I looked at the man in front of me.

He caught my eyes and smiled. I once thought he was handsome and charming. I was even slightly enamored by him when we first met. When I finally found his real truth, I realized that it was all just a pretty face, but his heart was black. He didn't know how to love.

He was the true definition of evil.

And that smile on his face, some women would fall for it. But I knew that smile. It was sadistic and filled with the promise of pain.

"Love, it's time for you to come home now," Alberto said, looking at me as he placed his hand out as if he expected me to take it.

I shuddered and hid behind Alessio, my hand going to his back, my fingers clenching around his jacket as I held on for dear life.

This couldn't be happening. I was supposed to be safe.

My breathing came out in hard pants as my chest grew tighter. I was losing it—losing myself again.

Alessio. Oh no. No. It wasn't supposed to happen this way. He wasn't supposed to find out my truth this way.

Everyone froze around me. Viktor, Phoenix, Artur, and Alessio. Silence. Utter silence. Viktor glanced down at me, his eyebrows furrowed. When he saw me cowering behind Alessio's back, he took a step toward me, protecting me.

Phoenix and Artur looked confused while Alessio stayed frozen. His muscles were tensed underneath my fingers, and I wished I could look into those eyes so he could see my real truth. That I loved him and never wished to betray him.

The air went from cold to deadly. It smelled like death even though nobody had died yet. It chilled me to the bones, and I shivered, fear slithering its way into my spine. My knees buckled, but I held on to Alessio, refusing to fall.

Nobody had died *yet*.

But there would only be one end. Bloodshed. War. We were all going to bathe in blood until one family would be left standing.

And in that moment, I wasn't sure which one.

The Ivanshovs or the Abandonatos.

"Take your fucking eyes off her," Alessio snapped. "And get the fuck off my property. You do not want to start war."

"I'm not here to wage war. As soon as I get what I'm here for, I will leave. This does not have to end in bloodshed, Alessio. Give me what I want and I'll leave without any disturbance," Alberto said calmly, as if he was discussing a business deal.

And that was when it happened.

Guns were drawn, and I was pushed behind. Viktor, Phoenix, and Artur pointed their guns at Alberto and his men. "Get out," Viktor growled. "Or I'm going to have your fucking brain splattered on the ground."

I trembled at the threat like it was said to me. This was going to end badly, and through it all, I was going to leave Alessio broken.

I couldn't leave him. I was his Angel. He needed me.

From my place behind their backs, I saw Alberto raise his hands up and let out a low chuckle. "Do you see my men pointing guns at you? No. As I said, I'm just here to take back Ayla—my soon-to-be wife. She comes with me, and no blood needs to be spilled."

No! I wanted to scream, but my voice was gone. I was paralyzed with fear. So much pain and fear. My heart was cracking under the pressure.

"Your what?" Viktor sputtered as he blinked down at me.

Alessio still hadn't said anything. He was quiet—so quiet. Why wasn't he saying anything? Why wasn't he yelling?

Say something, Alessio. Please. Say something.

"Oh, I see she hasn't told you yet. What a shame," Alberto tsked. "Well, let me indulge you then. The woman you are protecting behind you right now is Ayla Abandonato. The late Alfredo's daughter and only child. And also, my very soon-to-be wife. The Italian's queen. Your enemy."

"No," I whimpered. *No. Stop it!* I brought my hands to my ears and shook my head, but I couldn't block his words, his voice.

Phoenix stared down at me in shock, Artur glared, and Viktor just stared with his emotionless eyes. While Alessio—nothing. He gave me nothing. His back still faced me as he kept his eyes on Alberto.

He hadn't drawn his gun. No, he just stood there. Staring. Unmoving.

But I could feel it…the fury rolling off him. I knew he was begging for control. He was trying to keep the monster in.

For whose sake? I didn't know.

"C'mon now, love. Don't be shy. It's time for you to come home. You have wandered away for too long," Alberto said, his voice almost soothing, but I knew he was taunting.

THE MAFIA AND HIS ANGEL PART 2

I looked at Viktor, begging him with my eyes, saying the words I couldn't speak. *Please, don't let him take me. Please.*

Viktor shook his head and then looked at Alessio. His eyes went back to Alberto, glaring. "Only over my dead body will you take Ayla away," he finally growled menacingly.

"This doesn't have to be hard. Alessio, as a Boss, I'm sure your people are more important than just a measly whore who keeps your bed warm." Alberto chuckled.

His laughter rang through the air, and my blood roared. It felt like my ears were bleeding. His voice, his presence, his sadistic laughter, it was all too much for me.

His last words finally got a reaction from Alessio. But not one I expected.

"Viktor, get her inside," Alessio said, his voice calm, yet so cold and deadly.

Viktor nodded and took my arm, pulling me toward the gates. I saw Alessio, Artur, and Phoenix still standing, facing Alberto. But Alberto's eyes were on me, trained on my body and every movement I was making.

Viktor stopped at the gates, and I huddled closer to him, seeking protection.

"Get the fuck out of here, Alberto. This is the last time I am going to say this. It takes only one bullet to be fired and war will be upon us. Leave my property or my men will be forced to shoot."

Alberto raised an eyebrow and started to back away slowly. "You are right. We will let Ayla decide."

Alessio's fists tightened even further, his face murderous.

Alberto sent me a wink. "I will be waiting, love." With that, he got into his car, his men following behind as they drove away.

And then we were alone.

Alberto was gone, yet my heart pumped fiercely, fear still coursing through my body until I was weak in my knees. I was going to be sick. I bent forward as my stomach rolled, and I dry heaved in the driveway.

Alessio walked by me, leaving me there. Artur and Phoenix followed closely behind. "Alessio," I gasped through my dry heaving, my throat closing, tears stinging my eyes as I tasted the bitterness on my tongue. "Alessio…"

But he never turned. Viktor patted my back awkwardly until my stomach settled. He grabbed my arms again and pulled me inside, closing the gates behind us before locking it.

I shrugged off his hold and ran after Alessio. "Alessio! Please listen to me. Please."

But my legs weakened. I went down in a heap but struggled after Alessio. "Give me a chance to explain, please. I was going to tell you the truth. That's why I wanted to come back. Let me explain. Alessio!"

But he never looked at me. Not even once. None of the men turned. I was left on the ground, crying after Alessio, begging for him to listen.

"Alessio. Please," I whimpered. "Just let me explain."

Viktor stopped and turned toward me. "Let it go,

baby girl."

"No. Viktor, let me explain, please." But he, too, followed Alessio into the house.

And then I was left alone. I sank to the ground and sobbed. Wrapping my arms around my knees, I rocked back and forth, my mind quickly going numb, my body growing colder with each passing second.

You're my Angel.

The creek. The piano. Flowers. Alessio's smiles. Sweet kisses, gentle caresses, and softly spoken words.

I filled my mind with the good and tried to forget the bad. *It's okay, Ayla. You're okay. Everything is okay. Perfect. Complete happiness. Laughter, love, and beautiful smiles.* I floated and went to my happy place.

I rocked myself gently and smiled. I laid on the ground. Happy. I was happy. Alessio was kissing me. He was making love to me. We were happy.

We were at the creek, playing in the stream. Alessio was running after me. Laughter. Happiness. We were happy.

We were dancing. Alessio twirled me around the room. We were happy. I was his Angel. I was loved. We were loved.

Happy. Happy. Happy.

I smiled, pulling my legs to my chest. *It's okay, Ayla. You are happy. Everything is okay. Nothing is wrong.*

And then suddenly I was thrust back into reality. I didn't feel anything for a minute. I felt so cold.

But then my skin was on fire. I was burning. My

skin prickled as if thousands of tiny bugs were crawling under my skin. I scratched and scratched. I was sobbing again, my chest squeezing with so much pain, it was impossible to breathe.

I had to explain and make Alessio listen to me. Even if I had to resolve to beg on my knees, I would. But he needed to know the truth—from my side.

Swiping away my tears, I went to stand up but fell back down again. My legs wouldn't support me. My body was weak from my panic attack, and my vision was still blurred with dizziness.

So I crawled. I had to get to Alessio, no matter what.

When I reached the steps, I swallowed and wiped off the sweat on my face. Holding onto the banister, I stood up and walked up the three steps.

I stood in front of the porch and went to take a step forward.

But never got the chance.

Artur stood in front of me, blocking my way. I breathed out a sigh of relief. "I need to speak to Alessio. Please, let me in. Let me talk to him and explain," I begged, holding onto his arm.

But he sent me a glare so cold that I cowered away. Artur grabbed my arm roughly, and I squeaked as pain shot through my muscles. He pulled me away, and my knees buckled underneath me. But still he didn't stop.

He pulled me down the steps, and I shook my head wildly. "No, let me go. Artur, let me go! I need to talk to Alessio."

But he didn't stop. Instead, he pulled me toward

THE MAFIA AND HIS ANGEL PART 2

the gates, my legs dragging behind me as I tried to force him to let go.

He was stronger. I was dizzy, sick, and weak from my melt down. It wasn't a fair fight.

"No. Let me go. Artur! Stop!"

He did. I bumped into his back, and he swiveled around, his face filled with hatred and anger.

"Bitch! Do you really think Alessio wants to see you? After what you did?" he snapped, his lips curling up in disgust. "You are more delusional than I thought."

"No. Let me go!" I said, frustration and desperation building inside of me. "I don't care. I have to make him understand why I did it."

He laughed, shaking his head. "You are really delusional," he said, spitting at me.

I stood there, completely shell shocked by his action. He was dragging me again. I begged him to stop. I choked out a scream.

"You little whore. He doesn't want to see your face. Ever again. He wants you out of his life and far away from him," he uttered, breaking my heart even further.

This couldn't be happening.

I dug my nails into his arms and scratched, hoping Artur would let go. "No! He wouldn't do that. Alessio wouldn't do that."

Artur turned around and threw me over his shoulders. "No!" I punched his back repeatedly. "Let me go. I don't believe you! Alessio wouldn't say that. He wouldn't."

"Alessio!" I screamed, my voice hoarse. It was useless. My voice was scratched raw. I sounded like a newborn kitten.

"Artur, let me go. Alessio will kill you. Don't touch me. He wouldn't say such a thing. He would never cast me out of his life like that."

I wanted to believe the words I threw at Artur. But deep in my thoughts, maybe he was right.

I mentally screamed in denial.

I had to believe in Alessio. Even if he hated me, I was sure he would talk to me himself. Not send one of his men. But what if?

What if he hated me so much that he couldn't bear to see my face?

No. Alessio—the Alessio I knew, he would never do such a thing.

"You are lying. Let me go," I kicked at Artur.

"Your father killed his mother and sister. He hates you, Ayla. Deep loathing. If you come into his sight, he will kill you without a second thought. You would never get a chance to speak. He is not the man you think he is. He is a killer. And you are his enemy," Artur said, chuckling at the last words.

"Alessio!" I screamed, but my voice was low and croaky from my tears. He would never hear me.

"Do us all a favor and get the fuck out of here," Artur said, pulling me down. We were out of the gates now, and I felt a rush of panic.

I pushed at Artur. "If Alessio hates me and really wants me out of his life, he will have to say it to my face. Only then will I believe him. If he kills me, then so be it."

I tried to walk back in, but Artur grabbed my arm, pulling me away. "Fuck off, bitch." I struggled, not giving up without a fight. I had to

THE MAFIA AND HIS ANGEL PART 2

fight—for me, for Alessio, and for *us*.

Artur pushed me away, and I would have fallen if it wasn't for another set of arms.

NO!

His touch...my skin burned under it. My voice was gone again as I retreated into my head. I screamed internally. Screaming so much until it felt like my insides were going to combust.

His touch alone was enough to drive me insane.

My eyes widened, and I gasped loudly, my breathing coming out harsher as I felt panic claw at my throat. Fear slithered its way into my body and mind until my soul knew nothing but fear and pain.

His grip was strong, and I couldn't move away from him. I was paralyzed as I saw Artur walking backward, leaving me alone with the devil.

I tried to struggle, but my body wouldn't move. I submitted under the devil's hold because my body didn't know what else to do. It was so accustomed to submitting to that man, it was the only thing it was capable of doing.

My muscles tensed and locked until it hurt. Panic spread through me as I slowly started to go numb, unfeeling.

"She's all yours," Artur said before closing the gates.

And then I was alone. With Alberto.

I was too overcome with fear and pain. My head felt like it was going to explode in two. My heart was already broken. *How does someone live without her heart?* Because mine had shattered in thousands of pieces. I felt it shatter. My whole body and soul felt it.

And this time, I knew it was beyond repair.

Alberto's grip tightened, and my stomach dipped. I repressed the urge to retch as dizziness took over again. An obsidian darkness surrounded me, and I wanted to scream.

Alessio! But no words were uttered.

Alberto pulled me away, and when he pushed me into the car, I screamed.

"Alessio!"

But it was too late.

The door closed, and Alberto sat beside me. I crawled away from him, plastering myself against the door as the car started moving. No. No. No.

I pulled at the door, trying to open it, but Alberto wrapped his hand around my hair, roughly pulling away until my scalp burned under his assault.

He slammed my head into the door. Once. Twice. Pain splintered its way into my skull, and my cheek ached. I could taste blood in my mouth.

"You've been very bad, love. But it's time for you to come home now," Alberto said, keeping my cheek pressed firmly against the door. I winced as tears splashed down my cheeks.

He pulled me so that I was facing him. Alberto smirked, but his eyes were on fire. My blood ran cold.

My death had come sooner than expected.

"Time for you to go to sleep."

My eyebrows furrowed, and then I screamed when I felt a sting in my thigh. I looked down to see a syringe in his hand and the needle in my thigh. "No," I slurred.

His stares were cold and unfeeling, just like him.

THE MAFIA AND HIS ANGEL PART 2

The back of his hand smacked across my face, and I flew against the door, my head cracking under the pressure.

I was losing myself as darkness clouded my vision.

"*Alessio,*" I whimpered.

Alberto roared and pressed my face harder against the window. "You will learn to never say his name again. I think you forgot that he handed you over to me."

I tried to shake my head, forcing my eyes open even though I was slowly fading away.

"I think I've been too easy on you before. Now, you will feel what real pain is." Alberto whispered his promise into my ears, his nail digging into my cheeks painfully.

A wash of numbness filled me, and I shuddered violently, my body crumbling and weakening under his hold and the drug he gave me.

My eyes rolled into my head. This was it. My reality. My fate.

All I could do was cry and stay still as the drug took over and the dizziness threw me into a cloud of darkness and despair.

I submitted to the heavy hold that was pulling me under, and my eyes closed.

My final thought as darkness took over was Alessio.

I'm sorry, Alessio. I love you.

His name was a mere whisper in my head as I lost consciousness.

Alessio.

Chapter 28

Alessio

The sight of Alberto had caused a lava of rage to course through my body. But I had tried to stay as calm as I could.

My only thought was to keep Ayla safe. Far away from Alberto.

He couldn't know that she was my weakness.

But then he looked at Ayla like he knew her. Like she was something to possess. I wanted to gouge his eyes out, put a bullet right in the middle of his eyes. Only because he was looking at Ayla. *My Angel*.

What I never expected was the shock that came next. And the pain of betrayal.

I heard Ayla whimper behind me and felt her nails digging into my skin. I felt her panic. It was vibrating off her. The air surrounding us growing thick with her fear.

But only Alberto's words were ringing through my ears. Everything else was a blur.

THE MAFIA AND HIS ANGEL PART 2

The woman you are protecting behind you right now is Ayla Abandonato. The late Alfredo's daughter and only child. And my very soon-to-be wife. The Italian's queen. Your enemy.

Ayla Abandonato. A fucking Abandonato.

She lied to me. All this time, it had been a lie.

My shoulder ached with the tension, but I kept my face as blank as I could.

No weakness. Alberto didn't need to know how his words affected me. Ayla didn't need to know what her betrayal was doing to me.

I trusted her. I let her in.

She was my fucking Angel.

I swallowed the boulder of emotions that clogged my throat and stared straight into Alberto's eyes.

"Viktor, get her inside," I said, my voice calm yet the coldness and deadly warning was there.

The words came out instinctively. She was the enemy, yet my need to protect her never lessened. No matter how much my mind raged, I still felt for her.

She betrayed me, but she was still my Angel.

From the corner of my eyes, I saw Viktor pulling Ayla toward the gates. She was staring back at me, her eyes never leaving mine, begging me to give her a chance.

I saw everything there. Her pain. Fear. Panic. And lastly, her love.

My stupid treacherous heart hung on to it. I wanted to believe that look.

My decision might have been stupid, but it was the only one that made sense.

Giving Alberto my full attention, I sent him a chilling glare. "Get the fuck out of here, Alberto. This is the last time I am going to say this. It takes only one bullet to be fired and war will upon us. Leave my property or my men will be forced to shoot."

Alberto raised an eyebrow and started to back away slowly. "You are right. We will let Ayla decide."

I was tempted to shoot him right now. Put a bullet right through his eyes. But that would only bring war upon ourselves.

And Ayla would be right in the middle. Her safety couldn't be compromised.

My murderous intent must have shown on my face, because Alberto smirked and then glanced at Ayla, his look lecherous. "I will be waiting, love."

I felt Phoenix's hand on my arm, making me realize that I had reached for my gun. I was vibrating with the need to end the bastard's life. Slowly and painfully.

That day would come. Not now. But soon.

I watched the cars drive away before finally taking the courage to turn toward Ayla. I saw her bend forward, and she started to dry heave, hyperventilating right there in the driveway. Her small body was shaking violently, her sobs making my heart clench tightly.

I wanted to take her in my arms, hold her safely, and tell her everything was going to be okay. But I stopped myself.

I knew I would lash out and hurt her. And the last thing I wanted to do was hurt her…even though she was the reason for my pain right now.

So I walked away. From her.

I did it to protect her.

I had been shot before. Multiple times. But Ayla's betrayal was more painful than bullets piercing through my body.

She called out after me, my name on her lips. She begged me to listen, but I was numb. Too numb to care. To numb to understand her lies, her betrayal. I trusted her, but she didn't give me anything in return.

After giving her myself and opening my heart to her, she still lied.

But even through the tides of anger, I understood why.

I hated the Abandonatos.

And she was one of them. The daughter of the man who killed my mother and sister.

"Fuck!" I swore, punching the wall next to the door. She must have been scared. So damn scared. No wonder she never told any of us.

What about those who are innocent? Will they perish too? Just because they were doomed to be an Italian—an Abandonato?

Ayla's question rang through my ears, and I pulled at my hair in frustration, my fingers digging into my scalp. She wanted to tell me. So many times, she wanted to say it, but my hatred for the Abandonatos always stopped her.

I still remembered my words clearly, as if they were said the day before.

There is no fucking innocence in that family. They are all the spawn of the devil. They are tainted with my mother's and sister's blood.

How could I have expected Ayla to tell me the truth when those were the words I fed her?

You said you'd kill anyone in your path. But what about the innocent?

When realization dawned on me, I felt sick. She was talking about herself. She was the innocent.

I was running away from home when I found you and hid in your car. That's how we met. I'm not a spy, Alessio. I'm just someone running away from her nightmare, desperately seeking peace.

Everything she said came rushing back to me until my thoughts went wild. And that was when I lost control.

With a roar, I reached for the coffee table and flipped it over, sending it crashing into the wall. Hundreds of glass shards flew everywhere.

My hands clenched into fists, and I punched the wall again, harder than before. My skin over my knuckles tore, but that wasn't enough.

I was panting, fighting for breath, fighting against the monster that wanted to be unleashed.

The sudden rush was of realization made my head spin. My lungs constricted. "Fuck!" I bellowed.

The man I hated, the man I vowed to kill…my enemy, he was the one who had hurt my Angel. He was the one who caused her pain. The reason for her nightmares.

Alberto. He had ruined my Ayla.

My blood roared with the urge to kill him. To end his life. To end Ayla's nightmare.

Turning around, I saw Artur, Viktor, and

THE MAFIA AND HIS ANGEL PART 2

Phoenix standing there. Their faces were impassive as they stared back at me, waiting for me to give them orders.

But something else caught my attention. Someone was missing. My heart accelerated in panic as I glanced around the room almost furiously.

"Where's Ayla?" I growled, my knuckles aching as I tightened my fists.

Viktor's eyebrows raised in question, and he looked behind him. "She was right behind me," he grumbled, his face twisting with slight panic.

"You left her alone!"

I threw my fist, and it connected with his face. A crack resonated around the room, but I didn't care. "I left her with you. You were supposed to bring her inside."

I trusted Viktor to get her inside, to keep her safe while I tried to get myself under control.

"I thought she would follow. She's probably outside. Calm the fuck down," Viktor said, holding his bleeding mouth.

Artur came to stand beside me. "I'll get her, Boss."

I nodded, pulling away from Viktor. "Bring her inside," I ordered. Artur nodded and left without a glance. The need to protect her, shield her away from any suffering, was overwhelming. Alberto wasn't getting anywhere near her.

My head tilted to the side, and I speared Viktor with a glare. He glared back. "Are you done? Because you can't act like that when Ayla comes inside. You'll scare her to death."

I didn't say anything. Only because I knew he was right.

I had to get out of here, think clearly, away from Ayla so I couldn't hurt her.

Even though she was my Angel, she still betrayed me. My heart and mind were in a constant battle.

In that moment, I realized that I was more hurt that she lied to me than the fact that she was an Abandonato.

Ayla might have been an Abandonato, but she was innocent. She was another victim. And I couldn't hurt her for that.

I shook my head at that thought. That was exactly why I had to be heartless. Ruthless. That was why I never wanted to get close to her in the first place.

The human heart was a strange thing. It was treacherous and weak. It made us weak. It was easy for me to forget my revenge, only because what I felt for Ayla was more powerful.

What we had was more powerful than my need for vengeance.

I sank down on the couch and rubbed my forehead tiredly. How did this happen? One minute everything was perfect, and now…it was ruined.

What concerned me more was Ayla's feelings. How scared and worried she must have been.

"What are you going to do?" Viktor asked, sitting down on the sofa facing me. He regarded me with curious yet suspicious eyes. "With Ayla?"

I leaned forward, placing my elbows on my knees. "Is that even a question?" I hissed. "Do you really think I will hurt her?"

Viktor stared at me in silence and then shook his head. "I know you won't hurt her."

"And what if I did?"

I needed to know his answer. I needed to know where Ayla stood with my men, how much she meant to everyone.

I needed to know that when the time came, they would all stand in front her, protecting her.

"I would have had to go against you," he replied simply, shrugging his shoulders as if it meant nothing. But his eyes were intense and told me everything I needed to know.

My head turned toward Phoenix as I waited for his answer. He shook his head. "We can't let you hurt her, Boss."

I felt a sense of relief. They were Ayla's champions. If something happened, they would protect her.

But the relief was short-lived.

I saw Artur standing in the doorway. Alone. His face was forlorn, and when he caught my eyes, he looked down, shaking his head.

"Where's Ayla?" I asked, standing up.

"Boss, I'm sorry," he replied, keeping his head bowed.

"Where. Is. Ayla?" I asked through gritted teeth, punctuating each word as my heart accelerated almost painful.

"Boss, I tried to stop to her. I really did. But she left. With that fucking bastard. I couldn't believe my eyes, either."

"No!" I bellowed, rushing past him.

Panic rushed through me as I ran down the steps and into the driveway. The gates were closed, and I tore them open, but I was too late.

There was no sign of Alberto. No sign of Ayla. My Angel. She was nowhere to be seen.

I heard Viktor, Phoenix, and Artur behind me. The air crackled with tension.

"Ayla was just playing with you this whole time. She lied to us. That little bitch," Artur said in disgust.

Turning around, I grabbed Artur by the collar. "You are lying!"

It was impossible. Ayla couldn't betray me. She wouldn't betray me…not like that.

Artur winced as I pressed my fingers around his neck. "Don't ever call her a bitch! Where is she?"

"Boss, I saw Ayla going to him. She was in his arms," he wheezed as I pressed my fingers tighter around his throat.

I wanted to scream. Rage. Hit someone. I wanted to kill…I *needed* to kill.

"She betrayed you, Boss," Artur said, his voice hoarse.

And that was when I exploded. I lost it.

"Shut up! Shut the fuck up!"

Taking my gun from my waistband, I pointed it under Artur's chin. His head tilted up in surprise, and his eyes shone with sudden fear. "You are lying!" I growled, pushing the barrel into his throat. My fingers itched to pull the trigger and end his life.

He gulped hard and shook his head slightly.

I almost pulled the trigger then. If it wasn't for Viktor pulling me away, Artur would have been dead.

"Alessio! Damn it!" Viktor hissed in my ears. I glared at Artur as he coughed for air.

"Have you lost your mind? Pointing your gun at your man. We are a brotherhood, Alessio," he tried to reason with me. But I barely heard Viktor.

The only words that rang through my ears were Artur's.

She betrayed you, Boss.
She left. With that fucking bastard. I couldn't believe my eyes, either.
She was just playing with you this whole time.

"No!" I gripped my hair in frustration, in denial. "Ayla wasn't lying!"

It was a lie. Ayla wouldn't betray me. I didn't believe it. I couldn't believe it.

I was sixteen when I was raped.

He raped me on my sixteen birthday, and he continued to do so every single night for seven years.

My father never did anything. He never even paid attention to me. I was a loner, never allowed to leave the house. And then he handed me over to him. A cruel man who destroyed me.

He used to beat me. He would chain me to our bed and then whipped me if I did something wrong or what he perceived wrong.

Every word, every moment rushed back to me until I was blinded with grief. My lungs constricted as I fought for breath, my heart aching in the most painful way.

When Ayla was telling her past, I heard the truth in her words. Her pain-filled eyes, her nightmares, they weren't lies. They were real. Her suffering was real.

But why would she leave? With him…the same monster who destroyed her?

It didn't make sense. None of it made sense.

I refused to believe it.

Because I believed her. I believed in *us*.

"She didn't leave," I said, staring at the gates. "She wouldn't go back to Alberto."

"I agree," Viktor said beside me. "There's no way she would leave of her own will. I saw how scared Ayla was of him."

There was only one conclusion.

Alberto took her. Snatched her away right under my nose.

My eyes widened, and a sudden pain went through my chest and I almost doubled over.

My stomach lurched, and my hands shook beside me. I shuddered as I thought of the things Alberto had done to her. And now she was with him again. At his mercy. She had been thrust back into the darkness she'd been running from.

And it was all my fault.

I had one simple job to do. Protect her. But I failed. I failed my Angel.

"Are you sure you saw her leave with Alberto?" I heard Phoenix ask behind me.

"I saw her getting in his car," Artur replied.

"So it's possible Alberto had threatened her,"

Viktor added.

It didn't matter.

None of it mattered. How or why it happened.

The only thing that mattered was getting Ayla back safely. And making sure Alberto was no longer a threat.

In that moment, my vengeance was forgotten. The reason why I needed to finish the Abandonatos was forgotten.

It was replaced with another purpose.

Getting rid of every single person who had hurt my Angel. Slowly and painfully. Until they wished they had never laid eyes on her.

Chapter 29

I swiveled around and stalked back inside. My men followed close behind me.

"Boss, I'm so sorry. I didn't know. I thought—" Artur started but then quickly broke off.

I faced him, and he went to his knees, bowing his head, his gun placed in front of him. A posture of submission.

"I have failed you and Ayla. You have every right to take my life."

Bending down, I took his gun in my hand. "You are right. I can take your life right now. Only because you called my woman a bitch. You made a mistake, but that will be your last mistake."

I stood up to my full height, but instead of pointing my gun to his head, I gave him an order. "Stand up."

He stood up, facing me with his head still bowed down. "You have one more chance. Protect Ayla with your life and you will be forgiven."

I couldn't condemn him for thinking what any of us would have thought. It was easier to think that

Ayla had betrayed us.

But I knew…my Angel would never do such thing.

"Viktor, track her phone," I ordered. He nodded and took his phone out.

I rubbed a hand tiredly over my face as I looked around the room. "Phoenix, call in the other men. We are leaving as soon as we have Ayla's location."

I was still talking when I caught a glimpse of the cake Ayla baked for me the night before. Walking over to the dining table, my chest tightened with an unyielding pressure. All I could see was her sweet smiles. I heard her laughter, her melodious voice. And I felt her soft kisses.

When I reached the table, I froze, my eyes going to the item next to the cake.

I heard Viktor swear behind me before he spoke. "Alessio, her phone—"

I tried to suck in a breath, but I couldn't breathe. I clenched my fists together as my heart fell. Screaming out in rage, I took Ayla's phone and threw it at the wall.

Without thinking, I threw the cake too. It splattered against the wall. I couldn't stop. My anger was fueled further with the thought of my Angel being with Alberto and having no way to find her.

The thought of him hurting Ayla drove me insane.

My vision was covered with a red layer as I seethed. I destroyed everything around me. Nobody stopped me, because they knew I would destroy them too.

My body trembled with the need to kill. I was caught in the bloodlust.

There would be bloodshed. People were going to die, even those who were innocent. There was only death for those who would be in my path.

"This is war," I growled, my voice as sharp as razors. My chest was heaving, my breathing ragged as I imagined blood around me.

I wanted to watch Alberto's blood pour out his body as he breathed his last breath. I needed it.

My blood boiled under my skin, fiery with a searing burn, prompting me to kill. Death. The monster roared, and this time I unleashed it. I embraced the darkness inside of me.

Because this was war.

Alberto started it.

And I was going to end it.

Chapter 30

Nikolay

My car came to a stop in front of Alberto's beach house. I sat silently for a second, contemplating what to do and what was happening.

Whenever we had a meeting, he would call me to his clubs, but never to his estates. But now, I was sitting right outside one of his houses. He called me, asking me to meet him urgently.

And I came without a second thought.

Not because I wanted to. It was because I had to.

I couldn't stand his ugly face. Every time I saw him, I had to repress the urge to cut his fucking body into pieces and feed it to the dogs. My hatred toward Alberto held no bounds. I was disgusted by the very air he breathed.

And I wished that every time I saw him, I had the power to kill him and watch the life slowly leave his eyes as I ripped his fucking black heart out.

But I couldn't do any of that.

I leaned against my seat with a sigh. Taking a deep breath, I tried to calm my raging thoughts and the need for bloodlust. I was here, and I had to get my job done.

Although one question burned through my thoughts.

What was he doing in Florida? I didn't tell him about Boss's trip.

That was a big fucking coincidence that he would be here at the same time as Boss.

Shaking my head, I cleared my thoughts and stepped out of the car. The door was already opened, so I walked inside without knocking. I didn't have to. His men would already know I had arrived.

I saw a maid cleaning the kitchen, her back to me. "Where is Alberto?" I asked, my voice grating.

She jumped almost five feet in the air before turning around, her hand over her chest. "Umm...he was in his office the last time I saw him," she squeaked, her eyes filled with alarm.

"Where is his office?" She pointed silently to the end of the hall. Without a second glance, I followed her direction.

When I reached the end of the hall, I saw a man standing in front the door, guarding it. I nodded toward the door before speaking. "I need to see Alberto. He called me."

"Who are you?" he asked, his hand reaching for his gun.

"Nikolay."

Recognition flashed in his eyes. "He's not here. Boss went out about an hour ago. He had something

THE MAFIA AND HIS ANGEL PART 2

to take care of."

"I will wait for him," I announced, sending him a chilling glare, daring him to refuse me. The man huffed and opened the door for me.

"He should be back soon," he said, nodding toward the room. I went inside, and he followed me, closing the door behind him. Of course, he would follow me. No way would he have left me alone in Alberto's office. To him, I was an outsider.

What he didn't realize was that I was also the insider.

I didn't sit down. Instead, I paced the office.

Something felt wrong. Alberto would never call me to his house, especially if he wasn't here. And most importantly, what was he doing here? At the same time as us.

Did he have more spies than we thought?

I rubbed my hand over my head in frustration and tried to suppress the growl that threatened to escape.

I was still pacing when something caught my eyes. It was just a small glimpse, but it was enough for me to stop dead in my tracks.

No fucking way. Fuck no.

I stomped to Alberto's desk and took the picture frame in my hand. I thought it was my eyes playing tricks on me. Maybe it was. I blinked several times, but the picture was still there. *She* was still there.

I was looking into her green eyes.

Ayla.

My mouth fell open, but I quickly snapped it shut, my jaw grinding with the force. I stared at the picture, my mind going blank for a second.

"Who is she?" I asked out loud, although I already had my answer.

"Boss's woman," the man simply replied.

My fingers tightened around the picture frame. "What's her name?"

"Ayla Abandonato. The bitch ran away months ago. But Boss just found her. That's where he went. She was hiding with the fucking Russians all this time. Can you believe it?" he said in disgust.

My stomach dropped, and I froze, my muscles locking tight at his words. This couldn't be happening.

She was an Abandonato. And Alberto's woman. Was she the traitor?

My chest tightened at that thought. No. I didn't believe it. There was no way she would betray us.

I stared at the picture. Ayla looked so different here. Her eyes weren't glowing, like they did now. They were bleak, almost lifeless. She didn't have a smile. Her face and posture were stiff.

This Ayla looked like the one I had met the first time. When she was dirty, injured, and so fucking scared. The one who was broken.

Alberto was the one who broke her. He was Ayla's tormentor.

The man's voice sounded like he was under water as he continued to speak.

"Probably fucked every man there too. That's what she's good for. Though I'm not going to complain. Her pussy is one the best. She fit my cock like a glove."

My mind raged, and I saw red. Placing the picture down, I reached for my gun. He didn't have a chance to react or reach for his gun. I saw his eyes flare in surprise as I pointed my gun at him. And then I pulled the trigger.

One shot. One bullet, right in the middle of his throat. That was all I needed to kill him.

He sank to the ground soundlessly, his blood surrounded his seizing body. There was blood all over the office and the wall behind him, where some of his flesh had been splattered.

No one fucking talked about Boss's woman like that. I would never show mercy on men like him.

Without sparing him another glance, I walked out of the office and got into my car. My vision was blinded with Ayla's picture. The broken look on her face.

And then his words rang through my ears.

The bitch ran away months ago. But Boss just found her. That's where he went. She was hiding with the fucking Russians all this time.

"Fuck!" I bellowed, punching my steering wheel. I had to warn Alessio. I tore out of the driveway and called his cellphone at the same time.

But he didn't pick up. Which never happened. He always picked up.

My shoulders ached with tension, and my throat felt suddenly dry. I kept my eyes on the road and drove mindlessly while trying to call the others.

But nobody answered their phones.

I swore loudly, throwing my phone on the seat beside me. The road was packed. I would never get there in time. Alberto left an hour ago. He should have arrived by now. Or maybe he was waiting to attack?

That would have been the perfect time. There were not enough men to protect Ayla or Boss.

Fuck no.

I couldn't let that happen. Boss couldn't lose Ayla.

Not now. Not ever.

He wouldn't survive it. Because I knew, if Ayla lost herself, Boss would lose himself too—he would break.

And I couldn't let that happen.

I punched the steering wheel again, and pain shot through my fingers. Quickly making a U-turn, I changed the route. For the next thirty minutes, I broke every traffic rule.

When I reached the beach house, I stepped out quickly. The driveway was eerily quiet. But death hung in the air. It was almost chilling.

I ran up the stairs and went into the house but froze in my steps at the sight in front of me.

The house was a mess. Completely destroyed.

Phoenix and Artur were sitting on the couch, their heads in their hands, their posture defeated. Viktor was leaning against the wall, his eyes closed, his face twisted in pain.

Both of Boss's hands were braced against the wall. His face was turned away from me, but I could see his tensed shoulders. His whole body was rigid.

And I noticed something else, too.

Ayla was nowhere to be found.

The realization almost brought me to my knees.

I was too late.

Chapter 31

Ayla

My eyes blinked open as I slowly gained consciousness. My head throbbed, and my muscles ached. My whole body was hurting.

When my vision finally cleared, I let out a gasp. My body froze, and suddenly nausea assailed me. I had to swallow back the bile that was working its way from my stomach and into my throat.

I couldn't move my arms or legs. I felt trapped. I *was* trapped.

Alberto had me. I was completely at his mercy.

My chest tightened, and I choked on my sob. How did this happen? Everything was perfect, but I had been thrown back into the darkness again.

Tears fell silently down my cheeks as I thought about Alessio. I loved him so much that my heart ached at the thought of never seeing him again. He was my everything, and now I was alone again, without my savior.

I was living my nightmare again.

I tried to raise my arm but was horrified to find out that I couldn't. I tried to move my legs, but I couldn't.

They felt heavy, and there was no mistaking the coldness of steel wrapped around my wrists or ankles. I moved again, and the sound of metal jiggling filled the darkness.

I was chained.

Panicked, I tried to move. I wrenched my arms and legs but only cried out in pain when the metal bit into my skin.

I leaned against the wall and closed my eyes in despair. My hands and legs were manacled to a damp stone wall. I was shackled to the wall like a slave.

My throat constricted as I fought to breathe. My vision swam with dizziness, and my head tilted against the wall as I tried to keep my eyes open.

I heard footsteps approaching, and my stomach cramped. I whimpered in fear. My pulse thudded painfully against my temple and throat. My chest felt heavy under the pressure of my panic and fear.

I trembled against the wall, waiting for my impending fate.

And then suddenly, I wasn't in darkness anymore. The light was on, and my eyes closed instantly at the sudden glare. I flinched away and pushed myself harder against the wall, as if it could protect me.

I tried to cover my face with my hands, but they were yanked down cruelly. My eyes snapped open, and I was staring right into Alberto's eyes.

I cried out in pain as he tightened his fingers

THE MAFIA AND HIS ANGEL PART 2

around my arm. When he smiled, I flinched.

"Shhh, love," he said in my ear, his tongue licking down my neck.

Fear rendered me immobile. His fingers wrapped around my hair, and he pulled my head back until I was staring at him.

"Did you really think I wouldn't find you?" he hissed, his face red with rage. "You can escape, but I will always find you."

My heart sank. I knew this day would come. I was childish to think I was safe.

Alberto looked crazed as his hand twisted in my hair. I winced as my scalp burned like fire.

"Did you let him fuck you?" he asked, grabbing my chin. His fingers dug into my skin, and I had to bite my lips to stop myself from crying out. "Of course you did. He fucking touched you. Did you forget that you're *mine*?" Alberto snarled in my face. I cowered back and shook my head.

How could I forget? I was, after all, chained to my past. But for a small moment, I had let myself believe I was Alessio's.

Alberto stared at me for a second. He watched my tears slide down my cheeks, and I saw his eyes shining with delight.

He released me and stood up. I slumped against the wall, my body suddenly weak. Alberto walked backward and sat down on the chair placed in the middle of the room. He leaned back and crossed his arms over his chest, looking dangerously intimidating.

I quickly looked around the room, but it was empty. There were no windows, and the room looked unfinished.

When realization dawned, I sucked in a harsh breath. It wasn't a room. It was a dungeon.

My eyes snapped up. Alberto's lips curled as he speared me with a chilling glare. I trembled against his gaze and glanced down. I couldn't look at him. His face was a reminder of every bad thing that I had gone through.

"You ruined your father's plan," Alberto started. My eyebrows furrowed, but I didn't look up. "All this time, he kept you hidden so the Russians wouldn't find out about you. And now, they know about your existence."

I peeked up at him through my hair that was half covering my face. Alberto shook his head. "You were a fucking liability. A weakness. If they knew who you were, they would have come after you. Did you ever wonder why you were never allowed out of the estate?"

I didn't answer. It didn't matter what my answer was. Alberto would say whatever he wanted.

"Because you are a dead woman. You died in a fire twenty-one years ago."

My head snapped up, my heart throbbing at this new revelation. Alberto laughed at my expression, his face sinister. "But that's what the world thinks. Your death was fabricated, so your father's enemy wouldn't come after you."

Suddenly, his face changed. The anger was back full force. "But you fucking ruined all of that. You had to escape. And you had to end up with those Goddamn Russians. Now, they know the truth."

Shaking his head, he smiled. It was malicious,

and I shuddered. "But I think it all played out well."

I didn't understand what he meant. I only saw his smile. The same one that haunted my memories. I would never forget that smile.

Alessio. Where are you? I silently begged. I needed him. I felt like I couldn't breathe without him.

I saw Alberto get up from his chair and walk over to me. Kneeling down, he grabbed my face. "What are you thinking about, love?"

He tsked when I didn't answer. "Don't tell me you are thinking about Alessio?" he taunted to my face.

I swallowed hard as his words hit me right into the heart. He chuckled, his face right next to my ear. "Did you forget? He gave you to me."

No.

He didn't give me away. He loved me. I knew that. Alessio would come for me.

"He handed you to me like you were nothing. Do you really think he's coming to save you?" he whispered into my ears.

I closed my eyes tightly, trying to block his torturous words. I didn't believe him. I didn't.

I believed in Alessio. In *us*.

"Love, look at me," Alberto demanded.

I didn't have any other choice but to look at the devil. He had all the control. When I finally opened my eyes, I saw Alberto's face soften. His eyes changed to a lighter shade as he looked at me almost lovingly.

"Don't you see? I'm the one who cares about you," he said, trailing a gentle finger down my cheek.

Fear rocketed through my chest, squeezing me until I couldn't breathe. I knew what he was doing. Alberto always did that. He would change right in front of my eyes. Going from a monster to a gentle man.

He did that to play with my mind. To trick me into believing what he wanted. To make me believe he actually cared.

At the beginning, it worked. But now I knew the truth. It was all a game to him. There was not even an ounce of humanity in him. He was a monster.

"Everything I have done is for us. For you. I have always protected you and kept you safe so my enemies wouldn't hurt you," he continued.

I tried to shut him out. I really did, but his taunting words rung through my ears, refusing to leave.

"Alessio doesn't care about you. He never did. But I do. I'm here for you." Alberto leaned forward and placed a kiss on my cheek. His lips moved to my lips, and he kissed me. Almost sweetly and apologetically. "You're my queen."

I whimpered and shifted away. I thought he would hit me, but he didn't. Alberto rubbed a finger over my cheek instead. "You'll see that he never cared. He's not coming for you, Ayla."

I wanted to scream. *Stop it! Please stop it.*

He was lying. Alessio cared. I was his Angel. He would come for me. I trusted him.

Alberto continued to whisper in my ears as his hand wandered up my bare thighs. They went under my dress, his touch soft. But the softness was deceiving. The softness only held the promises of pain.

"It's okay. It'll be okay. Now that you are home, you are safe. He can't hurt you."

I squeezed my eyes shut when I felt a finger probing me through my lace panties. Pain. All I felt was pain. This couldn't be happening again.

Maybe it was just a dream. A nightmare. But I knew it was real. This nightmare was my reality.

He grabbed my thigh possessively, his fingers digging into my skin, leaving his marks. I sniffed as my tears continued to run down my cheeks.

I didn't say anything. I knew how it worked with Alberto. As long as I stayed quiet, it wouldn't be as bad.

And then suddenly the gentleness was gone. The back of his hand smacked across my face, and my head knocked against the wall. I screamed as agony pierced through my head and neck.

Alberto gripped my hair and shook me. He yanked me forward until the shackles bit into my skin painfully. I cried out again, the pain too intense for me to bear.

It didn't hurt just physically. My heart was hurting too. I was breaking inside, slowly losing myself to the darkness that surrounded me.

"Did you really think I would go gentle on you, love?" he spat into my face.

I shook my head, my stomach cramping violently at the unspoken promise in his words. My heart throbbed, and I was paralyzed.

His fist made contact with my face, and my lips cracked open. I didn't scream this time. I just waited because I knew what was coming next.

"You betrayed me, Ayla. You are making me do this. This is all your fault," he said against my neck as he ripped my dress.

I shuddered as his hands groped my body. As he touched me, Alberto placed kisses over my face. A mixture of gentle and pain. He was giving me both, trying to confuse me, trying to trick my mind.

"I'm going to fuck you and show you exactly who the fuck you belong to," he growled into my ears.

My heart sank, and my mind went blank.

I resisted at first. Something I had never done before. But that only angered him more. I didn't want him. I only wanted Alessio. I wanted my Alessio's touch. Instead, I was forced to feel the monster's touch.

I tried to be strong, but in the end, I was weak.

Alberto twisted me around until I was on my knees, my back against his front. He forced my face against the wall until I was trapped. I couldn't do anything, not with the chains wrapped around me so tightly.

He pushed my thighs apart, and I felt his tip at my entrance. "You are mine! Never forget that, Ayla. Mine!"

He slammed inside me, painfully and ruthlessly. I couldn't stop the scream that escaped past my lips.

I felt his breath at the back of my neck as he took me roughly and painfully. He pounded his cock inside of me repeatedly, his fingers wrapped around my throat the whole time, making sure I knew he was the one in control.

THE MAFIA AND HIS ANGEL PART 2

I was being cut from the inside. It felt like I was being prickled with glass shards. I was bleeding inside. My heart was bleeding. My soul was bleeding, begging for mercy. The pain was too much. I stayed silent as my body and heart broke into pieces. I felt disconnected.

It felt like this cruel punishment was never ending. He took me over and over until I slipped into the darkness.

And I knew this time I wouldn't be able to come back.

When he came with a roar, my head spun. Alberto slipped out of me, and I felt his cum slide down from the inside of my thighs, branding me in the most humiliating way.

My whole body was aching from his assault. I couldn't move so I just laid there, my head hanging limply against the cold wall.

I felt Alberto's lips next to my ears. "He's not coming for you. No matter how much you beg, he's not coming. He will never find you. Nobody is coming for you."

I closed my eyes, refusing to accept his words.

"You're a ghost, Ayla. A forgotten ghost. You always lived in the shadows."

His words impaled my heart in the most horrendous and painful way. Because I knew they were the truth.

But what made the pain worse was the realization that I would always live this way. In the darkness. Hidden with no escape.

I was truly a ghost. A forgotten one.

My eyes rolled into my head as I slowly

succumbed to the agony coursing through my body.

But even through the numbness, I still thought of Alessio.

No matter how impossible it was, I still wished I could feel him again and listen to his beating heart. Just one more time.

Just for one last time, I wanted to feel his beating heart.

Chapter 32

Alessio

I felt numb as I stepped out of the car. Standing in the driveway, I stared at the estate. The front doors were open, but my feet were rooted in place, refusing to move.

There was an ache in my chest. I left with Ayla but was coming back without her. At the thought of coming back home without my Angel and knowing she wouldn't be there to greet me or kiss me, the pain in my chest intensified.

Viktor came to stand beside me, and he waited. I felt Nikolay on my left side. And then Phoenix and Artur. Nobody stepped forward. They all waited for me.

No matter how much pain I was in, I was still a Boss—the King. I couldn't let myself get weak at a moment like this. Swallowing past the lump in my throat, I took a step forward and walked toward the door. Each step I took was heavy, a reminder of my failure.

I stepped inside, and as soon as I had walked through the doors, Maddie was on me. She grabbed my collar, her face a mask of anger and disbelief.

"Where is she?" Her voice was chilling as she screamed. "How could you have let this happen?"

Her eyes blurred with tears as she choked back a sob, her chest heaving with the effort. "You promised to protect her, Alessio."

I didn't say anything.

She was right. I vowed to protect Ayla, but I wasn't able to. My father was also right. I thought I wouldn't let it happen. I thought I was strong, but history was repeating itself.

The tightness in my chest was back again. Maddie released my collar, and she sank down to her knees, her anguished cries ringing through my ears.

"You promised," she sobbed at my knees. "You promised."

I heard another cry, and my head snapped up toward Lena. She was holding her chest, her eyes wide as she gasped.

"Lena!" Viktor rushed to her, pulling her to the sofa before she could fall over. "Call Sam," he ordered as Lena continued to gasp for air, her face twisted in agony.

"My sweet child," she whispered, her voice breaking.

This was all too much. All their emotions washed over me; disappointment, pain, sorrow so deep that my heart ached with it. I ran a trembling hand over my face, trying to stay calm. Trying to be strong for everyone.

For Ayla. She needed me strong.

Artur pulled Maddie into his arms. She buried her face into his chest as she sobbed. Swallowing against the lump of emotions around my throat, I shook my head and walked forward.

Maddie stopped in front of me. "Ayla might be an Abandonato, but she is innocent."

Her voice was a mere whisper, but it reached me. And the words were a straight blow to my heart.

"I know," I murmured, looking straight as I walked past her.

"Alessio, you have—" She broke off, her voice cracking. "I can't even imagine what she is going through right now."

My eyes closed, my fingers tightening into fists at the thought of Ayla being in pain.

"I will find her," I said, my voice gruff from the effort of keeping my emotions in check.

I will find her. It was a vow spoken out loud.

Maddie stepped in front of me, a single tear trailing down her cheek. "You promise?"

I broke my promise before, but not this time. So I nodded. Maddie seemed satisfied enough with my answer, and her eyes held no doubt. They only shone with absolute trust.

She stepped out of my way, and I continued upstairs. Walking down the hall toward my office, I only heard Ayla's beautiful laughter and sweet voice. She was everywhere yet nowhere at all.

A sudden surge of anger coursed through my body. Alberto had to die.

But first I had to find him. And the fucker was smart. A coward, but smart. The moment Ayla was in his trap, he went off the grid. Nowhere to be found.

It had only been hours since Ayla was taken, but it felt like years.

"Fuck," I swore, opening the door to my office, only to stop dead in my tracks.

Lyov was staring out the window, while Isaak's body sagged against the couch, his head in his hands as if all his energy had left his body.

I walked inside, analyzing both men closely. They hated the Abandonatos with a passion, but I wasn't going to let them stand in my way to find Ayla. Consequences be damned.

From the corner of my eyes, I saw my men following me inside. My expression stayed cold and emotionless as I faced my father and Isaak.

"I should have known," Isaak said, causing a cloud of confusion to settle around us. Lyov's back went rigid at Isaak's voice, his eyes closing tightly.

"She looked so much like Leila, but I didn't want to believe it. I refused to believe it," Isaak continued, his voice breaking over the last words.

Alfredo's wife?

"What?" I snapped, moving forward.

Isaak looked up, and I was shocked to see his eyes red. No, he wasn't crying. But the agony on his face spoke more than the tears would have.

"You knew Leila?" I asked when our eyes met. He flinched and stared at Lyov, who still hadn't turn around to acknowledge us.

"Yes. I knew Leila. I more than just *knew* her," he murmured.

Cocking my head to the side, I stared and waited.

I could have guessed the answer, but I needed to hear it from him. The truth.

My thoughts ran wild as I waited for Isaak to explain.

"To understand, you will have to know the beginning."

My eyes widened when I heard Lyov's guttural voice. "Tell him," he ordered without turning around.

Isaak stood up and paced the room. "After your mother's death, our only goal was to take down the Abandonatos. I was sent to find Alfredo's weakness."

He paused, taking a deep breath, as if it pained him to continue. "We thought Leila was his weakness, so for months I kept an eye on her. From far away. I watched her every move and waited. After weeks of watching, I started to see signs of abuse. Sometimes she would have a bleeding lip. Her cheeks would be red or a shade of purple. Once she was walking with a limp."

Why did that sound so familiar?

Ayla. Her name was a whisper in my head, and I clenched my jaw, my teeth grinding together.

"Every day, at the same exact time, Leila would go to a coffee shop. I watched her cross the street. I watched until I couldn't stay away anymore. She was so sad. So broken," Isaak continued. He had long ago stopped pacing. His eyes were now glued to the wall. He was lost in his memories.

"But she was never alone. She always had a baby in her arms. The only time I saw her smile was when she played with the small little bundle. I approached them, desperate to know the broken woman in front of me."

I knew where this was going, but I didn't stop Isaak. So he kept talking. And in doing so, his words stabbed at my already fragile heart.

"The baby's name was Ayla. Ayla Abandonato. She was the sweetest little baby. Only three months old when I met her." Isaak's voice slightly broke over Ayla's name.

My eyes snapped shut as I sank down on the couch.

"Leila and I got to know each other, but she didn't know who I was. Not my real name. We…we started an affair. It was forbidden, and we both knew it. But that didn't stop us. It lasted for several months. I watched Ayla grow. She took her first step in front of me, and it was toward me."

I heard Viktor swear, and Isaak paused. The room was suddenly filled with silence, and the silence was suffocating.

"What happened?" I asked, my voice harsh against the silent room.

Isaak took a deep breath before continuing. "Leila was mad when she found out the truth about me, but she understood why I did it. That night, we planned her escape. It was the only way to protect her and Ayla. But I was a little too late."

"Leila died in a fire," I said.

"No," Isaak suddenly growled. "She didn't."

My head snapped up toward him as he turned to face me. "I heard her die. I heard her screams as Alfredo killed her. Shot her. The bastard fucking called me and made me listen. Three gunshots and then there was silence."

Shaking his head, he ran a hand over his face, his body shaking. With anger. And deep sorrow.

"Leila had died, and I couldn't do anything. But I knew I had to get to Ayla. I promised Leila that Ayla wouldn't live the life that she did. Ayla would be free and happy. I vowed to protect her and take her out of that hell." Isaak broke off with a harsh, emotionless laugh.

He shook his head, still laughing. "I was too late. Again. Ayla—"

"—died in a fire," I finished off.

Everyone knew that story. Half of Alfredo's estate caught on fire. So many lives were taken, including his wife and daughter. That was the story, but it clearly didn't happen that way.

"Ayla was only a year old. I didn't believe it at first. But I saw her casket. It was so small. *She* was so small. She looked so fragile as she was lowered into the ground next to her mother," Isaak's voice was a mere whisper now.

I had known Isaak for many years, but I had never ever seen him so broken. I rubbed the back of my neck, trying to release the tension there.

It all made sense now. Why we never got anything on Ayla…no matter how intensive our research was. Why I never even thought for a moment that Ayla could have been an Abandonato.

She was a ghost. Alfredo had made sure of it.

"That fucking bastard," Isaak hissed, his eyes suddenly sparking fire. "He knew. He fucking knew I was coming for Ayla. She might not have my blood, but I loved her as my own."

"He made us believe that Ayla died. It was the only way to keep Isaak away. All these years we thought she was dead." Lyov finally spoke again when it became clear that Isaak couldn't say anything else.

There was only silence for a few seconds, until Isaak exploded. He reached forward and grabbed me, almost frantic in his actions.

"You have to find her. Please, Alessio. She won't survive there. Not again. We have to save her. We have to find her. She...she...you..." Isaak begged me, his breathing panicked.

My chest went tight, so tight that it was almost impossible to breathe. And the anger, it clawed at my body, laughing, taunting, shaking me, begging for release.

My fists shook as Isaak stepped away when I didn't answer him.

It was vicious cycle. Pain, suffering, and anger. It clouded us until we were blinded with it. But through it all, there was only one light.

Ayla.

Standing up, I walked to the large panel window. Lyov stood beside me, where he had been throughout the whole confrontation.

And then Viktor was beside me. Isaak on Lyov's side. Nikolay next to Viktor. Phoenix beside Nikolay and Artur right next to Phoenix.

A brotherhood.

Taking in a deep breath, I let it out slowly. When I spoke, my words rang with finality.

"I'm going to bring Ayla home."

Alberto didn't know what was coming for him.

He may have taken my Angel away, but I was coming for her.

I may have been a monster. A killer. Heartless. Ruthless. But what was worse for Alberto was that I was Ayla's monster.

I wouldn't stop until I had delivered all their corpses at Ayla's feet. My blood roared with the need to seek vengeance against the men who caused Ayla pain.

I would burn everything in my path to find her. It was the beginning of destruction. A bloodbath.

And I wasn't going to stop looking. Not until I found my Angel.

Chapter 33

My knuckles cracked when my fist made contact with his face. The sound was deafening in the silent room. I didn't feel anything, and the poor bastard at the receiving end of my furious fist was whimpering in pain.

When I pulled away and sat down on the chair, he looked at me through swollen eyes. His cracked lips were bleeding profusely, and his cheeks were red and oozing with blood from several cuts. They weren't deep, but they were enough to cause him blinding pain.

His mouth opened, but the sounds that came through his lips was almost too soft to hear. "If you're going to kill me, just do it. I don't know where he is."

It had been two hours since he was tied to the chair. One of Alberto's men. But he knew nothing of Alberto's whereabouts.

It had been one week since Ayla was taken away. It didn't matter that I had already killed eight of Alberto's men. Tortured them until they begged for death. No one knew where he was.

Reaching forward, I grabbed the index finger of his right hand. I looked into his eyes as I bent the finger backward. His body shook as he tried to escape my cruel ministration. But he had nowhere to go.

He was at my mercy.

I heard a pop sound; his finger cracked, his bone crushing. I let the broken finger go as he wailed. His screams still resonated around the room when I grabbed two more fingers, bending them into an impossible angle until I heard another crack. Or several cracks, I should say.

This time, the bones broke through the skin. They stuck out, taunting him.

"Where is he?" I said through gritted teeth.

"I don't…don't…kn…ow…" he sobbed, looking at his mutilated fingers.

Viktor wrapped his hand around the man's hair and pulled his head backward, his neck pushing painfully against the back of the chair. A wet cloth slapped against his face before he could protest.

Viktor held the cloth, heavy and wet with freezing water, over the fucker's face. He spluttered and fought against the invasion as Viktor pressed harder, stopping his circulation.

Then the cloth was gone. He panted for air but could barely breathe through his swollen nose.

"I'm going to ask one last time. Where is Alberto?" I snapped, pushing the chair away as I stood up.

He shook his head several times. "He…didn't tell…me…pl…please…beli…eve me."

My fist hit his stomach as Viktor placed the cloth over his face again. It was wetter this time, and I knew the water was filling his mouth and nose, suffocating him.

When I saw his body slowly giving up on life, I nodded at Viktor to take the wet cloth away. I loomed over the man's body, glaring down at him with all the hatred I felt.

My fingers wrapped around his hand, and I pressed hard, twisting until his wrist snapped under my hold. His eyes widened as a scream tore out from his throat.

"Please...kill...me..." he begged, struggling but too weak to fight.

He knew his death was coming. And he begged for it. What a fucking coward.

My eyes narrowed on him. It always came to this, Alberto's men begging me for death without giving me the answer I wanted...needed.

Alberto was smart. He went into hiding without telling anyone. I went after his right-hand men, and even they didn't know.

But there must have been someone helping him stay hidden this long. Whoever it was, I wasn't going to stop until I found him.

Pulling my gun out, I aimed at his knee. A shot was fired, a bullet piercing his knee cap. He screamed in agony, and I chuckled. I only chuckled on the outside—inside, my monster was roaring with laughter. It demanded more blood to be shed.

More blood from my Angel's tormentors.

Another shot. Another bullet. Right in his other knee. His scream pierced through my ears, but it wasn't enough. It was never enough.

I reached into my pocket and pulled out my spiral knife. The man's eyes widened, and he shook his head, his whimpers getting louder. He thought I was going to end his life easily.

How naïve of him.

Viktor smiled and pulled out his knife, too. One slice across his neck. Quick and swift. So deep that his blood poured around us and his bones were showing.

The man made a gurgling sound, blood oozing from the cut at an accelerating rate.

But it wasn't over. Not yet.

Holding my knife tight in my hand, I pulled back and then plunged it into his chest, right in his heart. His mouth fell open in a silent scream, his blood squirting around us. The floor was covered with it. The air smelled of death and the copper smell of blood.

I smirked as he convulsed and then collapsed against the chair, eyes wide open. They were full of fear until he was lifeless. Just another dead body.

Another step toward finding my Angel.

"Now what?" Viktor asked, his lips curled up in a sadistic smile. He rubbed his gloved hands together in anticipation.

"The next man on the list," I answered, my voice chilling. Anyone else would have pissed their pants at that tone, but not my men. After all, we craved the same thing.

The blood and death of our enemies.

Turning my back from the dead corpse in front of me, I walked out of the room. But not before I saw Nikolay taking his lighter out.

By the end of the day, the corpse would be nothing but ash.

As I stepped into the sunlight, I took a deep breath and closed my eyes. Like always, I saw Ayla's smile and shining green eyes. She radiated beauty.

I felt my lips tilt up at the thought of her.

I'm coming, Angel. Wait for me.

***

1 week later

I walked into the room, and the man trembled at the sight of me. He was on his knees, and Nikolay had his arms twisted around his back. Another captive. Another of Alberto's most trusted men.

"Let's see what you have to say," Phoenix said beside me.

"Please…I don't know anything," he begged.

My chest rumbled with laughter. What else could I have done?

I didn't even do anything yet, and he was already begging. I wondered what he would do when I got started.

"I…have…a wife," he stuttered, pleading me with his eyes. "And a daughter. Please, they need me."

Scoffing, I walked forward and pulled him up by the hair. "You should have thought about that before messing with the Ivanshovs."

Nikolay stepped away, and I slammed the man

against the wall. His head banged with a crack, and he winced.

"Where do you think Alberto would hide?" I snarled, my fingers wrapping around his neck. I pressed against his windpipe, my thumb moving up and down. He struggled to breathe, his face turning a shade of purple.

His fingers grabbed at my hand, pulling, scratching with the attempt to dislodge my grasp, but it was all for nothing.

I heard a gasp behind me and then a cry. Looking over my shoulder, I saw a horrified woman standing at the door; in her arms was a sleeping baby.

Ah. The wife and daughter.

I turned back toward my captive, and his fearful eyes met mine. He tried to glance at his wife, but my body was hiding his view.

His body started to shake from the lack of oxygen. But that wasn't all. It was also from fear. For his wife and daughter.

I couldn't help but smirk. Interesting.

"Come in, ladies. I'm sure you would want to stay with your husband as he takes his last breath. We wouldn't want him to die alone. Keep him company," I taunted without glancing away from the man's eyes.

Releasing my hold on his throat, I stepped away. He fell to his knees, and my heart soared with power. Yet another of Alberto's men on their knees, bowing down to me.

I turned around to see Phoenix escorting the woman and her baby to a chair. She sat down, but her whole body was trembling like a leaf.

"Who are you?" she whispered.

"I am your husband's executioner," I replied, my voice deadly. She flinched and held her baby tighter to her chest.

"But...he..." she stuttered, but I cut her off quickly.

"He deserves it."

Tears streamed down her face as she shook her head. "Please don't hurt him."

"Your begging only makes me want to hurt him more." I laughed, pointing a gloved hand at her husband, who was still gasping for breath.

Viktor chuckled, crossing his arms over his chest as he regarded the woman with keen interest. "Please keep begging. It'll only be more fun," he goaded.

"You're evil. All of you. Monsters. How could you do this?" she cried.

"Ah, I never said I wasn't evil." I shrugged when she shrunk back into her chair. Phoenix kept a hand on her shoulders, and she shuddered.

"I'm not that repulsive," he muttered under his breath.

Shaking my head at the poor frightened woman, I turned back toward her husband. I saw Nikolay holding a baseball bat. He shrugged. "We need to get creative sometimes."

And then he smacked the bat against the man's back. "Here you go, Boss," Nikolay said, giving me the bat as he stepped back.

"Are you going to talk or not?" I asked, looking at the man at my feet.

"I'm telling the truth. Alberto...didn't...tell

me…anything," he wheezed through the blood pouring from his mouth and nose.

My patience had run thin, and I snapped. I rammed the bat into his legs until I heard bones crunching. He screamed. His wife screamed. The baby cried.

But that didn't stop me.

It spurred me on. The bat came in contact with his stomach. His ribs broke under the solid wood, and his body convulsed in pain.

"Please stop. Stop!" the wife wailed.

Stop! Please stop! Ayla's voice resonated through my ears, and I stumbled back in shock. My chest grew tight at her voice as it rang in my head.

Angel. My Angel.

I looked at the man as he writhed in agony, his body beaten up and swelling under the pressure. I stepped away and faced the woman. She was sobbing heavily, and the baby continued to cry.

Phoenix caught my eyes, and he nodded. I didn't even have to say anything. He understood what I wanted. He grabbed the woman by the arm and started pulling her away and out of the house.

The wife and the baby would be given a safe place to stay. The innocents would be safe, while the evil would be chained.

"One last chance. Anything you might know. Tell me and I might let you go back to your wife and daughter," I hissed into his face.

It was a lie. He wasn't leaving this house alive. He knew it was a lie. We all did.

"I don't…kn…ow…I rea…lly don't know. But…please. Don't…hurt…my wife and daugh…ter."

I sighed and shook my head. I stood up and faced my men. Viktor looked pissed. Nikolay was ready to murder someone. Artur was glaring down at the man with venom.

Phoenix came back inside, and he rubbed his hand over his face, a sign of fatigue. We were all tired. Dead on our feet. But we were still not giving up. Not until we found Ayla.

I saw Viktor's eyes widening and then Nikolay's. "Alessio!"

Guns were drawn, and I swiveled around, my gun pointed at the man in a split second. Five shots rang through the air and the sound resonated around the walls of the house.

Five bullets.

And all five had pierced the man's body.

One in his chest, two in his stomach, one in his neck, and the last one between his eyes.

One bullet from each of my men. And one from me.

He sunk to the floor soundlessly, the gun he had drawn on me falling limply through his fingers.

"Another stupid man dead," Viktor spat.

Without a second glance at the dead body, I walked out of the house. My phone rang in my pocket, my eyebrows shooting up in surprise.

When I saw the caller ID was unknown, I picked up the call, knowing already who it was.

"I left another gift for you," I spoke before Alberto could say anything.

"Killing my men won't get you to me," he mocked.

"Maybe you should stop being such a coward and face me," I hissed through gritted teeth.

Every day I got a call from him. Every day he taunted me. And every day I was helpless as I listened to Ayla's cries.

If only his phone wasn't untraceable. The bastard enjoyed playing with me every day.

It was a game. We were both playing it. It was a dangerous game, and one of us was going to lose in the end.

And I was going to make sure it wasn't me.

"Ah, why would I do that? I'm enjoying my time with my woman here. We're making up for lost time." He chuckled cruelly.

My blood ran cold as my anger burned like lava. It burned under my skin, and my body shook with it.

"I'm not going to let you break her," I said, my fingers folding into a fist at my side.

"Ah," Alberto tsked and then laughed. "You're too late. I have already broken her. I have plucked every single feather off her wings. I took until she had nothing left to give, and still then, I kept taking."

My heart ached, my stomach rolled, and I almost doubled over in pain. Ayla. Ayla. My sweet Angel.

"So you see, in the end, I have won."

I refused to believe it. I just had to get to Ayla. I would cast away all her nightmares. I would take away all the bad memories. I had done it before. I would do it again until she'd be whole again.

"No," I snapped. "You haven't won yet. Your death is coming, Alberto. Start counting your days."

I hung up before he could say anything else.

Throwing my phone against the car, I closed my eyes.

I'm sorry. I'm so sorry, Angel. I'm sorry for keeping you waiting, but I'm coming.

Chapter 34

3 weeks later

I stared at the piano.

Ayla was sitting there, just like always. Her hair was down, flowing in beautiful soft waves at her back. Her eyes were closed, a small smile on her lips as she hummed and played the piano. For me. For us.

I smiled too. She was so beautiful. My Angel.

Ayla slowly glanced up, and her captivating green eyes met mine. She blew me a kiss, and I reached to grab it. She laughed, and I smiled again.

Suddenly the laughter stopped. Ayla stared down, and tears streamed down her cheeks.

No. Don't cry, I wanted to say. I reached forward, and just like that, my Ayla disappeared.

I closed my eyes tightly, my fingers tightening around the bottle of alcohol. My head spun, and the heartache never left me. I was drunk, like every other night.

I wanted to forget. But then I felt guilty and

ashamed. I *couldn't* forget.

Even though she was gone, Ayla never left me. Even when I was too drunk to remember my name, I never forgot Ayla. She was always there. I could feel her. Sometimes I saw her, too.

It had been five weeks since Alberto took Ayla away from me. Five weeks of looking for my Angel like a madman. But she was nowhere to be found.

I just wanted to touch her. Hold her. Kiss her.

I opened my eyes again and stared at the piano. The bench was empty. My Angel wasn't there. It hurt. It hurt so much that I couldn't breathe sometimes.

She was gone. And I was alone. All alone.

I craved her. I craved the peace only she could give. I craved her love.

But my Angel was gone. And without her, I was lost.

A broken, empty shell.

Ayla once said I was her peace. But she was mine, too. She was the light to my darkness.

But the light was gone, and only darkness surrounded me. I was used to the darkness, but now it only suffocated me. It only left me broken.

Standing up, I stumbled toward the piano. I touched the keys and thought about Ayla being there right now.

I can't live without you, Angel. I can't.

***

THE MAFIA AND HIS ANGEL PART 2

Viktor

2 weeks later

I opened the door to the piano room and sucked in a harsh breath at the sight that beheld me. It was the same sight as every night since Ayla had been gone, but it still shocked me to the core.

Alessio laid on the floor next to the piano, his body curled up in a ball.

I rubbed a hand over my mouth and face, trying to hold in the emotions.

I had never seen Alessio so broken. So disconnected from the world. So lost.

Walking forward, I knelt down and wrapped an arm under his arms, pulling him up. He stumbled, his eyes closed. "C'mon, big guy. Let's get you in bed," I muttered as his weight fell heavily on me.

I dragged him to his room and pushed him on the bed. Alessio didn't wake. Of course he didn't. He drank himself into oblivion.

After removing his jacket, I removed his shoes and threw them on the floor. Sweat broke out on my forehead from the effort of dragging Alessio and taking care of him.

When I was done, I pulled the comforter over the body. His eyebrows drew together in tension, and he mumbled something under his breath.

Moving closer, my heart stuttered when I heard what he was saying. I rubbed my chest, trying to get rid of the ache there.

"*Angel*," he whispered.

I sighed and kneaded the back of my neck,

rolling my shoulder, getting rid of the rigid muscles. What a fucking mess.

Alessio was the strongest man I knew, the most ruthless, yet here he was…broken over the woman he so desperately loved.

I didn't blame him, though.

It was impossible not to love Ayla. She brought light into the darkness of our world. She was *the* light.

I turned away from Alessio but stopped when I saw my father standing at the doorway. He stared at Alessio and then moved his eyes to me.

"I've done this so many times," he muttered. I cocked my head to the side, waiting for him to elaborate.

"For Lyov. When he lost Maria, he was exactly like this, and just like you, I had to take care of him. I had to help him pick up the pieces. But the problem is there are too many pieces. Lyov is still a broken man—" He paused, pointing at Alessio before continuing. "And now Alessio."

I looked back at the bed, and I saw Alessio struggling, as if he was fighting in his sleep. Nightmares plagued his sleep every night.

"That's why Lyov warned him. Don't fall in love. Don't let yourself get weak. That was exactly the reason why. I had been through it. Lyov had been through it, and all he wanted to do was save Alessio from the same suffering."

"We are going to find Ayla," I shot back, refusing to believe anything else.

He nodded. "I hope you do. For all our sakes. She needs to be saved, and Alessio needs her."

He turned to walk away but then stopped. Looking over his shoulder, he left me with words I didn't want to hear.

"Don't make the same mistake we did."

With that, he left. And I sank down on the bed.

My eyes caught the photo frame on the night stand. I took it in my hand and looked into the face of Ayla. She was laughing, her eyes shining with so much love.

Rubbing my thumb over her cheek, I looked back at Alessio and then glanced down at her face again.

"Sometimes, I wish you'd never hid under his bed," I whispered. "And we never knew you."

My father was too late to warn me.

Because I had already made the same mistake.

Chapter 35

Ayla

My body was strangely warm. I was floating, and a sense of peace surrounded me. My eyes opened, and I blinked several times, trying to get accustomed to my surroundings.

When my eyes finally adjusted to the light, I let out a gasp, my heart fluttering like the wings of a hummingbird.

I wasn't in the dungeon.

No, I was in a beautiful room. I sat up, and my eyes widened when I saw Alessio sitting next to me.

Alessio!

He was right there. Next to me. He found me! He came…he really came for me. Just like I knew he would.

My heart soared, and I jumped into his arms with a cry. "Alessio. I love you. I love you. I love you so much. Please don't leave me. Please," *I sobbed in his chest.*

"Shh…I've got you, Angel."

Oh, his voice. Those words. They were exactly what I wanted to hear. What I had been so desperate to hear.

His arms wrapped around me, holding me to his body. He caressed my hair and placed gentle kisses over my face, soothing all the hurt away.

"Alessio, you...found me." I hiccupped back a sob as he looked down at me with his captivating blue eyes, the ones I loved so much.

"I will always find you." Placing a kiss on my forehead, he let his lips linger there for a moment. "I'm sorry for keeping you waiting so long."

My fingers tightened around his jacket, and I shook my head. "You came for me. That's all that matters."

Alessio hugged me tighter. "I'm going to take away all the things Alberto has done to you."

I shivered in his arms at the mention of the devil's name. "He hurt me, Alessio," I admitted with tears streaming down my cheeks in a never-ending flow.

"I know. But he is never going to hurt you again," Alessio said, pulling away from me. He pushed me flat on my back and loomed over me.

"Where did he touch you, Angel?" he muttered, kissing my lips gently and so softly.

"Everywhere," I whimpered at the thought of Alberto touching me, defiling and humiliating me in the worst way possible.

"I'm going to take it all away," Alessio vowed before taking my lips. The kiss was slow and gentle. He kissed me with care, as if I was a treasure, a precious jewel, someone who deserved to be loved.

And slowly Alessio replaced Alberto's touch with his own. He traced my body with his fingers and lips. Slowly, softly, and gently. He explored my body with care and love. So much love.

But my heaven didn't last for long.

Because I was suddenly thrust back into hell.

My eyes snapped open when I felt a finger probe my entrance.

"No!" I screamed, my voice filled with horror.

"Hmmm…is that for me, love? Are you wet for me?"

Horrified, I froze, and numbness washed over me. Alberto cupped me roughly against my legs, his palm pressing hard against me. I flinched and shuddered in fear and disgust.

He was sucking on my nipple, biting and torturing the skin. Alberto slightly pulled away until he was looking down on me.

The smile on his face made my stomach roll until I thought I was going to be sick. It held so many promises. Dark promises. Every day was painful. Every day my body was abused. Every day my heart broke a little more. Every day I wished I was back in Alessio's arms.

And every day I hoped for Alessio to find me.

But he hadn't come for me. Yet. I still hoped. I still believed. In him.

Alberto pulled away and pushed my knees up until I was completely open to him. I bit on my lips to keep from crying or screaming. I had learned fast that fighting only made it worse.

The tears fell down on my cheeks, and I didn't

bother swiping them away. Alberto smirked at the sight of them, and my heart ached.

Weak. I was so weak. Alessio would be ashamed of me. *I* was ashamed of myself.

I was dirty. Used. A whore.

I was not an Angel. Not anymore.

Instead of moving on top of my body and taking me like he always did, Alberto pulled out his phone. His knees were holding my thighs apart and in place. His torso was holding my hips against the bed. I couldn't move. No, I was completely helpless underneath him.

He held the phone over me, right between my legs.

His next words sent me over the edge, and I was falling. Falling deep in the dark abyss.

"Why don't I send Alessio a picture, huh? Let him know that his woman is wet and dripping for another man."

My breath left my body in a loud whoosh, and I struggled to breathe. *No. No. No. Please no. Anything but this.*

I shook my head, or I thought I did. I felt too disconnected. Paralyzed by fear and humiliation. My breath was coming too fast, and my blood ran cold.

"No," I protested weakly, my voice barely coming out in a whisper.

My heart thundered against my chest almost painfully, and my mouth tasted bitter with bile. I was going to be sick. My stomach rolled and tightened.

Tears blurred my vision, and my lips quivered

with the effort to keep my cries in.

Alberto only laughed. When I saw the flash from the phone, I was suddenly snapped out of my haze, and I struggled under his body.

Alberto's nostril flared, and his lips pulled back in a snarl. He slapped me hard across the face, and I whimpered.

My body was already aching from days of abuse. How long had it been since Alberto took me away? A few days? Weeks? I didn't know. After all, I was trapped in the dungeon every day. I only knew darkness.

Except today. Today, I was in a room.

Was this Alberto's plan all along?

I pushed at his chest, but he was unmoving. *Let me go*, I screamed in my head. My voice was gone. My throat hurt, and I felt dizzy.

Alberto threw the phone somewhere on the bed, and then he was on me. I felt him near my entrance, and I closed my eyes.

My body filled with dread, and my throat was too tight. My chest ached with knowing what was coming. He brutally gripped my body as he aligned himself with me.

"You're mine," he hissed into my face.

I looked away from him, moving my face to the side. I thought of Alessio and our happy moments.

I heard his voice in my head, and I smiled.

I just want you to know that you are loved…you matter.

You bring happiness to others. You bring light, Ayla. You have people who care about you.

You are worth more than you think.

You are a fighter, Ayla. So keep fighting. Don't give up now.

Ayla...do you know how strong you are? You are the strongest woman I have ever met. Your strength shines brighter than any others.

Strong. Alessio thought I was strong. Even Nikolay and Maddie thought I was strong. But they were wrong. I wasn't. I was weak.

My eyes fell on the lamp, and for a brief moment, I heard Alessio yelling at me to fight.

Alberto pushed inside of me, and my already broken soul cracked further. But still I heard Alessio telling me to fight. Pushing me to fight.

I stared at the lamp as Alberto started moving inside of me. He was slower than usual, taking his time. I shuddered, my body itching with the need to hide and fade away.

Fight, Ayla.

Without thinking, I reached for the lamp. Everything happened so quickly. One minute Alberto was inside of me, and the next, I was smacking the lamp into his head. I hit his head twice, hard enough to make him bleed.

He roared in pain and pulled away from me.

My body felt light as soon as he shifted away, and without wasting a second, I was rolling off the bed. My legs gave out under me, and I fell down.

I could barely stand. My whole body was trembling. I crawled toward the door and was finally able to push myself on my feet. Stumbling forward, I reached the door.

But I was too slow.

Alberto was on me again. He grabbed my hair and wrapped it around his wrist before smacking my face into the door, right over the knob.

Pain splintered its way into my head and my skull. My neck ached with the impact, and my vision blurred.

Was my jaw broken? My cheekbone?

My whole face was hurting, burning like it was on fire.

The pain traveled down my spine until black dots appeared in front my eyes. I blinked, trying to clear them away, but the pain was too much.

He slammed my head against the door again, holding my cheek there. He pressed his knuckles into my skull, and I screamed as the blinding agony spread through my body.

Spots danced in front of my eyes with the searing pain. Red droplets fell in front my eyes. My blood.

"I thought you learned your lesson, but you clearly didn't," Alberto said. "How many times do I have to tell you that you can't run away from me?"

He chuckled, his chest moving against my back. "And why are you running? To whom? Alessio? Did you forget he gave you to me? He left you here at my mercy," he taunted in my ears.

Those were the words he fed me every day. But I didn't believe him. No matter how many times he said them, I would never believe him.

"Why are you running to him, huh? He doesn't care about you, Ayla," Alberto continued, his fingers getting tighter around my hair.

THE MAFIA AND HIS ANGEL PART 2

I closed my eyes and tried to block him out. But Alberto was a man impossible to block. He was a disease that infiltrated everywhere.

"He is probably buried balls-deep inside another pussy right now. That's how much you mean to him, love."

Stop it! I sobbed against the door. My heart cracked open, and the pieces flew everywhere. Empty. That was how I felt.

"Aww, does the thought of Alessio fucking another woman hurt?" he goaded, caressing a finger down my neck. "He can get any pussy he wants. You are not anything special, Ayla."

I sobbed harder, my head and body too heavy to do anything else. "Are you imagining it right now? Another woman's legs wrapped around his waist as he fucks her?"

For the first time, I begged.

"Stop it. Please…Please…stop…pl…please," I begged. Everything hurt. Even my soul was aching, screaming in pain.

Alberto gasped, but it was fake. "Are you begging, love? Well, isn't that a first. I've never heard you beg before. So beg. C'mon, beg me to stop."

"Please…"

"Alessio doesn't care about you," he whispered. "He doesn't. Because if he did, he would have come for you by now."

I tried to shake my head, but I couldn't.

"Of course, he isn't coming. He has probably forgotten all about you." He laughed, and I cried.

"He isn't coming for you. Forget him. Whatever

hopes you have, it doesn't matter. Because he doesn't care. It has been more than a month."

More than a month? No. This couldn't be true.

More than a month and Alessio still hadn't come.

He doesn't care about you.

He isn't coming for you.

Alberto's words rang through my eyes, and the tears blinded me.

What if I was holding on to a hope that wasn't even there?

"You are a ghost, love," he whispered before dragging my body away from the door. He dragged me by my hair and pushed me onto the bed until I was face down. I didn't fight him.

My body had given up as I slowly started to lose consciousness, the pain unbearable.

Alberto mounted my body, and as he slammed into me, I didn't make a noise. No sound at all. I thought about Alessio.

As he drove into me faster, Alberto taunted me in my ears.

But I didn't listen.

As I sank deeper in oblivion, I only thought about Alessio. *My* Alessio. My savior.

You're my Angel.

His voice was a mere whisper in my head, but I heard it. It was the only thing keeping me sane. Keeping me alive.

I lived for *him*.

Because I knew he was coming for me.

Where are you, Alessio?

Chapter 36

Alessio

2 weeks later

I stared at the pictures in my hand. Stared at them longer than I should have.

The pictures were shaking only because my hands were trembling. Anger had been a constant emotion inside of me since Ayla had been taken away. I lived on the anger inside of me. It kept me going. It kept me grounded enough to find my Angel.

But now, I was raging. There's a big difference between anger and fury. Anger was enough to make someone go insane. But fury, it made people psychotic.

And that was exactly how I felt.

I was past making sense. I no longer felt anything except deep loathing and fury. Nothing else mattered. The little humanity left inside of me was gone the instant I laid eyes on the photos in my hands.

Fury boiled inside of me as I imagined the multiple ways to mutilate Alberto's body.

My fingers tightened on the pictures until they crumbled in my fist. Closing my eyes, I threw the photo across the room, not caring where it landed. I just needed it out of my sight.

My jaw ground with the effort to keep myself under control.

Ayla's face flashed behind my closed lids, and my body tightened as a wave of pain coursed through me. Under the layers of fury, my heart was aching.

It ached so much I was suffocating under the pressure.

But the pain was nothing compared to what Ayla was going through. The thought was enough to drive me insane.

Through my rage, I heard the door open. My eyes snapped open, making contact with Viktor's as he stepped into my office.

He stopped in front of the door, his eyes moving to his feet. His eyebrows furrowed in confusion, and he bent down.

Viktor grabbed the photo firmly in his hands and stared at it. I knew what he was seeing.

The image of Ayla bare, her legs spread, her eyes frightened, filled with tears was forever etched in my memory.

A second passed. And then another. A full minute passed before Viktor finally reacted.

His face was red with anger. "What is this?" he growled.

"Alberto sent us a gift," I replied numbly, my voice a little hoarse from built-up emotions.

"I'm going to fucking cut his dick off and feed it to him," Viktor snapped, standing up to his feet.

I sat straight in my chair and leveled him with a glare. "He is mine to kill."

Taking a step forward, he stopped in front of my desk, his stare unflinching. "You are not the only one who cares about her."

"He. Is. Mine. To. Kill," I hissed, getting to my feet.

Viktor shook his head with a sigh. "I will never take that right from you. When we find him, he is yours to kill. But the rest of us will have a hand in it too."

We stared at each other. No words were spoken. The air around us filled with tension. It grew colder and heavier under our need for revenge.

"Fair enough," I replied. Viktor nodded and sat down on the couch, placing the heavy file he was holding on my desk.

"All the names that are connected to Alberto. His right-hand men. Their families are also listed. Everything there is to know about them," Viktor said, nodding toward the file.

I sat down and pulled it toward me. "We already got so many of his men. Nobody knows a thing. He was smart enough to keep his hiding place a secret. His men are a bunch of cowards. If they knew the truth, they would have told me for a chance to live."

"What about Enzo?" The same question had been brewing in my thoughts, but it was another dead end.

"From Nikolay's information, he went into hiding, too. He's Alberto's second in command. He knew he would be our target," I said, sitting back against my chair. The muscles in my neck were aching. Pressing my fingers against the back of my neck, I massaged the muscles, hoping to relieve the tension.

My body was weak from fatigue. If I kept going like this, I would be no use to Ayla when she was found.

"If we find Enzo, then it's another step closer to finding Alberto," Viktor muttered, a thoughtful look on his face. "Alberto has gone off grid, and his second in command is nowhere to be found. His empire is vulnerable, and he knows that. Even if Alberto didn't tell Enzo anything about his hiding place, he will have to contact him."

"His only communication to his empire is through Enzo," I added, sitting forward in anticipation.

"But we have to find Enzo first," Viktor said through gritted teeth.

If we couldn't find Enzo, there was only one person who would lead us to him. Or bring *him* to *us*. "His wife," I suggested.

Viktor shook his head. "She's out of the country."

"When will she be back?" I wondered out loud.

"I don't know. She left the same day Ayla was taken away. It was probably for her protection."

At the sound of Ayla's name, my heart stuttered, and another wave of pain crashed through me. My hands tightened in fists until my knuckles turned white.

I stared at the file in front of me. "One of these men, at least of one them, should know about Enzo's whereabouts. Or even Alberto's. This is our only option."

"We'll get to them. All of them. Everyone in this list will be questioned. We won't stop until Ayla is found," Viktor promised.

No. There was no way we were stopping. Ayla would be found. Today or tomorrow. Or the day after. But she would be found.

"What do you want to do after they're questioned?" Viktor asked. But he already knew the answer. He only asked because he needed confirmation. He needed a push, a new purpose again.

I stared at the photo frame on my desk. It was a photo of Ayla. Maddie took that picture a few days before Ayla was taken away from me.

She was laughing, her face had lit up, and her green eyes shone brightly. Her beauty, her smiles, her laughter, they were all mesmerizing.

"Kill them all," I whispered, still staring at Ayla's picture.

None of them were innocent. There was no innocence when it came to Alberto's men. I still remembered when Ayla was telling me about her abuse. How Alberto's men would rape her while the sick bastard watched.

I was going to avenge my Angel the only way I knew how.

I was going to destroy the Italians. One by one, until they bowed down to me. To Ayla.

Reaching forward, I touched Ayla's cheek through the photo. *Wait for me, Angel.*

I was snapped out of my thoughts when the door banged open. I looked away from Ayla to find my father and Isaak walking in.

Lyov was fuming, his chest heaving with each breath he took. "The Families are questioning your capabilities as the Boss."

Viktor swiveled around to face them. "What?" he growled, getting to his feet.

Lyov ignored Viktor's outburst. Instead, he leveled me with a glare, daring me to reply. But I had no answer. I knew it would come to this.

"While looking for Ayla, you forgot that you are the Boss of four Families. You are not taking care of the business or anything else. When there is a problem, you send them to Viktor. The Families have every right to question you as their Boss," Isaak added as he came to stand beside Lyov.

"You are the *Pakhan*. The Boss of the bosses. If it continues like this, they will lose faith in you," Lyov muttered.

"Like eleven years ago? When they lost faith in you? When you had no other choice but to make me the Boss, so that the Ivanshovs wouldn't lose the title?" I retorted with a shake of my head.

His eyes went wild at the mention of his downfall, when we almost lost everything. "I taught you better than this, Alessio," he growled, stepping forward.

"If you fail, like I did, we lose everything," Lyov snapped. He walked forward, stopping in front of my desk.

THE MAFIA AND HIS ANGEL PART 2

He bent forward until his face was mere inches away from mine. "If you continue this downward spiral, Solonik could take over as the Godfather. You fucking know that. He has been looking for every opportunity to do so, and now you are giving him an invitation."

The Russian Mafia consisted of four families. The Ivanshovs, Soloniks, Agrons, and Gavrikovs.

Each family had their own Boss, but I was the Boss of them all. The Godfather. The other families were underneath the Ivanshovs. But Solonik had wanted to take over. If Lyov hadn't handed this empire over to me, he would have been the *Pakhan* a long time ago.

And now he was looking for another opportunity, only because I'd proved myself weak.

Lyov grabbed my collar, pulling me forward. "I told you not to fall in love. And now you have become useless. I thought you were stronger than I was. Clearly I was mistaken."

Releasing my collar, he stood up, his gaze unflinching as he stared me down. "I'm taking over."

I wasn't surprised when the words were uttered. No, I knew it was coming. I expected it, and I was prepared for it.

But Viktor wasn't. "What?" he exploded, moving forward, but Isaak stopped him with a hand on his arm.

"You are useless while you look for Ayla. So it's better if you concentrate on finding her. I'll take care of the Families. When you find her and she is safe, you will have your position back," Lyov announced.

He didn't wait for my answer. Not that he cared. He walked out of my office, Isaak right behind him.

"Why didn't you say anything?" Viktor demanded as soon as the door closed behind them.

"It's better this way. I don't want to worry about the Families while looking for Ayla. She is my priority," I mumbled, my gaze drawn to her photo again.

There were a few minutes of silence between Viktor and me before I finally stood up. "Call the others. We have business to take care of."

Next man on the list. Another step toward my Angel. They were small steps, but I knew in the end, they would lead me to where I wanted. They had to. I wasn't going to stop until I had what I wanted, what I needed.

I walked out of the office with Viktor following closely behind. When my steps faltered in front of the room next to the office, Viktor walked away without another word. He always knew what I needed even without me saying it.

And right now, I needed privacy.

Opening the door of the sitting room, I walked inside before closing the door softly. The light was already on, although not surprisingly. Only two people were allowed in this room. If it wasn't me, then it was my father.

We just happened to be in the room at the same time.

He stood facing the wall, his hand behind his back, his legs shoulder-width apart in a defensive stance. Lyov looked very much like the powerful man he was known as.

But he was hurting inside.

I knew that because he stood staring at my mother's portrait. It was a family portrait, actually. The frame was big, taking almost half of the wall. My mother was sitting on a sofa chair, fit for a queen, wearing a beautiful golden dress. My father stood beside her, while a younger version of me sat on her lap. Her stomach was rounded with my baby sister.

Next to the portrait was another photo of my mother with my father standing beside her. But that was before I was born, just after my parents were married.

It was a tradition.

And I could almost see another portrait on that wall. Of Ayla and me, while she sat on the very same chair my mother did, looking very much like the queen she would be.

But the image was suddenly shattered by Lyov's voice.

"I miss your mother every day. Every day, I wonder why I'm still alive while she is gone. I loved her more than I should have." He paused and then chuckled dryly. "Who am I kidding? I still love her as much as I did before. That type of love never dies, Alessio."

He was right. It would never die. Several months ago, I would have laughed in his face, but not now. Because I knew how he felt. The pain of losing the woman you love with every fiber of your being.

"How much do you love her?" he asked suddenly.

I flinched at the question and stared blankly at the wall. "I will kill for her," I replied. "And I will die for her. Does that answer your question?"

No words were spoken at first. Only silence between us before Lyov finally continued in the same monotone voice, his back still facing mine.

My heart clenched at his words, and I rubbed at my chest, trying to get rid of the burning sensation. "You have that type of love. If I'm honest, I never wanted you to feel this way. When I first saw Ayla, I saw your mother. And I just knew it would be impossible for you not to fall. Now that you have fallen, there's nothing we can do."

I stayed silent, too overwhelmed with emotions to speak. But my father spoke enough for the both of us. "Just get her back, protect her with your life, and love her the way she needs and deserves."

"I will," I stated firmly, looking at the portrait of my mother and father. With a final glance, I turned around to walk out of the room, but Lyov's voice stopped me again.

"Your mother would be proud of you."

Letting out a shaky emotionless laugh, I shook my head. "Don't lie."

I heard him huff. When he spoke this time, his voice was heavy, laced with so much emotion that it made my heart ache. "If she found it in her heart to love me, a monster, then she would have loved you just as much, if not more. Your mother's heart was pure and so full with love. She would have wanted you to be happy. Nothing else mattered. Not who you are or what you do. Always remember that."

My chest tightened at his words. Without saying

anything, I walked out of the room. My heart was heavy, and it hurt. It hurt for many different reasons. But they all meshed together until all I felt was blinding pain. It hurt without Ayla. It hurt more knowing I was helpless.

But it also hurt because I always wanted to hear those words from my father. I had craved for those words and his support. And now that I had them, I didn't know what to do with them.

Shaking my head to clear my sudden foggy mind, I walked down the hall with only one purpose in mind. To find my Angel. That was all that mattered.

But even with my purposeful stride and determined mind, I couldn't shake away one thought.

In the sitting room, that was the most my father and I had spoken with each other in twenty-two years.

Chapter 37

3 weeks later

My head was buried in Ayla's pillow. It still smelled like her. I refused to have it washed. I needed something of her, and her sweet vanilla smell was the only thing left of her.

I inhaled and felt my eyes burn. I felt pathetic.

But I was too far gone. Almost three months without Ayla and I was slowly losing myself. Every day, it was worse. Every day, it got harder until I didn't know how to live anymore.

I forgot to eat. Sometimes I even forgot to sleep. Just stared at the wall, lost in the memories of my Angel.

I never stopped searching. Not a single day. But no matter how much I searched, how far I looked, she was nowhere to be seen.

It was as if she never existed. Never here. Sometimes I wondered if it was all a dream. I wondered if she had really been here. With me.

But she *was* here. I could still smell her. See her

sometimes. Hear her laughter and sweet voice. She was everywhere but still gone.

And I was empty without her.

Was that how my father and Isaak felt?

The whole house had been in a despairing mood. Nobody really talked. We all stopped caring about everything else. The only one we cared about and thought about was Ayla.

Maddie lost a friend who was more like a sister. To Lena, Ayla was a daughter. Another child to pamper and love. My men felt like a failure.

While I lost the woman who was my everything.

With a sigh, I rolled to my back and stared at the ceiling. Through my pain, I thought about what Ayla was going through.

Her pain was no comparison to mine. It hurt more knowing that she was hurting. My pain didn't matter, but hers did.

I felt her pain, and it was enough to break me.

Alberto used to call, but it had been three weeks since his last call. Three weeks of nothing but silence from the other side.

I realized that I was somewhat thankful for his daily call. At least I knew Ayla was alive. Now, I didn't know. I knew nothing, and all I could do was hope.

But hope was such a silly emotion. How could I hope when I felt so helpless and hopeless? It was all jaded hope.

Instead of hoping, I chose to believe in our love. Maybe it was strong enough to keep Ayla alive.

I knew that when I found her, Ayla would never be the same again.

But I also knew that when the time came, I wasn't going to give up on her. I would heal her again, like I did before. I would teach her how to live again, how to smile, laugh, and love again.

Alberto may have clipped her wings, but I was going to make sure she would fly again.

***

2 weeks later

I stood in the driveway and watched Nikolay going through the lock, and then the door opened. I walked inside the house, my men following behind me.

The house was quiet, almost seeming empty. But the woman in the living room betrayed the perception of the house being empty.

Her back was to us, and at the sound of our footsteps, she swiveled around quickly, her hand going to her chest in panic. Her eyes flared in fear, and she took several steps back, hitting the wall behind her.

"Hello, Anna," I started, walking further into the house, making the air seem more dangerous and deadly.

Anna trembled against the wall, her whole body quaking with terror. To say I was surprised that she came back was an understatement. She must have known what to expect the moment she stepped foot back into New York, but she still returned.

And now she would lead us right to Enzo.

"How was your trip?" I asked, taking a seat on

THE MAFIA AND HIS ANGEL PART 2

the sofa in front of her. I sat back and crossed my ankle on my opposite knee, watching her reaction like a hawk.

"You...what...are...?" she stuttered, looking wildly around the room and at my men. She looked for an escape, but there was none. Not this time.

It didn't stop her from trying, though. She ran into the kitchen, and I sighed in frustration.

"I don't have time for a game of cat and mouse, Anna," I called out loudly enough that my voice echoed across the walls.

I heard her scream, and she yelled at someone to let her go. Rubbing my face in frustration, I waited for her to come back to the living room.

I turned around to see Nikolay dragging her back as she flailed. Anna threw her body on the ground, trying to stop Nikolay. Instead of stopping, he just grabbed her arm, dragging her body across the floor.

"No. Let me go! Don't hurt me, please," she whimpered as Nikolay deposited her in front of me.

"If you cooperate, I won't hurt you," I replied stoically, leveling her with a glare.

She flinched and scrambled backward. Shaking her head, she whispered, "I don't know anything about Ayla."

My eyebrows raised up high in surprise, and a heartless chuckle vibrated from my chest. "How do you know I'm here for Ayla?"

Her eyes widened, and she snapped her mouth shut. Too late. She was already caught.

"Where is your husband? Tell me where Enzo is, and I will let you go," I snarled, sitting forward so that my face was mere inches from hers.

She shook her head repeatedly. "I don't know. I really don't know. Please, I'm telling the truth."

"I really hate when people lie," I tsked before sitting back, giving the frightened woman some breathing space.

"I'm not lying," she begged, her eyes wide with fright. She looked at my men, her eyes begging, as if asking someone to help her.

But no one was going to help her. She was at my mercy.

"I know the things you have participated in. Every single detail. You might have an innocent face, but you are far from innocent," I hissed, my voice getting louder with each word.

Enzo was part of the human trafficking business with Alberto. What surprised me was when I found out his wife was part of it, too. She trained the victims to become slaves.

It made me sick to think that a woman would do that to another. It made my heart ache to know that Ayla could have been one of those victims.

Her shaking worsened, her face crumpling as tears slid down her cheeks. It didn't faze me one bit. Her fear was useless, and she was helpless.

"Start talking!" I bellowed. Her back straightened as she flattened herself against the wall, cowering in the corner. When she said nothing, Nikolay stepped forward and pulled her up.

Viktor brought a chair and placed it in front of me. She fought Nikolay as he pulled her down on the chair. She screamed and cried when Viktor tied her body to the chair, rendering her useless and at our mercy.

"Please don't hurt me," she whimpered in horror when I took my gun out. "Please. Believe me, I don't know anything."

"I'm not going to hurt you," I simply replied, my voice as emotionless as before.

"Have mercy," she begged when I stood up, towering over her much smaller body.

"As I said, I'm not going to hurt you," I scoffed at her attempt to beg. If only she would talk.

Leaning forward until our faces were close, I continued. "I will never hurt a woman."

It was the truth. I would never hurt a woman or even lay a hand on them in an attempt to kill them. It wasn't how my men and I worked.

Her body sagged against the ropes, and a look of relief flashed in her eyes. "You won't hurt me? You will let me go? Please, I don't know anything."

This time I smiled. A cold, heartless smile.

Her eyes widened. The look of distress on her face almost made me laugh. How naïve of her. Panic and horror painted her face as she trembled with the uncertainty of her fate.

I waited.

One second. Two. Three. Four.

With each passing second, her panic grew.

Five. Six. Seven. Eight.

She cried silently. I just smiled, or was it a half sadistic smile? Probably.

Nine. Ten. Eleven. Twelve.

I heard the door behind us open. It closed with a bang. I heard the sound of high heels clicking against the hard floor.

"Did someone call me?" the intruder said to my back. I felt the smile in the intruder's voice.

I didn't answer. My gaze stayed on Anna, unflinching. Although she was looking behind me now. Her already wide eyes widened more.

"I said I wasn't going to hurt you. But that doesn't mean someone else can't," I murmured so only she could hear.

"No, no, no," she whispered in alarm as I pulled back, my back straightening as I stood to my full height. "Who are you?" Her voice trembled, but the words were spoken clear enough for everyone to hear.

"My name is not important."

The words were softly spoken, but the voice held such dark promises. I took a step back and watched Anna shake in fear. Dread filled her expression, and her lips quivered with the effort to keep her tears at bay.

I turned around and faced the intruder. The side of my lips tilted up in a small smile.

Only she would dress up for a job like this. Black leather jacket. Tight black leather pants. Red heels. The hood of the jacket was over her head, covering half of her face. It was used to camouflage her appearance.

One second passed. Another.

She lifted her hands up and pulled the hood down, showing her face. Her face was as flawless as ever, with her lips painted red. Only this time, she looked different. Her expression showed no emotion.

Blonde hair fell down her back as she looked

THE MAFIA AND HIS ANGEL PART 2

straight at the tied-up woman behind me.

A smile spread across her lips, although it was nothing close to welcoming or gentle. No, it was a sadistic smile. A predator ready to hunt its prey.

The woman standing in front of me looked very much like the killer she was.

Nina.

She worked undercover for me, but she was also a killer. A trained assassin. Someone who did my dirty work.

And by dirty work I meant torturing the answers out of women who refused to cooperate.

She took a step forward. Another. A few more steps until she walked past me and stood in front of Anna.

"What you need to know is that by the time I'm done, you won't remember *your* name. Or the difference between living and dead," she started, her voice low and deadly.

Leaning forward until their faces were close, noses almost touching, Nina's lips curled up. "I am your worst nightmare, baby. I am what you call…Death."

Those were the same lines she fed her captives. They would tremble in fear and sometimes piss their pants. The reaction she got from Anna was no different.

Nina was good at her job. Better than most. She did her job with a passion.

Nina had the same darkness that my men and I had in us. She craved blood. She had the need to kill.

"Your tools and everything you need are in the

bag next to your feet," Viktor announced, finally speaking up.

"Thank you," she replied, not glancing away from her captive.

Shaking my head, I rolled my shoulders, trying to relieve the tension there. "She's all yours," I muttered before turning around and striding away.

I walked out of the house with my men following closely behind me.

Nina worked alone, not that she needed help.

Nikolay closed the door as I leaned against the wall. "So?" Viktor asked.

My reply was simple. "We wait."

That was exactly what we did. We waited.

It was mostly quiet, but if I listened carefully, the muffled screams could be heard. They filled our ears as we stayed by the door. It shouldn't have taken her hours to break Anna—but knowing Nina, she was just taking her time and enjoying this.

I could imagine what was going on in there, but I stopped thinking after a few minutes. Nina liked to get creative. She always surprised us, but whatever she did was always effective. At the end of the day, we got the answers we needed, and that was all that mattered.

How we got it didn't matter.

After three hours, although I was surprised Anna lasted this long, the door finally opened. Nina walked out, looking fresh and surprisingly decent from what just occurred inside.

But then again, Nina was a clean assassin. As clean as a killer could get.

She stopped beside me, her face impassive as she

stared straight ahead. Her sadistic smile was gone and now replaced with a more contented, relaxed one.

Nina removed her black leather gloves. They were most definitely stained with blood, but the thing with black was that the blood we spilled never showed on it.

She passed the gloves to Phoenix, who was standing beside her, her eyes on her hands as she inspected her nails.

"I need another manicure," she muttered and tsked.

Shaking my head, I glanced at the door.

She noticed where my attention was and sighed. "Enzo is hiding at the Black Club."

My eyebrows furrowed in question. "The MC?"

"The one and only. They work for Alberto. Undercover. No wonder they're helping hide Enzo," Nina replied with an exaggerated huff.

"Anna finally admitted it?" I asked quietly.

Nina nodded. "It took me a little longer to break her." She shrugged before continuing. "But no matter how long it takes, by the time I'm done with someone, they are always left broken."

That was true. Nina was good at what she did. She liked to call herself *Death*. She earned that name, though.

"She is pretty loyal," Nina added. Unfortunately, when it came to life and death, her loyalty flew out of the window.

"Is she alive?" I asked, although I already knew the answer.

"Well, she was when I left...I thought it would

be nice to let her think about her life. I was in a generous mood, lucky her. But she stopped breathing about two minutes ago," Nina replied dryly, looking down at her watch.

Viktor scoffed. "Generous mood," he muttered under his breath.

Nina heard and sent him glare. "All of a sudden, I'm not in a generous mood anymore. Don't test me, Viktor."

She turned back to me and lost her glare in the process. Her face was still cold, but there was a hint of sympathy in her eyes, if it even was possible for her to feel anything.

"About Ayla, I'm sorry," she said regretfully. "I know what type of man Alberto is. I saw how he treats the women in the clubs, and I can't imagine what Ayla is going through right now."

My chest tightened at her words, and my body grew cold. Shaking her head, Nina glanced down before continuing. "I also owe her an apology. For what I said. Although I didn't really mean what I said. I was testing her. To see if she was strong enough."

Viktor shook his head and huffed. The others rolled their eyes. Nina glared, her eyes shooting venom.

"Oh please, all of you know that I could have broken her body in half before she even had a chance to lay a finger on me," she hissed, her anger evident. "That's enough to prove I didn't mean it."

I closed my eyes with a tired sigh. "You can apologize to her when she's found."

When I opened my eyes, I saw Nina nodding.

THE MAFIA AND HIS ANGEL PART 2

When we fell into silence, she stepped off the porch. "If you need any other help—for anything—just call," she said, her back straight, a look of determination and true loyalty on her face.

"I hope you find her soon," Nina mumbled before walking away. "She deserves more than the life she got."

I struggled to breathe, my chest heaving with the effort to be in control. I stared at Nina's retreating back, and after a few minutes, I finally found myself calming down.

Although my blood still roared with the need to kill, I kept the rage underneath the layers on my skin.

I glanced back at the door. I should have just walked away and let Phoenix take care of the cleaning, but curiosity got the best of me.

I stepped back into the house and was assaulted with the smell of blood. I stared at the woman tied to the chair. Or what was left of the woman.

I felt no pain. No remorse. No emotions at all.

I approached her slowly and stopped a few feet away.

Viktor swore behind me. "Fuck yeah. Now that's what I call art."

"Creativity at its best," Nikolay added quietly. Phoenix and Artur chuckled.

I just stared. Her head fell limply against the back of the chair, her body sagging as her blood poured around her.

She was missing all the fingers on her right hand. All her nails from her left hand. Her missing fingers were on the floor in a pool of blood. She was missing an eye.

It looked like it had been carved out in the most painful and horrifying way. Not that I was surprised. Her other eye stared straight ahead, lifeless. The light had left her. Her face was covered in blood; her clothes were soaked with it.

The smell of death hung in the air. An unfortunate death for an unfortunate situation.

Warring emotions raced violently through my mind, but I quickly tamped them down. Now was not the time to get weak over a death.

"Phoenix. Artur. Clean up," I ordered, turning away from the lifeless woman.

I walked out of the house and took a deep breath as soon as I hit the fresh air.

I felt Nikolay and Viktor beside me. "What's next?" Viktor asked.

"The Black Club," was my only answer.

Chapter 38

It didn't take us long to find Enzo after receiving his location. It went down more smoothly than I thought. A small fight, a few guns drawn. Some bullets flew around us, and then I was dragging Enzo out of the club.

And now he was tied to a chair, locked in my basement.

He had been interrogated for hours, but I still hadn't gotten the answers I needed.

He didn't know where Alberto was.

I thought he was lying, but the truth was written all over his face. He really didn't know. His fear betrayed his tough armor. He was scared.

Alberto was a smart man, but how long would he stay hidden?

I sat in front of Enzo as he coughed again, spitting a broken tooth. Blood dribbled and slid down his chin. He breathed heavily, his chest heaving almost painfully. Each intake of air appeared difficult for him.

He let out a small laugh, and my eyebrows shot

up in surprise. His laughter sounded funny, almost forced. Leaning forward, I waited for him to talk.

"Why don't you ask Nikolay?" he wheezed.

My spine straightened, and my muscles tightened over his words. "You are so sure…of yourself, but your most…trusted man…is a traitor. Ask…him…"

His head dropped, as if speaking those few words had tired him out.

Nikolay, who was standing behind him, wrapped his fingers around his throat and squeezed. Enzo struggled to breathe, his face growing red and purple. I even saw the blood vessels break across his skin.

When his eyes started to lose focus, I raised my hand, and Nikolay immediately let go. A laugh suddenly bubbled out of my chest. It was a low chuckle, but it sounded deadly and cold. Dangerous even.

I gave Enzo time to struggle through his breathing before speaking. "He is not the traitor," I replied calmly, sitting back in my chair.

Enzo's head snapped up as he coughed repeatedly. His eyes flared with surprise. "He…is…He is…spying…on…you…for Alberto."

"Wrong," I muttered back. "He isn't. Too bad for Alberto he thinks that."

"Wh…at?" Enzo sputtered, confusion written all over his bloody face.

Instead of answering, I stood up. Frustration built up inside of me as I walked out of the room. If Alberto's men thought Nikolay was the traitor, then they didn't know who the real traitor was.

Another smart move from Alberto. Someone from my estate was working for Alberto, but nobody else knew that except Alberto.

"Fuck!" I bellowed, punching the wall. I heard my knuckles crack, but the pain didn't faze me. It only pissed me off more.

"What do you want to do?" Nikolay asked quietly. He was always calm, always ready for the next step.

"Don't kill him. Not yet."

Enzo was Alberto's second in command. Alberto was going to need him. After all, his empire was currently at the hands of Enzo. Alberto would need to contact Enzo one day soon.

And when he did, we would be ready.

I closed my eyes and leaned my forehead against the wall.

Ayla's face flashed behind my closed lids. The same sweet smile. The sound of her laughter.

Only this time, I heard her whisper. Three forbidden words.

I love you.

The words were never uttered between us, but it was there.

For the first time, I wished she said it. I wished I had those words to hold on to while my Angel was gone.

Chapter 39

Ayla

1 week later

What's my name?
I tried to remember. I tried to whisper my name, but my lips wouldn't move.
What's my name?
I asked myself that question a few times, trying hard to remember. But everything was a blur. Nothing made sense. I couldn't remember my name…my life…or anything.

I was just numb. Lost. I didn't feel.

I didn't know where I was. It was always dark, with just a little bit of light. The cold seeped into my skin until I would shiver uncontrollably.

My name. I had to remember my name.

Ay…A…it started with an A.

Al…Ay…Ay…

Closing my eyes, I laid down on the cold ground and pulled my knees to my chest. My memories were all broken, shattered around the place.

Ay...Ayla...

Ayla.

It sounded correct. Familiar. It sounded like *me*.

Ayla.

My name is Ayla.

I hung onto this new revelation. Ayla. My name was Ayla, and I had to remember. I couldn't forget again. It was a routine. I would remember but then forget it again.

My name is Ayla.

As I repeated the phrase in my head, I heard a whisper. It was all in my head, but the whisper continued. It was one word. Two Syllables.

It wasn't my name.

But it sounded so right. Like I needed to know it.

Every time I tried to remember my name, the word *Angel* was always a whisper in my head.

Ayla. Angel. Ayla. Angel.

I didn't make sense, but I repeated it over and over again in my head.

Who was I? I didn't know.

Where did I come from? I didn't know.

I was living in a blur. In a pitch-dark world. I was nothing. I felt like nothing. I was just an empty vessel.

How long has it been since I was locked in this dungeon?

The days and nights blended into each other until I lost count. Days, weeks, months?

I wished I knew, but the devil made sure I was left in the darkness. He had stripped me of everything, even my memories.

Curled against the wall, with the shackles around my ankles and wrists, I rocked back and forth. My eyes closed as I slowly fell into oblivion, another dark abyss where there was no escape.

I woke up to the sound of the door opening. It banged shut, and I opened my eyes to see the devil approaching me.

I waited for his command, my body and mind ready to do his bidding.

He held a bowl in his hand, and the smell of food filled my nostrils. My stomach tightened as hunger suddenly assaulted me.

He didn't feed me on a regular basis. Sometimes, I would go days without food, until my stomach would cramp so painfully that I found it hard to breathe.

He would leave me on the cold ground until I trembled so hard that it felt like my insides were shaking.

The bowl was placed on the ground between us. He kicked it away a few feet.

"Eat."

He kept his eyes on me when the single word command was given. The tone of his voice held a hint of rage, but it also held no space for questions.

I sat up and stared at the bowl a few feet away from me. Without wasting another second, I got to my knees obediently. That was what he wanted.

And I gave it to him. Only because I needed the food he was offering me.

I felt the cold hard floor under my knees and palms as I crawled toward the bowl. My dignity was long shredded to pieces. My soul was crushed, and my heart had fractured.

I had nothing left. I was the definition of an empty shell. The devil made sure of that.

When I bent down to eat, he kicked it a few feet away again. I crawled again. He kicked the bowl again.

This process was repeated once again until I had used all the length of my shackles, and I was straining against them to reach the bowl.

Still on my knees, I bent down and licked the soup. Trying to get as much into my frail body as possible. My stomach rolled as the warm liquid filled my mouth.

It was tasteless, but I still ate. It was the only thing I could do.

My body shook every time I swallowed. When I heard the devil unzipping his pants, my mind went blank, and I waited for what was to come.

I continued to eat as I felt him behind me. I still ate as he bent over me, molding his body on top of mine. If I stopped eating, he would hurt me more.

I felt his heavy length at my entrance, and I closed my eyes. He pushed inside, only penetrating slightly. It was all a game for him.

I continued eating, taking as much liquid as I could into my body.

He pushed into me slowly until he was buried deep inside. I pressed my hands harder into the floor, trying to keep myself upright.

His fingers dug into my hips, and I almost winced in pain. My shackles rattled as he started to thrust inside of me, going deeper and faster each time. An almost feral growl erupted from his lips as he bent my body to his will.

He shoved inside me forcefully and painfully. It felt like my body was splintering in half as he took me again and again.

I stared at the soup, my eyes blurred, my mind numb, my body empty.

My stomach rolled painfully. My throat went tight as I tasted bile on my tongue. My mouth was filled with a bitter taste, and I dry heaved into my soup.

As he finished inside of me, I couldn't help myself. I retched, my body heaving as I threw up. The vomit trailed down my chin and neck.

The dungeon already smelt bad, but the vomit only added to the horrendous smell. It was enough to make me throw up again.

The devil laughed. His laughter echoed into my ears. My body hurt. Everything hurt.

As he pulled out of me, I fell to the ground next to my bowl. I laid my cheek on the ground, right where the vomit was. I tried to breathe, but it was too hard.

I felt crippled with pain.

The devil laughed as he left the room. Even when he wasn't there anymore, I still heard his laughter. My ears rang with it. I would never forget his laughter.

I didn't know how long I stayed in that position. When my eyes started to droop, I got to my knees and crawled back to my spot next to the wall.

I laid down and curled into myself, closing my eyes.

I tried to go somewhere in my mind, a place

where I could escape this nightmare. But I couldn't remember anything.

No, that was a lie.

I remembered something.

Even when I would forget my name. Even when I had forgotten everything, there was something I didn't forget.

Blue eyes. Bluish-steel colored eyes.

A face with those blue eyes would always flash behind my closed eyes. Although the face was blurred, I always saw the eyes.

It was the only constant thing in this nightmare.

Sometimes, I would see a hint of a smile on the face. A lot of times, I tried to concentrate harder, and occasionally I could almost see the man behind the blue eyes.

When everything else was broken memories, the man with blue eyes was my savior. I called him my savior because he kept me from completely losing myself.

I didn't know who he was, but while I had forgotten everything else, there was something stopping me from forgetting him. And those blue eyes.

My mind wouldn't let me forget him. Whoever he was, wherever he was, he probably didn't know it, but he was my savior.

It was strange that while I didn't know anything, he was there. Always in my thoughts.

Who was he to me? I wondered.

With my eyes closed, I heard a voice calling out to me. The man with blue eyes was calling out to me.

I was surprised when I heard him say *Angel*. He was calling *me* Angel.

Was that my name? Angel?

No, my name was Ayla.

Confused, my head started to ache, but I still forced myself to remember.

The piano. White flowers. The forest. A river.

They were all just blurred images in my head. They flashed behind my closed lids before I had a chance to understand them.

Alessio.

The name was a whisper in my mind. I heard laughter. And the name Alessio.

Alessio. I felt it in my heart.

Sweet kisses. Gentle caresses. Loving eyes.

The memories were all broken puzzles that didn't make sense.

But one thing for sure was that with all the shattered memories that assaulted me, the man with blue eyes was always there. In every single piece of memory, he was there.

Alessio.

Was that his name?

It felt…right. It felt like…him.

My savior finally had a name. Alessio.

With my eyes still closed, I slowly sank into another pit of darkness. Sleep took over my body as I slowly succumbed to my tiredness and pain.

And as every time I fell asleep, the man with blue eyes met me in my dreams.

Alessio.

With his name a mere whisper in my mind, I fell asleep against the cold hard floor with the shackles around my wrists and ankles.

Chapter 40

Maddie

I looked at the clock in the living room. It was 9:30 p.m. The men were still not home. I grew worried as each minute ticked by.

I hoped that tonight was the night they would bring Ayla home.

So I sat on the sofa in my nightdress with my robe around me. I waited. I prayed that by some miracle Ayla was going to appear in front of me, safe and sound.

But again, tonight that wasn't the case.

The men walked through the doors, and I jumped to my feet, looking wildly around them for any sight of Ayla. When I saw their heads hung down, their shoulder sagged with yet another night filled with defeat, my throat closed up.

My chest tightened, and I almost fell to the ground. Despair filled me, and my cheeks were already wet with my tears.

I cried as Alessio walked past me without a

word. A few minutes later when his roar of pain echoed around the house, I sobbed.

Nikolay walked away. And then Viktor. No one said a word.

Phoenix stayed at the door, his face drawn in with sorrow. That was when I noticed the blood on him. My eyes widened, and I scrambled toward him in panic.

"Phoenix!" I gasped, my arms moving over his body, looking for the wound. "What happened to you?"

My tears blurred my vision. With the thought of Ayla in pain and now Phoenix being hurt, I was slowly going crazy.

He grabbed my hand, holding it still over his chest. "Shhh…I'm okay, Maddie. It's not my blood."

He palmed my cheek, softly rubbing his thumb over the skin. I should have pulled away. It was wrong for him to touch me like that. It was more wrong for me to care the way I did.

But I found that I couldn't move away.

"You're not hurt?" I whispered, looking at his blood-covered suit.

He shook his head. "No."

The air left my body in a loud whoosh, and I sighed in relief. But the relief was short-lived when I heard Artur's voice behind me.

My eyes went wide, and I quickly pulled away from Phoenix. He didn't let go of my head.

I turned my head to see Artur staring at us. His eyes showed what he felt. He looked at me as if I betrayed him.

My heart ached at the thought of hurting Artur. Looking back at Phoenix, our gazes met. He begged me with his eyes.

But I couldn't give him what he wanted.

I glanced down at our intertwined hands and slowly pulled away. He grasped me more firmly, but I twisted my hand until I was free. Without looking at him, I stepped back and turned toward Artur.

I walked straight into Artur's arm and buried my face into his chest. Taking a deep breath, I inhaled his familiar scent. This was what I needed.

He swept me up in his arms and carried me to his room. As soon as the door closed behind us, he had me against the wall, his lips on mine.

Artur kissed me furiously as he pushed us toward the bed. I fell down on the soft mattress as he settled on top of me. Before I could think, he had me out of my nightdress until I laid bare underneath him.

His kiss was bruising, his hands hard against my skin. His touch wasn't searching. He didn't touch me to bring me pleasure.

Artur seemed almost lost in his mind.

"Artur?" I questioned.

He didn't answer. Instead, he continued to trail kisses down my neck. I should have felt good, but this time, I just felt cold. Almost disconnected.

"Artur? What are you doing?"

When he ignored me, my panic grew, and I pushed against his shoulders. "Artur, stop."

He didn't. He kept kissing down my stomach until his face was between my legs. The Artur touching my body wasn't him.

THE MAFIA AND HIS ANGEL PART 2

My nails dug into his shoulder as I pushed him hard. "Artur, stop!" I called out louder.

His head snapped up, his eyes laced with a mixture of lust and anger. He looked confused for a second and then cocked his head to the side, giving me a heated look.

"You're scaring me. What's wrong with you?" I said, pulling away from him. I grabbed the comforter and pulled it to cover my body.

His expression changed to a remorseful one, his eyes flashing with regret. Artur raked his fingers through his hair almost angrily, although this time he appeared angry at himself.

"Talk to me," I begged, looking at the man I loved struggle with something inside his head.

He flopped down on the bed beside me, staring at the ceiling. Rubbing a hand over his face, a small growl vibrated through his chest.

"Fuck! I'm sorry. I'm so sorry, Maddie. I don't know what's wrong with me. It drives me fucking crazy when I see *him* touching you," he replied through clenched teeth. "His hands were on you, and I wanted to slice them off his body."

The image made me go cold. "Artur," I snapped.

He turned to face me. We stared at each other in silence before he finally brought his hand up. He palmed my cheek gently, a soft look in his eyes.

"I hate that he had you first," he whispered.

I flinched at the reminder and pulled away from him. "You promised that you would never bring this up. It's in the past. Leave it there, Artur. You have me now. I chose you."

"I know," he murmured.

"Then stop thinking so hard. Please, Artur. Don't let Phoenix get between us. I left him in the past, and you need to do the same thing," I begged.

Even as I said the words, my mind screamed lies. Did I really leave Phoenix in the past? Was I really over him?

I loved Artur. I chose him.

But when I thought Phoenix was hurt tonight, it felt like my heart was going to split into two. How was it possible to still feel that way after so many years?

"I'm sorry, Maddie."

I stared down at Artur and felt my heart expand just a little bit more. This man has stood beside me when I needed him the most—when Phoenix wasn't there for me.

Artur was there for me when Phoenix left me broken.

Leaning forward, I kissed Artur slowly. He groaned into my lips and returned the kiss with the same fervor. When I pulled away, a small smile played across my lips. My heart didn't feel as heavy anymore.

Moving my fingers through his hair, I smiled down at him. "I need the bathroom. Be right back," I mumbled before jumping off the bed.

I closed the door behind me and went to the sink. Staring at my reflection, I quickly combed my hair. And then washed my face.

I wrapped the white robe around me and took a deep breath.

I pushed hard...harder than before. I pushed Phoenix out of my head and heart. I refused to think

THE MAFIA AND HIS ANGEL PART 2

of him. Of *us*.

Artur was the one I needed. The man I loved. Now I just needed the courage to tell him. I had dragged this out for too long. He needed to know how I truly felt.

Since Ayla's kidnapping, we had drifted apart, but I needed *us* again.

I also learned that love shouldn't be kept to ourselves. Alessio and Ayla loved each other, but they never had the chance to say it. My heart ached for them, for what both of them were going through.

I didn't want the same between Artur and me.

We didn't need the words, but I wanted to say it. I didn't want Artur to think that I didn't love him enough. He had to know how much he meant to me.

Because anyway, we were about to take another step in life. Together.

Closing my eyes, I took a deep breath. When I felt my racing heart start to calm down, I opened my eyes and smiled at my reflection.

Without a second glance, I opened the door but stopped dead in my tracks. My heart stammered to a stop.

"Don't worry. They won't find Ayla."

My eyes widened, and I stayed completely silent. I was even scared to breathe. Artur's back was to me as he faced the windows, his phone next to his ear.

My chest tightened when he continued to talk. "It's been almost four months, and they still haven't found her. All thanks to me."

My fists tightened. *No*. This couldn't be happening. Not Artur.

He listened to the other person and then replied, "I know how to do my job. I'll make sure they don't find you."

Even though he was whispering, the words echoed through my ears loudly. My heart raced and pounded like a drum. The veins in my neck throbbed as my body grew cold with panic.

And anger. So much anger. The fury built up inside of me like hot lava until I was ready to explode.

"I have to go. Don't call me again. It's too much of a risk," he mumbled before hanging up.

I stayed partially hidden behind the door, my legs feeling suddenly weak.

Artur was the traitor?

I didn't want to believe it. My mind fought violently against me. It couldn't be true. I tried to force the thought out of my mind, but how could I when the truth was right there in front of me?

I heard him talk. He admitted it clearly. How did I not see that before? How did I miss it?

Tears of anger and frustration blurred my vision. But I was also hurting at the thought of Ayla being in pain because of the man I loved.

The bastard. How could he?

Alessio would never let him live. Hell, *I* wouldn't let him live.

Stepping forward, I marched toward Artur. He heard my footsteps and quickly swiveled around, surprise evident on his face.

"Maddie?" He swallowed nervously but quickly hid it with a seductive smile.

When I stopped in front of him, I drew my fist

back before slamming it in his nose. "You fucking asshole."

He stumbled back in surprise before quickly straightening up. His eyes went wide. "What the fuck, Maddie?"

"I heard you," I hissed. There was a flash of horror on his face, but it was quickly gone, and he regained his composure.

"What are you talking about?" he asked, feigning innocence.

That little shit. It wasn't going to work on me. I raged inside. My skin prickled with it, like flame dancing underneath. My body shook with my fury.

"Don't act innocent, Artur. You are crazy!"

The innocence façade was suddenly gone, and he glared down at me. "Keep your voice down."

I scoffed and took a step back. "You betrayed us," I said to him.

When he didn't even convince me otherwise, I laughed humorlessly even though the tears spilled down my cheeks. "How could you?" I choked. "After everything Alessio has done for you, this is how you repay him?"

His face was a mask of rage. "He didn't do anything for me!"

I stumbled back from his outburst. "You are so stupid. Why? Why did you do it?"

"Is that really a question, Maddie? You're acting like the stupid one here," he hissed.

My eyes widened when realization dawned. "God, I am so disgusted right now. Your father was a traitor, and so are you!"

"He killed my father!"

"Because he was a traitor! And Alessio pitied you. You were left on the streets to die, and he gave you a home. He thought you were different. He trusted you," I argued past the lump in my throat.

Shaking my head, I took several steps back. "You made him trust you. Was that your plan all along?"

When he didn't say anything in reply, I had my answer.

"You disgust me!" I spat at him.

I swiveled around to walk out of the room, but Artur's voice stopped me. "Where are you going?"

Turning back around, I leveled him a glare. "Away from you! I can't even look at you right now."

He was a traitor, but I wasn't. If he thought I would keep quiet, then he was so wrong.

I was in pain at Artur's betrayal. It was hard to breathe, but it only got harder when he reached behind his back and pulled his gun out.

He pointed it at me. "Another step and I will shoot you."

Fear slithered its way through my body, and sweat broke out on my skin. I stood frozen, debating if I should make a run for it.

Artur glanced between us, and his expression softened just a little. "Maddie, I don't want to hurt you."

A sob escaped my lips. "Betraying my family hurts me, Artur. This is hurting me more than you can ever think."

Regret flashed across his face. "Maddie…"

My sniffles filled the room. I rubbed my chest,

trying to get rid of the ache there. "What about Ayla? What did she ever do to you? How could you do this to her?"

Artur shook his head. "She just happened to be in the middle. Alberto wanted her, and I wanted my revenge against Alessio. He was invincible, but then Ayla came into his life. She's his weakness. What better way to destroy Alessio than destroy his only weakness?"

I gasped at his cruel words. Never had I expected to hear such words for Artur. Where was the sweet man I knew?

My shaking began again, only this time it was a mixture of fear and anger. Anger at Artur for being so heartless. "Ayla is innocent. You condemn her to the very monster that destroyed her. You knew the things that were done to her, yet you still sent her there."

Artur shrugged. "It was two birds with one stone."

"She doesn't deserve this. What you have done to her is enough to make me hate you with everything that I am." My voice was filled with hatred and utter despair.

My skin felt raw as panic coursed through my body. I felt suddenly dizzy as the world tilted around me. I had to get to Alessio.

I moved a step back, but Artur caught it. His eyes widened. "Maddie, don't make me do this," he warned, his eyes begging me.

In that moment, I wondered if he really would shoot me. The thoughts accelerated in my head. My heart hammered in my chest, and my stomach rolled. As my stomach tightened painfully, I knew I was going to be sick.

I glanced beside me toward the dresser. My gun. Just a few steps and I could reach for my gun. I glanced back at Artur and thought of ways to divert his attention.

Licking my dried lips, I swallowed past the heavy lump in my throat. "What about us? Did you ever love me, Artur, or was that fake too?"

He quickly shook his head. I saw his arm drop just a little. "No. We are real, Maddie," he admitted in a quiet voice.

I took a step toward the dresser. He didn't seem to notice, so I kept talking. "What will happen now? To us? To me?"

The tears fell down my cheek as I waited for his answer.

"Come with me. Run away with me, Maddie," he replied. His voice was so soft, sweet even, as if he was making love to me.

Another step toward the dresser.

But this time he noticed, and the gun was pointed directly at me again. "Don't move, Maddie. Don't make me hurt you."

I was only two steps away from the dresser—from my gun. My hands shook by my side as my stomach lurched with tension.

"Will you really shoot me?" I asked, my body slowly starting to go numb.

I took another step. Artur didn't answer.

But when a gunshot rang through the room, I had my answer.

I didn't feel it at first. I stumbled back when the

THE MAFIA AND HIS ANGEL PART 2

bullet made contact with my body. But I was too surprised to feel it.

One second passed. Two. Three.

And then I was hurting all over. My shoulder burned like it was on fire. My skin felt raw, and I almost retched as pain raked through my shoulder and traveled down the length of my spine.

I looked at the left side of my shoulder, where blood poured through my robe and the bullet had pierced my skin.

Artur made a regretful moan. I looked up to see him stepping toward the open window. Knowing that he intended to do, I jumped into action.

Adrenaline pumped through my body, and I reached for the drawer, pulling my gun out. I pointed it at him at the same time as another gunshot echoed around the room.

As a second bullet pierced my body, I fell to my knees. Pain. So much pain. It was an excruciating burning sensation, and this time I felt it in my stomach. I looked down to see my robe quickly getting soaked with my blood.

No. Please no.

I was frozen on the spot, and my body continued to pulse in agony. I was quickly losing blood. It wasn't just my body hurting. My heart and soul had shattered in that moment.

I cried out as my body convulsed in pain. I felt warm. Too warm. I was burning. My vision blurred in front of me and I called out.

"Alessio!"

I saw Artur quickly moving toward the window. Acting on reflex, I pointed my gun and pulled the trigger.

I missed.

The bullet hit the window, and the glass shattered, throwing shards everywhere in the room.

Artur climbed out of the window, and as I fell on the ground, curling into a fetal position, I screamed again.

"Alessio!"

My heart stuttered a few times. When I saw Alessio running inside the room, followed by the others, I didn't know whether to cry or be relieved.

There were gasps of surprise and looks of shock. Alessio knelt down beside me and pulled me into his arms. "Maddie?" he choked.

"Artur…" I gasped through the pain. "He…is…the…the…traitor…spy…"

Alessio's expression thundered with fury. I kept talking, knowing I had little time left.

"He…knows," I broke off when a fiery pain coursed through my body. I felt blood dribble in the corner of my lips.

I was going to die. Tears slid down my cheeks as I tried to speak. "He…knows…where…Ayla…is…"

Alessio bellowed something. I saw Viktor running out of the room. Nikolay jumped out of the window.

I stared back at Alessio, this time my body shaking with how heavy my sobbing was. Placing my hand over my stomach, right over where the bullet went through, I closed my eyes.

"My…baby…"

My heart had shattered the moment I realized I

THE MAFIA AND HIS ANGEL PART 2

would never see my baby. I only found out the day before. But now, I had lost him before I even had a chance to see him.

I didn't even know if I was having a girl or a boy. It was too early.

Opening my eyes again, I saw Alessio staring at me with a horrified expression. "Baby…my…baby…" I cried in his arms.

Behind his back, I saw Phoenix running into the room, followed by my mother. His face was a mask of horror as he ran to me, falling down to his knees next to Alessio.

He pulled me out of Alessio's arm, who stayed frozen, his eyes empty and soulless. He was in shock.

I looked away from Alessio and up at Phoenix. When I saw tears in his eyes, my already bruised heart broke a little more.

I had never seen Phoenix cry. Ever. But right there in front of my eyes, I saw him break.

"Maddie," he choked, pulling me to his chest. "Where's Sam?" he bellowed.

"Maddie, hang in there. Okay? I'm right here," he said against my cheek.

My fingers tightened around my stomach as the pain intensified until I found it harder and harder to breathe.

Phoenix placed kisses over my face, and I cried silently.

I was stupid…so so stupid.

"Don't leave me, Maddie," Phoenix whispered, kissing my lips gently.

Why did I stay away from him for so long? Why

did we break each other?

My heart continued to ache as blackness slowly surrounded me, pulling me further under.

I brought my hand up and cupped his cheek. I tried to smile.

I wanted to give him my smile. He loved my smile.

But my lips felt stiff. I tried to speak, to tell him the truth.

Staring into his eyes, I pressed my palm against his cheek, willing him to understand what I couldn't say.

I love—

My hand fell away, too weak to hold it up any longer. I lost sight of Phoenix and everything else as I was thrown into pitch blackness.

I went numb. All feelings were gone. Nothing hurt…I felt nothing.

As I succumbed to oblivion, I wished I had a chance to say those words to the man I truly loved.

I love you.

Chapter 41

Alessio

The sound of a gunshot was a shock through my body. Everything was silent, cold, as I stared at the piano thinking about Ayla.

And then the silence was gone. Replaced with the sound of a gunshot. I heard a scream. Then another gunshot.

Everything else happened in a blur. My feet acted of their own accord, and I was running out of the piano room without a second thought.

Another painful scream. Maddie's voice. It was Maddie's voice.

I followed the scream toward the end of the hall, my heart racing wildly in my chest. I heard footsteps behind me, and without looking, I knew it was Viktor and Nikolay. They were a few rooms away from mine. Without a doubt, they must have heard the gunshot too.

My feet slightly faltered to a stop when I realized the scream was coming from Artur's room. I felt my eyes widen in panic and picked up my pace. Was the estate under attack?

Fuck no! Not again!

My hands tightened in fists as my body went tight with alarm. I rushed to open the door, my eyes wildly searching around the room, looking for the threat.

The first thing I saw was the broken window, and just for a brief moment, my mother's face flashed in front of my eyes.

This moment. The gunshot. The screams. It felt so familiar.

My eyes snapped to the floor when I heard a pained whimper. My muscles locked tight as my body went rigid at the sight in front of me.

I almost stumbled back in shock but stopped myself in time as I stared at Maddie in complete horror. My eyes followed the pool of blood surrounding her, and my stomach rolled.

Blood wasn't something new to me. I was accustomed to blood and the horror that came with it. I made people bleed. I laughed when they bled. Hell, I took pleasure in seeing them begging for their lives as they bled to death.

No, I wasn't scared of blood. It wasn't why my stomach rolled and my knees felt weak.

It was this moment, this feeling of *déjà vu* that made me sick. I saw this when I was seven, when my mother took her last breath.

And now I was seeing it again.

I rushed to Maddie's side and knelt down beside her before pulling her into my arms. "Maddie?" I choked.

THE MAFIA AND HIS ANGEL PART 2

Her next words were filled with pain, but I heard them. Clear as day. They brought another type of pain in my chest. Pain and then anger. So much anger.

"Artur..." she gasped through the pain. "He...is...the...the...traitor...spy..."

Maddie winced as her body convulsed. She stared at me with frightened eyes, begging me. I didn't have to see my face to know my expression thundered with fury. I felt it vibrating through my bones.

Maddie kept talking even through her labored breathing.

"He...knows," she broke off and her face twisted, sweat breaking out on the skin of her forehead. Blood dribbled in the corner of her lips.

Tears slid down her cheeks as she tried to speak. "He...knows...where...Ayla...is..."

Ayla. At the sound of her name, my heart picked up a beat. My arms tightened around Maddie.

The numbness was gone. My mind was clear once again. Instead of the coldness seeping through my body, all I felt was burning anger.

"Get him!" I bellowed. I saw Viktor running out of the room. Nikolay jumped out of the window.

I felt hot, my skin itching with the need to kill. To make *him* bleed.

Artur, one of my most trusted men. How did I not see it? I trusted him, yet he betrayed me. For how long?

He was dying, cold, homeless, starving. But I picked him up, gave him a home. A family. Even when his father was a traitor, I believed in him.

Stupid. So fucking stupid. I didn't trust people easily, but trusting Artur had been a mistake. A big fucking one.

Shaking my head, I looked down at Maddie. She had to pay the price. Ayla had to pay the price of my stupidity.

Maddie cried in my arms, her entire body shaking with how heavy her sobbing was. She placed her hand over her stomach, right over where the bullet went through.

Closing her eyes, she whispered. Her voice was low, her words so softly spoken. "My…baby…"

What—?

I stared at her, completely horrified.

I heard her wrong. My mind was playing tricks on me. I wanted to ask her, try to clear this confusion, but my tongue felt heavy.

She opened her eyes again. "Baby…my…baby…" she cried in my arms.

There was no mistake. No confusion. My mind wasn't playing a trick on me. I heard it clearly, and it hurt. The words hurt, and I couldn't imagine how badly it was hurting Maddie.

My lips didn't move. I just stared. Even when Maddie was taken from my arms, Phoenix screaming, crying, begging her not to leave him, I didn't move.

My eyes slowly made their way to Maddie's stomach, where she was bleeding profusely. There was no way the baby would make it. It was impossible.

Would Maddie even make it?

I didn't fucking know anything.

THE MAFIA AND HIS ANGEL PART 2

I was snapped out of my thoughts when Sam came running into the room. Phoenix carried Maddie to the bed, and I quickly got to my feet.

My blood roared at the unfairness. No, it roared with anger, with the need for answers. I was raging, my body shaking with the force of my fury.

My eyes moved around the room, making contact with Viktor as he rushed into the room again.

I saw the fury, impatience, and worry in his expression. I also knew he was wrestling for control. I was too. We all were.

Artur wasn't going to make it out alive.

Viktor stared at me and gave me a single nod before walking out again. One nod was all it took to drive me to the point of insanity.

Artur had been captured, and my control had snapped.

Giving Maddie a final glance, I walked out of the room. I didn't call Phoenix. There was no point. He wasn't going to leave Maddie's side now.

Making my way to the basement, I let the fury boil. I let myself feel the anger, knowing it would serve me well later.

Only the anger would keep me going. There was no time for weakness. I pushed the image of Ayla frightened and hurt, Maddie bleeding and close to death, to the back of my mind.

Viktor was waiting for me in front of the door, his expression fierce. He didn't say anything. There was nothing to say. One of our own betrayed us. Someone we trusted and treated as a brother.

But we couldn't dwell on that betrayal now.

There was no time for it. Our only purpose was to get answers and find Ayla.

Viktor opened the door, and I walked inside, my stride confident and purposely. Slow even through my anger.

Artur was tied to a chair, facing me. His head was cast down, but I knew he heard me come in. The way his body tightened gave him away.

Nikolay was standing behind him, a murderous look on his face.

I walked forward, stopping just two feet away from Artur. The room was filled with silence. No words were uttered, but the air was heavy and tensed. Almost suffocating.

I let the silence drag for a few more minutes. Artur grew more tense. It was all a game, a game of dominance, and in that moment, I held the power and Artur was just a pawn.

When I felt myself barely hanging on the thin thread of control, I moved forward. I'd give him credit. He didn't move or flinch.

Grabbing his chin, I raised his head. He stared at me blankly, completely void of emotion. Fueled by deep hatred and anger, I pulled back and punched him. I heard his nose crunch under the force of my knuckles.

I craved his scream, his blood. When he didn't make a sound, I punched him again, harder than before. There was a very satisfying sound. Another broken bone. This time he winced, his eyes shutting tight in pain.

I grabbed his throat and squeezed, watching him fight for his breath. His face turned a shade of red and then purple. The cells broke across his skin, tiny red dots as his wide eyes stared at me in panic.

The whites of his eyes turned red as he suffocated under my grasp. His pupils enlarged, and I smiled, watching him struggle for his life, for another gasp of air.

The corner of his mouth was swelling, and there was a laceration over his cheekbone. His nose was already swelling, turning an ugly shade of green.

I pressed my fingers just a little harder, feeling his windpipe. He choked against the pressure building in his throat as it traveled up into his face.

I fought against the urge to laugh at his suffering.

Ayla was suffering because of him. She was innocent, yet paying for something she didn't deserve. All because of this man in front of me. Whatever was going to be handed to him would never be enough. I would never be satisfied.

When I saw Artur's eyes rolling back into his head, I pressed one more time before releasing him. His head fell forward, and he coughed dangerously, desperately gasping for his next breath.

His whole body shook with the effort to take in as much air as he could.

When I noticed him getting in control of his labored breathing, I grabbed his hair and pulled his head back. I held his neck against the back of the chair and glared.

"Why?" I simply asked.

One word. One question. Artur was one of my men. He understood how I worked. He understood what I wanted without even asking.

I thought the betrayal would hurt. It did hurt, but

I was mostly consumed by anger. The fury clouded my vision and every other emotion.

I had to find Ayla, and Artur was my only hope. The thought of her being in danger and hurt because of someone I trusted sent a wave of pain through my body.

Was it my fault? It was a constant thought in my mind, something that slowly killed me every day since she was taken from me.

"Why the fuck did you do it?" I snarled into his face. He didn't flinch, but the way his eyes darted to the side betrayed his fear and pain. I knew my gaze promised violence and revenge. My voice shook with it.

When he didn't answer, I punched him again, quickly losing my patience. "Answer me!"

There was a gash next to his eye, and he winced when my punch landed on it. It looked like Nikolay had already done a number on him.

I looked down at my hand and saw his blood. I wasn't wearing my gloves, and in that moment, I didn't want to. I wanted to see his blood on my hands, knowing that he was suffering and in pain.

At the thought of Ayla, I landed another furious punch on his face. I felt my jaw tighten and heard my teeth grinding together. If I could, I would string him up by his fucking intestines for what he had done.

Artur coughed and choked, spitting out the blood that accumulated in his mouth. He glanced up at me through swollen eyes. "You killed my father."

Oh, I knew this was coming. There was only one reason why he would betray me.

THE MAFIA AND HIS ANGEL PART 2

His father betrayed my life, my father, and when I took over as Boss, I killed him. Without any remorse or even an ounce of guilt. I left him on the cold ground, bleeding to death. When I came back at night, his body was already gone and buried.

Artur had been kicked out of the house. He was seventeen. When I found him a few days later, he was starving. Homeless. And alone.

I brought him back into my house. We were friends, brothers not my blood, but still *brothers*.

I never thought it would come to this. But all this time, I was getting betrayed. For ten years, he betrayed me.

Shaking my head, I pulled away. With my hands behind my back, I glared down at Artur. He finally flinched under the weight of my murderous stare. I felt the corner of my lips twitch with satisfaction.

"You were the traitor all this time?" Viktor growled behind me.

Artur glanced at him and then chuckled. He broke off and whimpered in pain before replying. "Yeah. All this time…it…was me…but…you were too…blind…to see it."

Nikolay's face thundered, and he reached forward, punching Artur in the stomach. He doubled over in agony and wheezed through his broken nose.

"Fuck," he muttered under his breath.

Rubbing my face in frustration, I took a deep breath. I couldn't kill him. Not now. Not until I found Ayla. And I knew he wasn't going to tell me easily.

My fingers itched with the need to kill him. But

for now, I was going to hurt him until he would feel the weight of the pain he caused my Angel.

"Why Ayla? Your enmity was toward us…not her," Viktor asked, coming to stand beside me.

Artur shook his head. "You are…right. My enmity was with you." He broke off and gasped. Sucking in a deep breath, he continued in a low painful tone. "I didn't even know who she was until the day we went to the beach. Alberto might have trusted me, but he was smart. I was never allowed into his house. Only his clubs. But that day, he called me to his house. I saw Ayla's picture there. I put two and two together, and there you go. She was an Abandonato."

"That doesn't explain why you handed her over," Viktor snapped. When I saw him moving forward in anger, I grabbed his arm, stopping him.

Artur continued speaking. "Alberto wanted her back, and I wanted to make you pay. It was easy. Two birds with one stone. The best way to bring you down was by hitting you with your weakness. And she was your only weakness."

I stayed silent, forcing my anger into control. If I moved, I would kill him.

"For years I waited, planned. I looked for your weakness. You were a strong motherfucker. Your motto was kill or be killed. And then Ayla came into your life. It was almost too easy," Artur said through his harsh breathing.

I saw his lip twitch in a small smile as he chuckled dryly. "You only made two mistakes. The first one was to trust me."

He took a deep breath before delivering the final

blow. "The second was falling in love with Ayla. So, you see, in the end...it was your...fault. You let her...become your weakness."

Viktor reached forward and pummeled Artur with three furious punches. "You fucking bastard!" he roared.

He reached back for another punch, but Nikolay was quicker. I closed my eyes, taking a deep breath. When I heard Nikolay's voice, my eyes snapped open.

"Did Alberto know I wasn't betraying Boss?" he hissed into Artur's ears.

Artur laughed through his pain. "Fuck...yeah...he knew everything. It was our plan. We'd make you think he believed you, while I was behind your back, giving him the correct information. How did you think he always knew your moves when Nikolay was giving him false information?"

"So it was all for nothing?" Viktor snarled, pulling away in frustration.

Artur nodded. "It...was...obvious. Nikolay was...too...loyal. Even when he was...close to...death...he never spilled...anything."

He paused, taking in desperate air through his compressed lungs. "He...knew you...would never betray Alessio." Glancing back at Nikolay, he smiled through his broken lips. "You are...like...a...fucking loyal dog."

Nikolay's eyes glowed fiercely with fury. "You little shit," he spat.

"It doesn't matter anymore," I finally spoke. "Where's Ayla?"

Nothing mattered. Why Artur betrayed me or how…only Ayla mattered. I fucking hated that I depended on Artur to find her, but there was no other way.

He raised an eyebrow at me. "Did you…really…think…it would be this…easy?"

This time, a smile crept his way across my lips. In no way was it a gentle smile. No, it promised only pain.

"No, I didn't think it would be easy." I shrugged a heavy shoulder, leaning forward until our faces were mere inches apart. "It's not going to be easy for *you*. Not at all."

I leaned back and nodded at Nikolay. He pushed a white cloth into Artur's mouth and stepped back, looking at his handy work.

Viktor walked over to the back table and came back with his favorite equipment. Clippers. They usually chopped off the fingers clean and without much effort.

Nikolay also came back with a spiral knife. My favorite.

He handed it to me while I watched Viktor get to work. It started out slow. A few punches, choking Artur, and when he still didn't talk, Viktor moved to the nails.

It hurt like a son of a bitch. Artur's screams were muffled by the cloth, but the way his body trembled, it was obvious he was in terrible pain.

He hadn't lost any fingers yet. Only three nails.

I raised my hand, and Viktor immediately stopped. Nikolay tore the cloth from Artur's mouth, and he screamed as the pain coursed his fingers and traveled its way through his body.

His hand was strapped to the arm rest, and I saw the way his fingers shook. They were covered in blood, and I chuckled at the sight.

"You want to talk now?" I wondered, looking at his bloody mess.

"Fuck…you…" he wheezed.

"No? You don't want to?" I taunted. "Okay then. Enjoy."

Viktor held the clipper over Artur's index finger, just below the first knuckle.

He waited. Waiting was a form of mental torture. The best way to break someone. Waiting made them tense, more alarmed, and their fear would hold no bounds.

I counted the seconds in my head.

One. Two. Three. Four. Five.

Artur screamed. He bellowed so loud my ears rang. His pain was music to my ears, and I sat down on the chair behind me.

"That was barely a finger," Viktor muttered as he stared at the bloody knuckle on the floor.

"Make sure he doesn't bleed to death," I snapped. We weren't done with him yet. Not until we had our answers and Ayla safe in our room.

A few minutes passed, another finger lost. One on each hand.

I waited to see if he would talk, but Artur stayed stubbornly quiet. Shaking my head to repress my frustrated growl, I got up and Viktor moved out of the way.

Leaning forward, I grabbed Artur's chin. "If you talk, this is going to be easy on you," I warned.

"I…know…you…" he gasped. "Doesn't…matter…if I talk…or not…I won't…make…it…out alive…either way."

I cocked my head to the side, regarding him with curious eyes. "Smart. You're right. You won't make it out alive either way. But I'll make your death quicker if you speak."

Another lie and he knew it.

When he didn't speak, I sighed just for a good measure. Taking my sweet time, I strolled around his chair, giving him some time to catch his breath.

I stopped in front of him again. He was staring at his feet, his swollen lips set in a tight, stubborn line.

I lightly dragged the spiral knife down his cheek, not enough to break his skin. But it was enough to let him know what was about to happen next.

When the knife reached his other cheek, I pressed it harder, and blood oozed through the broken skin. He winced but stayed quiet, biting on his lip to stop the scream.

I knew the spiral knife burned where it cut and Artur was probably in agony.

I dragged the knife to his neck, leaving trail of blood. The skin turned red, and I pulled away. His breathing was harsh and labored. Each breath appeared difficult to inhale and exhale.

I moved the knife to his thighs, making cuts as I went. The cuts weren't too deep, just enough to cause pain that would be unbearable after a few minutes.

"Are you ready to talk now?" I asked after his screams calmed down.

He hissed and glared at me. I shook my head.

THE MAFIA AND HIS ANGEL PART 2

Nikolay paced the floor while Viktor got to work again.

Two more nails and fingers.

And then I made cuts over his body.

Sometimes we walked out of the room, leaving Artur alone to breathe through his pain. And then we were back. It kept going like that…for hours. Until I started to feel helpless and completely hopeless.

The next time we walked into the room again, Artur's head was hanging low. It was already morning. For an hour, I paced outside Maddie's room, debating if I should go in or not.

But guilt weighed heavily on my heart. Instead, I stayed outside.

Then, I was in the piano room, wishing Ayla was there. Another pang of guilt. Another wave of pain.

After an hour of wallowing in self-pity, I walked away and made my way into the basement.

The fury was back in full force. The air smelled of blood. It felt heavy with death and uncertainty.

I stared at Artur, waiting for a reaction from him. When I started toward him, he slowly lifted his head. His face was almost unrecognizable. Swollen, red, a mix of green and purple. Several cuts. Some deep, some barely there.

He stared at me through swollen eyes, and I saw his jaw working. He opened his mouth, but no words came out.

He tried again, but it sounded like some gurgling noise. Artur tried to clear his throat and coughed a few times before taking a deep breath.

I saw his throat moving as he swallowed and

then tried again. "She…"

My eyes widened, and I stepped forward. "Where is she?" I demanded, my heart accelerating and beating as wildly as a caged bird.

"She…is…" He choked before continuing slowly. "Is…at…my house."

"Your house?" Viktor growled.

Artur nodded slowly. "That's…where…Alberto…is hiding.…My house…he u…ses it…hiding…place."

I raked my fingers through my hair and swiveled around, punching the wall. All this time. She was right under our fucking nose.

"Move out," I ordered Viktor and Nikolay.

"For your sake, I really hope she's there," I told Artur.

He stared at me blankly, but I saw something in his eyes. It almost looked like regret. "She…is…there."

"Why are you telling us that now? Why wait until you are half dead?" Nikolay questioned.

I wondered the same thing. Artur didn't answer. He glanced down, and I saw his lips move. No sound was made, but his lips told me what I needed to know.

Maddie.

With a deep breath, I nodded toward my men. They walked out, and with a final glance at Artur, I walked out too.

We met with Phoenix in the hall. He glanced at the closed door, his eyes murderous. "Is he alive?"

"He is. Don't kill him yet," I ordered. Just in case he was lying. When Ayla was found, then his death would be signed.

I took a step forward but stopped. "How is Maddie?"

Phoenix let out a pained groan, his face twisting. "Sam took the bullets out. She...is okay."

Taking a deep breath, he stared at the wall, his eyes filled with so much pain. "But...but the baby didn't make it."

Even though I knew the baby wouldn't make it, hearing the words was still a blow to my chest. I looked down, wishing this wasn't real. I wanted to tear Artur apart piece by piece.

"Was it yours?" I asked quietly. They thought it wasn't obvious. But it was. For years, even after whatever happened between them, they still cared. Maybe still loved each other.

Phoenix clenched his fists, and I looked up again. Closing his eyes tightly, he shook his head. "No," he choked. "No...Maddie...she never..." He paused, taking a deep breath. "Maddie never cheated. She would never do that. The baby was Artur's."

With a heavy heart, I nodded at Phoenix. "We found Ayla's whereabouts."

He looked at the door. "I can't leave Maddie."

"I was never going to ask you to leave Maddie. The rest of us will go."

He sent me a grateful look, and I walked away. Making my way upstairs, I stopped in the living room when I saw Nina walking into the estate.

She rushed over to us. "Nikolay called."

"What are you doing here?" I asked, wiping my hands with the towel Viktor handed me.

"He told me Artur is the traitor. That little shit," she growled, her eyes sparking fire.

"He told us where Ayla is," Viktor muttered.

Nina's eyes widened. "He did? Where is she?"

"Artur's house," Viktor replied. There was no emotion in his voice. No light. No anger. Nothing. I felt the same way.

"I'm coming," she announced.

"Seriously? Like this?" Viktor retorted, pointing at Nina's outfit.

She looked down at herself. "Those heels are killer heels. They might come in handy. Who knows?"

"You will be a liability," Nikolay argued. "We don't have time to save your ass."

Nina cocked her head to the side. "Really?"

It happened fast. But the next thing we knew, Viktor was on the floor with Nina's legs wrapped around his neck.

"What the fuck was that? I didn't say anything," Viktor snapped.

"Still think I'm a liability?" she spat, her voice holding venom.

She got up and looked at me. "Another body to protect Ayla," she added, raising an eyebrow at me. She knew I couldn't refuse that. "I think you will need a woman with you when you find her."

Viktor stood up and glared at Nina's back. "Bitch," he mouthed.

Staring at Nina, I saw her resolve and finally nodded. She was right. The more bodies to protect Ayla, the better. And Nina was far from a liability. She was more of an asset. A killer who could easily

THE MAFIA AND HIS ANGEL PART 2

take anyone.

I walked out, followed by Nikolay, Viktor, and Nina. A few of my men were already waiting next to the cars. I got in without a word while Viktor took the driver's seat.

The drive to Artur's house was tense.

When the car came to a stop, I quickly stepped out. This time, Nikolay and Viktor took the lead, while Nina and I stayed in the rear.

Nikolay crashed the door open, and we were inside in mere seconds.

As soon as we stepped inside, guns were blazing and bullets were flying.

The fucker! He was ready, and he wasn't alone.

His men surrounded the house, and I quickly ducked, avoiding a bullet which could have pierced my head. I growled in frustration and shot at the man in front of me, my bullet going right through his heart.

I didn't have time for fucking child's play.

Turning around, I fired at any men who came into my path. Bullets in their legs, some in the neck, and a few in the head.

Through it all, Alberto was nowhere to be found. A coward. Of course, he was nowhere to be found.

When most of his men were down, I nodded at Viktor and Nikolay. They searched through the house as I continued to gun down the rest of the men, Nina beside me doing the same. She was ruthless in her attacks. Her bullets pierced their bodies with an astonishing ferocity.

I saw a man standing in front of me, pointing his gun at my chest. I pulled my trigger, but nothing happened.

A gunshot echoed across the wall. I expected a fiery pain in my chest, but when I saw the man drop dead, I glanced at Nina beside me.

She rubbed her gun against her leather pants and sent me a wink. "You're welcome."

Viktor ran down the stairs, his expression frantic. "Ayla is not there."

Nikolay came to stand by my side. "I searched the first floor. She isn't there, either."

"What?" I bellowed, my body shaking with panic, fear, and lastly rage.

"Look everywhere! She has to be here!"

I looked wildly around the living room, moving from the kitchen to the dining room. Then the bedrooms upstairs. I searched every corner of the house.

When I didn't find her, I searched again. Frantically. Desperately. I searched again and again. She had to be here.

My Angel was nowhere to be found. Again.

I was standing in the middle on the living room, my head pounding, my chest aching. She wasn't here, but I felt her. It was an unexplainable feeling, but as soon as I had stepped in the house, my heart had accelerated. Almost as if it knew Ayla was here.

I felt her. My skin prickled with a strange sensation, and I closed my eyes. No, she wasn't here. We looked everywhere, but she wasn't here.

My heart felt heavy in my compressed chest, my lungs hurting as I breathed through the agony of failing yet again.

THE MAFIA AND HIS ANGEL PART 2

Ayla. Ayla. Where are you?

I heard a scream.

"Boss!"

"Alessio!"

My eyes snapped open, and I stared at a man pointing his gun at me. I didn't have a chance to raise my gun or even move out of the way. I tried to duck, falling to the ground, and then the gunshot rang through my ears.

A few seconds later, I felt a searing pain run through my right leg. "Fuck!" I bellowed.

I heard a shout and then a scream of pain behind me. I looked down at my leg to see it bleeding where the bullet had gone through.

Still on the floor, I turned around to see Nina pulling out her heel from the man's chest. "Fuck you! Those were Louboutin heels. Now it's covered in your dirty blood."

She glanced back at us. "You okay, Alessio?"

"Just a nick," I muttered back. It was lie. The bullet had gone through my leg and was now lodged inside.

Nina noticed us staring, and she glanced back at her bloody heel. "What? I told you it comes in handy. I was out of bullets."

"So you just throw your heel at a man, hoping it kills him?" Nikolay asked as I stood up, ignoring the burning in my leg.

"Pretty much," she replied, taking off her other heel and standing up barefooted.

"What do we do?" Viktor asked me, his expression forlorn.

I ignored his question, my eyes roaming around

the house one last time. We looked everywhere. Did Artur lie?

Or maybe Alberto had already taken Ayla away? I had never wanted to hurt someone so bad in all my life as I did right there.

I let out a harsh, barking laugh. It was empty, void of any emotion. I was going to lose my mind if I didn't find Ayla soon.

I limped away, but my feet twisted in the rug, and I almost went down. I quickly straightened myself and glanced down at the fucking rug, wanting to tear it apart with my bare hands.

But something else caught my eye, and all thought of tearing the rug apart was gone.

The rug was bunched around my feet, and underneath was a wooden door. My eyebrows furrowed in confusion, and I pushed the rug away completely.

I heard Nina gasp.

The rug wasn't there for decoration. It was there to cover something—to hide a fucking door in the floor.

Viktor swore under his breath, looking at the closed door.

"There's no basement. We checked," Nikolay added, his eyes wide.

"What the fuck is this door then?" I growled. Without waiting for an answer, I bent down and opened the heavy latch. When it came undone, I pulled the door open, and it hit the floor with a loud bang.

"Stairs," Nina muttered. "What the hell? It leads to a basement."

THE MAFIA AND HIS ANGEL PART 2

I didn't say anything. I couldn't even if I tried. My tongue felt heavy, my body numb. She was in there. I knew it. I felt it.

Nikolay came to stand in front of me and turned his phone on, putting on the torch. I took the first step, my heart racing, pumping wildly.

We descended the stairs in the dark, only Nikolay's and Viktor's phones used as flashlights. As soon as we reached the landing, Nina pressed her hand against the wall, looking for a light switch.

A few seconds later, the basement was illuminated.

The basement was incomplete. No wall or tiles. It looked more like a fucking dungeon.

My legs trembled as I took a step further inside. Another step. A few more and I stopped.

A foul smell touched my nostrils, and I shuddered. The smell was horrible. It was almost impossible to breathe. It smelled like days of piss and vomit. Ayla. Was my Angel here? In this place?

My heart squeezed painfully, and I stepped forward on shaky legs. The further we ventured in, the worse the smell got.

I heard Nina gag behind me. "I think I'm going to be sick," she gasped.

"Fuck, what is this?" Viktor growled.

I wasn't dying. I was very much alive, but in that moment, it really felt like I was dying. The thought of Ayla being in a place like this was almost unbearable.

When I finally reached the far side of the basement, I stopped dead in my tracks, my stomach twisting painfully.

"No," I whimpered, my eyes widening at the sight in front of me.

When I heard them swear behind me, I knew they were seeing what I was seeing.

She was turned away from us, facing the wall. I didn't see her face, but I knew it was her. I felt it in my heart.

She was there. My Ayla. She was right there in front of me. She was lying on the cold hard floor, pushed against the wall. There were chains around her ankles and wrists.

And she was barely covered, her white dress ripped until nothing covered her body.

"No. No. No!" I rushed forward, ignoring the burning ache in my leg. Falling down beside her, I was too afraid to even touch her body.

Ayla looked so fragile. So small. So broken. She'd lost weight, some of her bones practically showing. I reached forward and gently pushed her greasy hair out of her face.

Her face was covered in dirt, and it appeared slightly bruised.

"Ayla?" I whispered brokenly, softly touching her cheek. So cold. She was so cold, freezing.

My heart stuttered, and I frantically looked behind me. Their faces were masks of horror. "She's cold. She's so cold," I repeated.

I looked back at Ayla, my mind and heart going crazy. Agony coursed through my body. It hurt. Everything hurt. It wasn't my leg, but it was my heart that hurt the most.

My Ayla. My sweet Angel.

She laid frozen, so still. Too still.

THE MAFIA AND HIS ANGEL PART 2

I felt my heart break. When I lost her, I thought I was in pain. But now…now I knew what real pain felt like.

And my Angel went through worse than that.

"Angel," I whispered, leaning next to her ear. "It's me. Alessio. I'm here now."

A small guttural cry escaped my lips when she didn't answer. I was desperate to see her beautiful green eyes. To hear her sweet voice.

I needed her.

And I knew, she needed me just as much, if not more.

I couldn't protect her. I'd failed her, and the thought felt like a bullet through my heart. I had been careless, and she had to pay the price.

My eyes pricked with unshed tears, and I slowly leaned forward. As gently as I could, I wrapped my arms underneath Ayla.

I gathered my Angel in my arms and pulled close to my chest. Her hair was matted with vomit and other things I didn't even want to think about.

I rocked back and forth, holding her to me, begging her to open her eyes.

I gently pressed my arms over her body, looking for any other bruises. My vision blurred as everything hit at once. All her pain and suffering. Her face was turned toward my chest, and I placed a kiss on her nose. "Angel," I whimpered.

My eyes followed my hands.

Oh fuck no. Fuck no! No!

My heart stuttered painfully. I forced myself to breathe. I shook as my eyes took in what I was seeing.

My stomach cramped, and I held Ayla tighter to my chest.

This couldn't be happening. Not my Angel.

My eyes stayed fixated on her body—her stomach.

"No," I whimpered, shaking my head wildly.

My eyes went to her face again. She was still unconscious.

My Angel. My beautiful Angel.

My eyes moved to her stomach again. Her round, rigid protruding stomach.

This time I let out an enraged roar that echoed through the stone walls.

END OF BOOK 2

Alessio's and Ayla's story continues in Book 3, The Mafia and His Angel: Part 3

Acknowledgements

I remember in the last book, I thanked my parents first. They are the reason why I am here today, writing. They made me realize that I loved writing. If it wasn't for their constant push, years ago, I wouldn't have written the first word of a rough short story back when I was still in high school. I wrote my first word, and since then, writing has become my obsession. So I would like to thank my parents *again* for making me realize that writing is my passion. Since the release of book 1, they have stayed with me, supported me, opened my eyes to many things and they have taught me better. I am so thankful for everything they stand and for making me the person I am today. So thank you Ma and Pa.

To Vivvi. My girl. My boobito. You are everything. I can't go a day without texting you, and I know you are pretty much as obsessed with me as I am with you (; Thank you for being there for me. Thank you for always pushing me up when I am falling down. Thank you for loving my characters, my babies just as much as I do, if not more. Actually, saying thank you is not enough. You are my soul sister. And I am so glad I found you.

A biggest thank you to my publisher. Thank you for giving TMAHA a chance. I am holding my book right now, because you think it is worth it. So thank you.

To my editor, Toni—you rock! I am so glad we worked together on this book. You truly did wonders. Thank you.

Thank you to everyone else who had a hand in making this book—my proofreader, formatter…you guys are a star.

To Deranged Doctor Design—Thank you for such a kickass cover. I couldn't stop staring at it! I had to hold my screech in when I first saw it, because I was at work.

To the bloggers and everyone who took their time to promote TMAHA, you are awesome! My big thanks to you.

And I wanted to leave this for the end, because this is the important part. A huge thank you to every single one of my readers. My lovelies. If my parents are the reason why I started writing, then *you* are the reason why I am still here. In this moment, holding this book. Your never-ending support and love has taken us on this path. From the first word to the last, you have been here with me. I am proud we took this journey together. Together, we dreamed about holding TMAHA one day, thumbing through the pages. *We* did it, lovelies. Thank you for standing with me, even through my craziness. To all the fan accounts and groups out there, thank you! All the beautiful edits and posters you have made, they are my inspiration and motivation. I am going to say it loud and clear. "You freaking rock!"

About the Author

Lylah James lives somewhere in Canada. She is usually pretty busy but she uses all her spare time to write. If she is not studying, sleeping, writing or working – she can be found with her nose buried in a good romance book, preferably with a hot alpha male.

Writing is her passion. The voices in her head won't stop and she believes they deserve to be heard and read. Lylah James writes about drool worthy and total alpha males, with strong and sweet heroines. She makes her readers cry – sob their eyes out, swoon, curse, rage and fall in love. Mostly known as the Queen of cliffhanger and the #evilauthorwithablacksoul, she likes to break her readers' hearts and then mend them again.

FOLLOW LYLAH AT:

Facebook page:
https://www.facebook.com/AuthorLy.James/

Twitter page:
https://twitter.com/AuthorLy_James

Instagram page:
https://www.instagram.com/authorlylahjames/

Goodreads:
https://www.goodreads.com/author/show/16045951.Lylah_James

Wattpad account:
https://www.wattpad.com/user/HumB01

Or you can drop me an email at:
AuthorLylah.James@Hotmail.com

Or check out my website:
http://authorlylahjames.com/

You can also join my newsletter list for updates, teasers, major giveaways and so much more!
http://eepurl.com/c2EJ4z

Printed in Great Britain
by Amazon